DEADLY SILENCE

A DETECTIVE JANE PHILLIPS NOVEL

OMJ RYAN

D1419859

INKUBATOR
BOOKS

1

She hadn't changed much. Older, of course, and a lot heavier than when he had first known her. Since she wore a hat and scarf against the winter weather, most of her face was covered, but there was no denying it was her. Even as a young girl she had carried herself apologetically, and the years seemed to have amplified her timid posture. She scurried along the dark street now, as if hoping to avoid human contact.

She did not notice him step out of the alleyway and slip in silently behind her. It wasn't the first time he had followed her home.

The walk from the church to her house took the usual five minutes. This evening, though, with the bitter wind biting to the bone, she appeared to be in a hurry. Careful not to get too close, he watched from the opposite side of the street as she fumbled with her keys on the doorstep of the large Victorian terraced house, a moment later stepping inside. A creature of habit, she busied herself switching on lights and closing the curtains in the front rooms before heading into the kitchen.

At the rear of the property, he positioned himself in his

usual spot, in the shadows of the alley that ran along the back of the house. While the homes on either side enjoyed open-plan living rooms that opened onto smartly decked gardens, hers remained locked in the past, tired and dishevelled, in need of some TLC. Despite her insistence on closing the front curtains, the kitchen shutters always remained open, and for the next hour he watched her potter about before eating her evening meal alone at the breakfast bar.

He checked his watch: 7.30 p.m. With the school run complete and the majority of commuters already home, this was the perfect opportunity. Slipping on latex gloves, followed by a pair of leather ones, he returned to the front of the house and checked to see if the street was empty.

With a final glance, he walked up to the front door and pressed the old metal bell, which rang feebly in the hallway. He waited, attempting to appear as casual as possible, all the time careful to keep his face hidden from sight.

He heard footsteps in the hall, then the heavy lock released as she pulled the door open on its chain. 'Can I help you?' she asked, staring quizzically through the gap.

'Susan Gillespie?'

'Yes?' She looked him up and down. 'Have we met?'

He smiled warmly. 'It's been a long time Susan, I'll grant you. Have I really changed that much?'

She continued to stare out at him, looking confused.

'Surely you remember me and my pyjamas? You and the gang loved them, as I recall.' He chuckled. 'Please, Susan, don't leave me hanging here.'

Her expression changed, replaced by a slow dawning of recognition. 'Winnie...is that you?'

'The very same.' He doffed his cap and bowed theatrically.

'Well, I never. It must be twenty years since we last met.'

'Twenty-eight, actually.'

Susan stared at him uncertainly. 'Would you like to come in?'

He smiled. 'I thought you'd never ask.'

She unchained the door and ushered him into the hall, where he waited patiently for her to lock it again. 'Can't be too careful these days.'

'Quite.'

She squeezed past him and headed for the kitchen, 'Would you like a cup of tea?' she asked over her shoulder.

'Coffee, if you have it.'

'I don't drink it myself, but I think I still have some in the cupboard. Noel likes it. You remember Noel, don't you?'

'Yes, of course.'

He followed her into the kitchen. He had only ever seen glimpses of it from outside, but after so many nights watching from the alley, he knew the layout well. Still, the house itself appeared much larger inside than he had expected, almost too big for one person.

With her back to him, she continued to chatter, busy in her search of the coffee. 'I'm sorry I didn't recognise you, Winnie. You look so different. I don't mean to be rude, but you were a chunky monkey, weren't you? Now you're built like an action hero.' She turned to face him, a wide grin on her face.

He returned her smile. 'Many hours in the gym.'

Susan opened a cupboard door. 'The coffee's in here somewhere.'

He pointed to her left. 'What about that one?'

She followed his direction and stepped over to the farthest corner, exactly where he wanted her. He removed the leather gloves. Glancing over at the window, he took what he needed from his jacket pocket and stepped forwards.

'You must be psychic.' Susan grabbed the jar of coffee from the top shelf and turned to face him.

'Something like that.' His words sounded muffled through the surgeon's mask pulled tightly across his face.

For a moment Susan looked confused, then terror filled her eyes as he raised his right hand towards her face. She tried to speak, but was immediately silenced as he pumped two large sprays from the dispenser directly into her nose and mouth. A second later, he stepped forwards to catch her as she dropped like a stone towards the floor.

IN THE LIVING ROOM, his final preparations were complete. He dragged an old armchair in front of his victim, who he'd cable-tied to a chair he'd retrieved from the kitchen.

Still unconscious, she sat slumped in the middle of the dimly lit room, the single lamp casting long shadows across the floor. Taking his seat, he inspected the transparent plastic bag in his hands with forensic attention. He pulled it back and forth, testing its strength. He was sure it would do the job. He checked his watch: almost 8.30 p.m. *Time flies when you're having fun.* Exhaling heavily, he sat in silence and waited for stage two to begin.

Sometime later, Susan began to stir. When she realised where she was, she bolted upright, shock written on her face.

'Welcome back, my dear.'

She stared at him wild-eyed. 'Wh-what is this? What are you going to do to me?'

'Exactly what you did to me.'

'But I didn't do anything, Winnie.'

'Precisely, that's the whole fucking point. And don't call me Winnie. I always hated that stupid nickname.'

Susan remained silent, continuing to stare at him fearfully.

'Are you scared, Susan?'

A tear rolled down her cheek. 'Yes, I am.'

'*Good*,' he purred as he leant in and wiped the tear away. 'They say animals can smell fear, but do you know, I swear *I* can taste it.' He licked his finger.

Susan began to sob uncontrollably. He smiled as he heard liquid dripping noisily onto the carpet. 'Same old little Susie. Crying and wetting herself.'

He walked over to the fireplace and picked up a photo of an elderly couple in his gloved hand. With his back to her, he examined it closely. 'I remember this used to be your mum and dad's house. Is this them?'

Susan nodded.

'What happened? Did you lock them in a home?'

Susan controlled her tears long enough to speak, 'They died within twelve months of each other. Mum went first, and Dad couldn't cope.'

'Died of a broken heart, did he?' he asked sympathetically.

Susan started sobbing again.

He put the picture back on the mantelpiece. 'I never knew my father,' he said coldly, then walked back over to her. He stood behind her and took out the plastic bag again, then held it above her head. 'Right, Susan, it's time to tell me the truth.'

He pulled the bag over her head so that it covered her nose and mouth. Standing over her, he watched in awe as she writhed in panic, the plastic forcing its way into her airway. His heart raced, and adrenaline surged through his body as he held it in place.

After fifteen seconds, he pulled it off. Immediately, Susan gasped for air, spit running down her chin.

'Come on, Susan...*the truth*.'

She was crying like a child now. 'The truth? About what?'

'About why you didn't do anything, that's what.' He pulled the bag over her head again, holding it longer this time. Her screams were muffled as she involuntarily sucked the plastic in and out of her mouth, her legs kicking against the carpet.

Finally, he pulled it off, 'Tell me the truth, Susan. Why didn't you do anything to help me? We were supposed to be friends.'

He waited for her to speak as she desperately sucked in air. 'I-I couldn't,' she wailed. 'He told me I'd be next if I told anyone – I was terrified of him.'

Holding the bag taut, he stood in fury as the words landed. '*You* were terrified? How do you think *I* felt for all those years?' He pulled the bag over her head once more.

Her whole body fought for air, every muscle straining in the hope of finding oxygen. He watched coldly from above, his jaw tightening before ripping the bag away just in time.

She heaved and gasped, her mouth dripping with saliva, and she began bawling like a distraught child. 'Please, you have to believe me. I did try, once. But he was too powerful. I'm so, so sorry.'

He stood in front of her, then knelt to stroke her cheek gently. 'Yes, he was powerful...and evil. And *you* did nothing to stop him.'

'I know I did wrong. I should have spoken out.' She broke down again. 'Believe me, I ask God for forgiveness every day.'

'Oh, it's a little too late for prayers, Susan.'

'I'm begging you, please let me go. I won't say anything, I promise.'

His voice was almost tender now. 'I know that, Susan. *You never do.*'

He pulled the bag over her head one last time and held it there as her body thrashed from side to side. As he stared into her eyes, the energy coursing through him was almost over-whelming. As her lungs finally ran out of air, she stopped moving and her body came to a complete rest. With his hands still gripped tightly around the plastic, he was aware of a deadly silence that now permeated the room; it was almost deafening.

He turned his gaze back to Susan. Her dead eyes stared through the condensation that clung to the inside of the bag. He checked her pulse to be certain she was dead, then withdrew a roll of black duct tape from his pocket. It was time for stage three.

2

Detective Jane Phillips slammed on the brakes, narrowly missing an oncoming car as she attempted to cross a busy junction. She had suffered one of her flashbacks and hadn't seen him until it was almost too late. The wound in her chest chafed against her seatbelt, a constant reminder of her terrifying ordeal just six months ago. She wasn't right yet, and she knew it.

Sticking to the speed limit, she drove the remaining ten minutes without incident and arrived at the house shortly after 3 p.m. She killed the engine and sat for a moment, breathing deeply. 'Come on, Jane, get a grip of yourself.'

Putting on her game face, she stepped out of the car and strode over to the SOCO tent, where she pulled a set of protective overalls over her charcoal trouser suit and black boots. For convenience, as ever, her hair was tied back against her head.

She stepped through the front door and walked hurriedly down the hall. Jones and Bovalino had already arrived. She was late again, which would almost certainly cause problems with her new DCI.

In the lounge, she was confronted by the body of a woman

slumped in a chair. Her face was covered by a plastic bag secured around her neck with a cable tie. Four strips of black gaffer tape had been used to create an X over each eye.

Jones and Bovalino were inspecting the room. Their white protective suits appeared incongruous to the rest of the scene. Jones's wiry frame was drowned out by the baggy material, while the man-mountain that was Bovalino looked like a huge balloon, filled to breaking point.

'Jesus, Bov, could that suit be any tighter?' she said as she approached.

Both men turned to face her. 'Guv,' they said in unison.

She lowered her voice. 'Where's Brown?

Jones pointed across the room. 'In the kitchen with Evans.'

'Jesus, Evans doesn't mess about, does he?'

'Just been made up to senior CSI,' Jones replied. 'Trying to get on the right side of Brown.'

'Does he have one?' Phillips gazed around the room. 'Do we know who the victim is?'

'Susan Gillespie,' came the sharp Glaswegian tones of DCI Brown, emerging from the kitchen. 'Detective *Inspector* Phillips. How good of you to finally join us.'

Reluctantly, she apologised. 'Sorry sir, I got held up.'

'Of course you did.' Brown's dislike of Phillips was so evident that even Susan Gillespie might have noticed it.

Brown had taken charge of the team after Phillips had been demoted to inspector following the Marty Michaels case. Despite catching the mastermind responsible for a killing spree that had shocked Manchester, she had broken the law in doing so. In such a high-profile case, an example had to be made. Vigilantism would not be tolerated in the force.

Now she reported to DCI Fraser Brown. Originally from Glasgow, he had transferred to the Northwest fifteen years ago, and he and Phillips had clashed many times. Their contempt for each other was widely known, and evident for all to see.

Brown stepped closer, his lack of height making him look ridiculous in his billowing SOCO suit. Phillips believed his small man syndrome was one of the many things that made him so unpleasant.

'Right, now we're all finally here, let's get on with solving this case, shall we? Jones, what do we know so far?'

'Well, sir, there's no obvious signs of forced entry. There's two coffee cups and a biscuit tin next to the kettle. Nothing appears to be missing, and there's no outward signs of a struggle. From what we can see, there's no indication of rape or sexual assault.'

'We'll know for certain once we get her on the slab,' Evans chirped in, clearly trying to make an impression.

Brown ignored him. 'What do we know about the victim?'

'Forty-three. Single, lives alone. No pets.'

'Who found the body?' asked Phillips.

'Her brother,' said Jones. 'When she didn't turn up for work at the family accounting firm, he called around and let himself in with his key,'

'Approximate time of death is early evening last night,' Evans cut in.

'Could it be a sex game gone wrong?' asked Bovalino.

There was a pause, then Jones responded, 'We'll need to check her sexual history. Maybe the brother can give us some idea of the kind of life she lived behind closed doors.'

Brown rubbed his chin, attempting to look intelligent. Phillips had seen him do it a thousand times. Each time, she had to fight the urge to slap his hand away.

'Right,' he said. 'Phillips, you carry on here with Jones and Bovalino. I have to get back to the station and brief the Chief Super. This is not your run-of-the-mill murder case, so we need to manage it carefully. If one sniff of this gets to the press, there'll be panic across the city. We can't have innocent women murdered in this manner.'

'How do we know she was innocent, sir?' asked Phillips.

'Does she look like a criminal to you, DI Phillips?'

'Well, admittedly, she's not wearing a mask and carrying a swag bag.'

Jones and Bovalino attempted to stifle their childish grins, which didn't go unnoticed by Brown.

Phillips continued. 'Isn't it a bit early to make assumptions on who Susan Gillespie was and what might have brought the killer to her door?'

Brown stepped in closer to her. She was at least two inches taller than him. 'Don't get funny with me, Phillips. Instead of acting up in front of the gang, why don't you use that smart mouth of yours to find our killer, and *fast*. I don't want a case like this hanging over my head. And not a word to the press, you got that?'

Phillips stared him in the eye. 'Yes, sir.'

Brown wagged a finger at Jones and Bovalino. 'And the same goes for you two clowns.'

'Sir,' they both replied as Brown turned and made his way outside, shouting for Evans to follow him.

'Prick,' mumbled Phillips.

'Jesus, Guv. Why do you do it?' Jones asked in his South London drawl.

'Do what?'

'Wind Brown up like that? It's not going to help you get back to DCI any quicker, is it?'

'I know. He just gets to me, that's all. Such a bloody weasel. He's been here less than an hour and already he's making assumptions about the victim. He'll do anything to get the case closed and off his desk.'

'True, but he is our boss. It doesn't help any of us if you two are constantly at war.'

'Okay, okay, I hear you. I'll try to rein it in. Promise.'

'Good. Thanks, Guv.'

The three stood in silence, staring at Susan Gillespie's body. Then Bovalino finally spoke. 'You're right though, Guv.'

'About what, Bov?'

'He is a prick.'

Phillips burst out laughing. She playfully slapped Bovalino's cheek. 'You don't say much, Bov. But when you do – it's always worth hearing!'

_____

3

Susan Gillespie's brother lived just a short walk from Susan's house. Unlike the grand Victorian family home she had inherited, Noel had bought new build. Judging by the colour of the brick and the height of the hedges surrounding the garden, it had been constructed at least twenty years ago. A black 3-series BMW sat on the drive. As they walked to the house, Phillips noted the private plate, 'NG 58'.

At that moment her phone rang, and she tapped Jones on the shoulder, signalling for him to wait. She stepped away to take the call, and returned to the driveway a minute later.

'Everything all right, Guv?'

'Yep. I just needed a quick word with Don Townsend.'

'*The hack* Don Townsend?'

'The same.'

'What the bloody hell are you doing with a shark like him?'

'Don't worry – I know exactly what he's like. As the saying goes, "keep your enemies close" and all that.'

Jones shook his head, 'He's bad news, Guv. Nothing good can come from it.'

'Actually, it can. That little snake has just agreed to help me with a police finance issue.'

'Finance issue? Since when have you been interested in budgets?'

'I happen to think funding is something all officers of Her Majesty's police force should take an interest in.'

Jones looked at her sideways. 'What are you up to, Guv?'

Phillips smiled. 'Nothing. Merely ensuring the public know how hard their local coppers are working, day in, day out, to keep them safe.'

She reached the front door and rattled the metal knocker.

Noel Gillespie answered almost immediately, and as the door opened, Phillips was struck by his haunted features. From the limited intel she had, she knew Noel Gillespie was a couple of years older than Susan, but for a man in his late forties, he looked a lot older.

'Mr. Gillespie?'

'Yes?'

'DI Phillips and DS Jones.' Both flashed their credentials simultaneously. 'May we come in?'

'Of course.' Gillespie moved back inside, and Phillips and Jones followed him through to the lounge room. 'Can I get you some tea?'

'That would be lovely,' said Phillips. 'Jones will give you a hand.'

With the clatter of mugs and spoons ringing from the other room, Phillips took a moment to survey the space. Judging by the plethora of family photos adorning the walls and various surfaces, Gillespie was a family man with two teenage girls. Mercifully for them, both looked like their mother, who was surprisingly attractive considering Gillespie's hang-dog appearance. A well-ordered bookcase in the corner of the room was partnered by a cabinet bursting with DVDs. Neither contained anything that jumped out; just a variety of popular fiction, kids' books and mainstream movies.

'You still taking sugar, Guv?' asked Jones, re-entering the room ahead of Gillespie.

She turned to face him. 'Given up.'

In truth, she had never taken sugar. She and Jones were playing out a routine they'd established long ago for home visits. While he kept the person of interest out of sight, she had a quick look around for anything untoward. The innocuous question warned her of the person of interest's returning. So far, this time, she'd found nothing of note.

Gillespie chose the armchair, so Phillips and Jones took a seat on the adjacent sofa. After a few polite sips of tea, Phillips carefully placed her mug on the small table to her left. Jones followed suit and pulled out his police notepad and pen.

'Mr Gillespie —'

'Please, call me Noel.'

'Noel. Can you tell us how you came to discover your sister's body today?'

Gillespie took a deep breath and exhaled, steadying himself.

'Take your time, Noel.'

'Susan didn't show up for work this morning, which wasn't unusual, as she often suffered from terrible migraines and IBS. When she was particularly stressed, her attacks would come quite regularly.'

'And had she had these attacks recently?'

'Yes. A lot of our work comes from SMEs, and tax returns for them need to be in before the end of the month.'

'SMEs?'

'Sorry, Inspector, industry jargon. Small to medium enterprises. Businesses with less than two hundred and fifty employees, and a turnover ranging from twenty thousand all the way up to fifty million. Having said that, those kinds of clients are out of our league.'

'I see.'

Gillespie continued. 'We're pretty manic at the moment, and Susan never was good with stress'

'And what did your sister do for the business?'

'Office manager. Kept us all on track.'

'So, if the absences were a regular occurrence, what made you check in on her this time?'

'She was off ill quite a bit, but I nearly always got a text first thing to explain why. Very, very occasionally she wouldn't text until late morning if it was a migraine. Looking at the screen would make it worse, you see. But today I hadn't heard anything, and it was after lunch. So I rang the house phone. It's next to her bed. Even when she was very poorly, she would always pick up. When she didn't, I got worried and went round, and...' Gillespie's words tailed off.

'We're very sorry for your loss, Noel. We know this can't be easy for you, but if we could just ask a few more questions, we can get out of here and leave you in peace. Is that ok?'

Gillespie nodded, lifting the shaking cup to his mouth.

'Did your sister have any enemies that you know of?' asked Jones.

'Susie? No way. She was such a gentle soul.'

'And she didn't owe anyone money?'

'God, no. She never borrowed a penny in her life, and was totally against gambling. Said it was sinful. She wouldn't even do the lottery.'

'And what about boyfriends?'

'She didn't trust men. Not sure why, but she never had any boyfriends that I can remember.'

Phillips shifted slightly in her seat. 'Noel, I'm sorry, but I have to ask: did she ever pay for sex?'

Gillespie looked shocked. 'Susie? She was a virgin, Inspector. Devout.'

Jones looked up from his notepad. 'A Catholic?'

'Yes. She didn't believe in sex out of wedlock and was virtually married to the church. I used to call her "Sister Susie"; the amount of time she spent at church, she may as well have been a nun.'

Phillips changed tack now. 'Can you tell us what you know of her movements yesterday?'

Gillespie drained his mug and set it down. 'She came in early – about eight – because she was organising a cleaning group at the church from 4 p.m. Susie being Susie, she felt guilty about leaving early; but then again, she felt guilty about pretty much *everything*. Forty years-plus of Catholicism can do that to you. I knew how much her work at the church meant to her and had no issue with her taking time out for it. But still, she *would* insist on coming in early and working through lunch to make up the hours.

'Yesterday was no different. She managed to clear her desk and left the office around two. Told me she had a few errands to run, stuff to send at the post office, then the dry cleaners to pick up an order and home to change into her cleaning clothes. As far as I know, she cleaned the church and went home.'

'And you didn't speak to her after she left the office?'

Gillespie dropped his chin to his chest before shaking his head. 'No. I had my head in work all afternoon...' Tears formed. '...maybe if I had, she'd still be alive.'

Phillips reached out and placed a reassuring hand on his wrist. 'Please don't blame yourself, Noel. This wasn't your fault.'

'I can't get rid of that image of her with the bag over her head. Who would do something like that to my little sister?'

Phillips held his gaze. 'That's what we're going to find out.' She stood, Jones following her lead a second later. 'If you think of anything else, no matter how insignificant, please call me. I'll leave my card here by the phone.' She placed a reassuring hand on Gillespie's shoulder for a moment before heading for the front door.

4

B ack at Ashton House Police Headquarters, Phillips sat
at her desk and tried to figure out if Noel Gillespie's
grief was genuine or not. It had appeared so at the
house, but something had been gnawing at her on the drive
back, something she couldn't quite put her finger on. Looking
around the room, she wondered if the sterile workspace they
now called home could be affecting her instincts. She remembered the original Greater Manchester Police HQ at Bootle
Street – a grand, white stone Victorian work of art in the heart
of the city. As grubby and run down as it had been at the end of
its life, it had possessed a certain romance and aura; a proper
old-school nick where you felt like a real copper. She had loved
it from the moment she stepped inside as a uniformed police
constable over fifteen years ago. By comparison, the 'state of the
art' building that now housed the GMP – on an industrial
estate in Failsworth, six miles out of Manchester – was a soulless block that could easily be mistaken for an insurance
company's HQ. Looking around the room, pausing to watch
Jones and Bov hunched over their PCs writing up overdue
reports, she couldn't help but wonder if modern spaces such as

these were counter-productive when it came to catching criminals.

Leaning back in her chair to think about the case, she allowed her gaze to drift out through the window, zoning out, almost trance-like.

Jones prodded his partner. 'Bov, she's got that *look*.'

'You're right. She's onto something, Jonesy.'

'What is it, Guv? What are you thinking?'

Snapping back into the room, Phillips turned her attention back to the boys. 'What are you two gabbing on about?'

'You had that *look* on your face. You know, when you're putting something together.'

'It's probably nothing, Jonesy, but the brother's registration plate. Did you see it?'

'Private, wasn't it?'

'Yeah, but not the type you'd pick up for five hundred quid from the DVLA. It was shorter than that, "NG 58". I don't know that much about them, but I'm sure you'd be looking at thousands for a plate like that. The car must only be worth twenty-five K and looked pretty basic, so why not spend the extra cash on the next model up? Doesn't that strike you as a bit extravagant – particularly for an accountant?'

Bov turned his computer monitor to face Phillips. 'Just looking here, Guv, you're right. There's a similar style plate for sale, just shy of ten grand.'

'Exactly. Maybe it's nothing, but you know that feeling you get when something just *doesn't* fit?'

'Instinct, Guv. It's what makes you such a good copper,' said Jones.

'Sadly, not in everyone's eyes.' She pointed to the DCI's empty glass-walled office at the end of the room. 'Where is Brown anyway?'

Bov glanced at the ceiling. 'He's been up there at least half

an hour. I'd say he's probably elbow deep in the Super's arsehole by now.'

'You're not kidding. He's got his head so far up her backside,
she can brush *his teeth* at the same time as *her own*,' said Jones.

All three laughed.

Phillips's face straightened first. 'Heads up, he's back. And
he's got company.'

Jones and Bovalino turned to see Brown entering the squad
room with a young, suited man in tow. He was mixed-race, tall
and slim, with a police ID on a lanyard around his neck.
Walking in front of him, Brown looked even shorter than usual.

'Gandalf and the hobbit,' Bov muttered under his breath as
Brown arrived.

'Right, you lot.' Brown addressed the three. 'This is DC
Entwistle. As of today, he'll be joining the team.'

Phillips couldn't hide her surprise. 'Joining *this* team? In
what capacity?'

'As a detective. Why else would I be giving him to you?'

'But I have all the detectives I need on my squad, sir.'

'That's just it, Inspector. It's not *your* squad anymore, it's
mine, and Entwistle is the newest edition. He's a criminology
graduate, not to mention a gun with social media and digital
technology. He's forgotten more about computers than you lot
will ever know. His ability to track victims and suspects' digital
footprints will save this department a fortune in man hours.
That's your desk over there, next to DC Bovalino.' Brown
pointed to the empty space next to the big Italian. 'This here is
DS Jones, and you've already met *DI* Phillips. I'll leave you in
their capable hands for now.' Turning on his heels, he headed
for his office.

Entwistle offered his outstretched hand. 'DI Phillips, it
really is an honour to meet you.'

Phillips ignored him, instead following Brown into his office and slamming the door behind her. 'What are you playing at, Brown?'

'You will address me as Detective Chief Inspector, Guv or Sir. Have you got that?'

'Have it your way, *sir*. We don't need fresh-meat detectives on this team, and you know it.'

'Personally, I've never known a squad that *doesn't* need more detectives, whatever their experience level.'

'We run a tight ship here and we don't need to babysit any rookies. Especially not on the Gillespie case. It's far too important.'

Brown appeared even more smug than normal. Placing one hand in his pocket, he inspected the fingernails on the other. 'This news may not have filtered down to *your level* yet, but the Chief Super has just asked me to take on the role of diversity ambassador for the GMP. Entwistle's appointment makes the right impression in my new role.'

'You're bringing him in because he's *black*?'

'Mixed-race, actually.'

'Black, mixed-race, does it matter? Do you ever stop playing politics?'

'This is the modern world of policing, Phillips. Battles are won in the boardroom now.'

'You're just doing this to piss me off, aren't you?'

Brown took a seat in the oversized black leather chair delivered just yesterday. 'If you think I'd waste my time coming up with ways to piss you off, then you flatter yourself. Having said that, if Entwistle joining the team means you would like a transfer, then just say so and you're gone.'

'You'd like that, wouldn't you?'

'Very much indeed. I may have inherited you, but it doesn't mean I have to keep you. I don't like your methods and I certainly don't buy into the "heroine" bullshit you've been peddling. You harboured a fugitive and got yourself shot by a psycho. There's nothing heroic about that.'

'I've paid for that mistake. You know that better than anyone.'

'Yes I do, *Inspector*. Personally, I think you got off lightly with just the demotion. If it wasn't for the whole thing playing out in the media, with you somehow considered a hero by the public – you'd be in a cell right now, just like Chief Constable Blake.'

Phillips struggled to keep her disdain for Brown in check. '*I did what was right.* An innocent man came to me looking for help. What was I supposed to do? Abandon him?'

'You were *supposed* to follow procedure. Bring him in. Not run off like some vigilante. Your actions resulted in the deaths of two people and almost got you and Michaels killed in the process. Dead bodies. Is that what you call good policing, Phillips?'

Ready to blow, she just managed to stop herself. 'Just because I don't play politics doesn't make me a bad copper. My team get results!'

'Yeah? Well, you'll get even more with Entwistle on the team, won't you? It's about time this squad stepped into the digital world.'

'We already have.'

'Really? Have you seen Bovalino using a PC?' Brown pointed towards the team, who had obviously heard him through the glass and turned to look. 'It's like watching a gorilla shoving rocks around a boulder.'

Phillips glanced to her left and caught Jones's eye for just long enough. The look on his face told her she couldn't win. It was time to back down.

'Entwistle is the first step in the right direction for this squad. You and your two cronies will give him your full support. Do I make myself clear, *Detective Inspector*?'

'Crystal.'

Phillips headed for the door before Brown stopped her in her tracks. 'Oh, and I forgot to ask: do you like what I've done with *your* old office?' There was a wide grin across his face.

Phillips surveyed the room briefly. 'Yeah, it's good to see you've lowered the furniture to the right height.'

5

From his position in the darkened garden, he marvelled at the fact that, in a crime-riddled city such as Manchester, most people hadn't invested in security lights. What's more, they appeared happy to go about their business with the curtains or blinds open, in full view of anyone wishing to watch from outside.

Standing in the freezing cold shadows of the tall trees surrounding him, he observed her evening routine once again, conscious of his hot breath visible in front of him. No matter how many times he stood in this exact spot on her lawn, staring through the kitchen window, he never failed to marvel at the way she moved around the space with a rhythm that was beautiful, almost theatrical. Time had been kinder to her than Gillespie, yet still her clothes, thick glasses and limp hair made her look older than her years. Maybe that was part of the problem with her marriage?

He checked his watch: 8.28 p.m. Right on cue, her husband walked into the kitchen, just as he did every night. Placing his bag on the bench, he loaded it with a thermos flask and a box of sandwiches freshly prepared by her. The usual chatter ensued before he slipped on his heavy winter coat and scarf, kissed her on the cheek and headed for the front door. A heavy thud echoed through the night air as it closed. A moment later, the car engine rumbled to life, followed by high-pitched reversing tones, before he engaged drive and headed for his night shift at Manchester Airport.

Just like that, she was alone until 7 a.m. the following morning, with only her decrepit chocolate Labrador for company. If she really knew where her husband was spending the night, she might not be so keen to see him go. After all, *she* wasn't the only one he'd been watching the last few weeks.

He looked on as she busied herself with the washing up, clearing away the remnants of the evening meal. She was a traditionalist, washing everything by hand in the sink in front of the window. Now, vigorously scrubbing a large pan, she looked up and stared out into the garden. For a moment, her eyes appeared to fix on him. His heart jumped and he held his breath, waiting for her to acknowledge him. Evidently, she could see nothing more than her own reflection in the glass. Still, something had clearly spooked her, for she reached over and closed the blinds to the outside world.

'I'm afraid they won't help you, Dee-Dee,' he whispered into the silent garden.

DESPITE THE COLD, an hour passed surprisingly quickly as he maintained his position in the shadows, listening to the sounds of the surrounding streets and households going about their business. As was the case each evening, the back door opened at 9 p.m. and the old Labrador hobbled into the garden to relieve herself before retiring for the night. He had grown fond of the old girl, and genuinely enjoyed the few moments they shared during his visits. Cautious at first, a few doggy snacks had broken down the barriers, and now she lay happily on her back as he stroked her belly, legs splayed, face content.

At 9.05 p.m. on the dot, the back door opened and the chocolate Lab returned to the house. The kitchen light went out. Then, a moment later, the upstairs landing light came on, followed by the one in the bathroom. He could see her preparing for bed on the other side of the frosted glass. With no knowledge of her bedtime routine, he imagined her desperately scrubbing her skin, washing away the grime and grit that had blackened her soul for so many years. Soon he would help her find a purity she had never known.

The toilet flushed and, as water rattled down the drainpipe, she switched off the bathroom light and headed for her bedroom, which overlooked the back garden.

Another ten minutes passed before her bedroom light flicked off, plunging the property into complete darkness.

He closed his eyes, painting pictures in his mind of what lay ahead. Not long now, Deidre McNulty. Not long now.

6

Phillips unlocked the heavy front door and stepped inside the warm red brick terraced house, throwing off her shoes and coat in the ornate entrance hall. Making her way through to the large extended kitchen-diner, she was greeted by Floss, her blonde pedigree Ragdoll cat, snaking between her legs, purring loudly with delight.

'You're a sight for sore eyes,' she said, picking her up and cuddling her tightly. 'Why can't humans be as nice as cats, hey?'

She placed Floss back on the floor and opened the fridge. She pulled out a ready-meal Lasagne, a tin of expensive Waitrose cat food and a bottle of ice-cold Pinot Grigio. She bent over and filled the bowl under Floss's prodding nose.

After she despatched the Lasagne to the microwave, she grabbed a long-stemmed glass, poured herself an extra-large measure, and made a mock toast. 'Here's to another day above ground, Floss. And to the wonderful world of police politics, of which I am a master, or should that be *disaster*?'

Gulping down the cold liquid, she drained the glass, loudly wiping her mouth like a thirsty child on a hot day. Floss finished her food and looked on as Phillips poured a refill. 'I know, Floss, I know. Drinking on a school night isn't good, but *you* try working with Brown. The man's a total idiot. All he cares about are statistics and budgets. He doesn't give a shit about the victims and catching the bastards that are out there, killing people's daughters, sisters and mothers.' She took a large mouthful. 'He just wants a nice, neat, *cheap* result to show off to the Chief Super. And don't even get me started on her. The way she smiles in a briefing – as if she truly cares – when actually she's taking mental notes of how she's gonna screw you at the first chance possible.' Another gulp. 'Clowns, the pair of them – like Crusty and Sideshow.'

The microwave pinged, signalling it was time to eat. Grabbing a fork, she peeled off the plastic film, placed the container straight onto a tray and headed into the living room. She switched on the TV.

Surprisingly hungry, she demolished the meal in no time before retrieving the remaining Pinot from the fridge. She drank it quickly and allowed herself to relax into the large couch. A few minutes later, she was fast asleep.

Floss's rough tongue licking her fingers eventually woke her. Lying face down, she felt cold, wet saliva on her cheeks. Lifting herself up, she noted the wet patch on the blue cushion. 'Classy girl, Jane,' she mumbled, sitting up.

Blinking her vision into focus, she stroked Floss, who had jumped into her lap, and stared at the familiar face on TV. It was Marty Michaels, delivering a re-run of his morning magazine show that aired daily on Sky. After cutting short his self-imposed hiatus following their macabre experience, Marty had recently signed a big-money TV contract, plus landed a book deal to tell his side of the story. Despite the horrific events, he had added even more weight to his formidable reputation, star status and power. After almost losing *everything*, Marty was back at the top of the celebrity tree, raking in millions in the process.

She looked down at the cat purring loudly in her lap. 'If ever there was an example of how times change, *Marty* is it. A murder suspect six months ago...now the nation's TV darling with people lining up to hear about the sex crimes and murders. Whereas I – in the exact same time – have gone from an ambitious, successful murder squad DCI to a powerless, disillusioned Detective Inspector, working for a *total* wanker.'

If the cat was listening, she wasn't showing it.

'You know, almost every day, without fail, I wish another SIO had taken the call that morning. That someone else – anyone but me – had been given the so-called "case of a life-time". That investigation was supposed to cement my reputation and fast-track my career. Instead, it almost cost me my life and flushed my career down the toilet.'

She switched off the TV and checked her watch. It was 3 a.m. 'Time we were in bed, Floss. Come on.'

7

Bovalino watched with bemusement as Entwistle grappled with the multitude of wires under the desk next to him, intermittently sticking his head up to type something on either his laptop or the tablet locked into the docking station. After ten minutes of mumbling and tapping, the new recruit finally signalled everything was working to his satisfaction.

Bov compared Entwistle's gleaming kit to his own ageing PC. 'How come you've got all the new gear, then?'

'Dunno. The guv ordered it for me.'

'Phillips did?'

'No, Brown. He told me he wanted some digital expertise on the team and asked me what I needed. This is it.' Entwistle smiled broadly.

Bov leaned across the desk. 'Listen 'ere, son—' His accent was thick Mancunian. '—let's get one thing straight from the off. There's only one "Guv" round 'ere, and that's Phillips. Brown may be the boss, but she's the guvnor. You can call him anything else you like, but if I hear you call him "Guv" again,

I'll take that posh laptop of yours and stick it up your arse. You got that?'

Entwistle raised his arms in defence. 'Jesus, yeah, I got it.'

Bov held Entwistle's gaze for a long moment before turning his attention back to his own desktop PC and typing slowly on the keyboard with two fingers.

A minute passed before Entwistle dared speak again. 'Bov?'

'Hmm?' the big man replied without taking his eyes off the screen.

'What's your theory on the Gillespie murder?'

'Too early to say.'

'It looks ritual though, doesn't it? I mean, it has all the hall-marks of a symbolic killer, right?'

Bov looked up. 'And you're basing your thoughts on what exactly?'

'Well, the way the body was placed. Tied to a chair in the middle of the room, facing the TV. The see-through plastic bag over the head so she could see her killer, but then the black Xs placed over the eyes. No signs of sexual assault—'

'Says who?'

'Well, we won't know for sure until the post mortem, but there doesn't seem to be any signs of it.'

Bov leaned back in his chair and folded his arms, 'Did I miss something? I don't remember you being at the crime scene.'

'Er, no, but the guv – sorry – *DCI Brown* said it was unlikely.'

'And you believe everything he says, do you?'

Entwistle looked confused. 'He's the SIO in charge of the investigation. Surely he knows what he's talking about?'

'How long have you been a copper, Entwistle?'

'Twelve months next month.'

'So, you have extensive experience, then?'

'Not exactly, no, but I do have a first class criminology degree.'

Bov laughed. 'So what you're saying is that, in between getting pissed and parading around in fancy dress at uni, you managed to get to a few lectures on "textbook" crimes, did you?'

Entwistle blushed. 'Look I'm not suggesting uni compares to real life—'

'Good.' Bov leaned forwards again. 'Cos it doesn't. In real life we don't have the luxury of distance, pontificating or navel gazing. We have to deal with the reality of murder and its devastating effects on the victims and their families. That's why we never jump to conclusions, we never assume – ever – and we always keep an open mind. Do you understand?'

Entwistle nodded.

'How did you end up here, son?'

'I was on the people-trafficking team over in Leeds and my DCI was mates with Brown. I did a piece of work last year tracking a gang through social media. Brown found out about it and said he needed someone like me on his team.'

'Did he, now? Look, let me give you some advice, son. I've been doing this almost twenty years, and during that time I've learned that there are two types of coppers in this world: those who look for the simplest solution to a case, and those who never jump to conclusions. They think outside the box and will not rest until they get the right result – not just the easiest or quickest. You need to decide which kind of copper *you* want to be. Quick and easy, or thorough and determined?'

'Thorough and determined, every time!' Entwistle said enthusiastically.

'Really? I'll remind you of that as this investigation unfolds. Because not everyone upstairs appreciates that approach. It's not always easy to be that kind of copper round 'ere, let me tell you'.

'I'm determined to be the best copper I can be.'

Bov nodded slowly. 'We'll see, but for now you can start by

forgetting all that criminology bollocks and crack on with the task in hand. Track Gillespie's phone on the day she died.'

'On it like a car bonnet.'

Bov shook his head, half smiling. 'Jesus. Give me strength.'

8

P hillips jumped in the passenger seat of the unmarked Ford Mondeo, the sickly smell of ancient cigarette smoke still clinging to the upholstery. Jones sat behind the wheel and she passed him a hot cardboard cup. 'One peppermint tea for Jonesy. God knows how you can drink that stuff.'

Jones smiled. 'I'm an ex-smoker who drinks like an Irishman at a funeral. It's my way of apologising to my body. Besides, coffee is like ingesting liquid stress.'

Phillips took a sip of her skinny latte, and chuckled as she glanced back at the coffee shop where she'd just bought their beverages. 'You've gotta laugh, don't you? Barristas earn just over minimum wage, and yet they ponce around with all the swagger of bloody rock stars.'

'What do you expect? You live in Chorlton, for God's sake. One of the "wankiest" places on the planet. *Everyone* round here takes themselves seriously.'

'Everyone? Are you including me in that?'

Jones looked Phillips up and down. ''fraid so, Guv. *You* are a bona fide "Chorlton Wanker"'.

'Piss off!' She punched him playfully on the arm. 'All right, let's go. The post mortem is at nine-thirty. We've got half an hour to get to the MRI.'

'Gotcha.' Jones placed his cup in the central console, then pulled away from the herb, heading for the Manchester Royal Infirmary and Susan Gillespie's post mortem.

He was soon navigating his way through the backroads of Chorlton towards Whalley Range. 'So what's the deal with you and Brown, Guv? I mean, I know he's not our kind of copper, but we've dealt with his type before. They come and go on their way up the ladder, but Brown seems different. I've never seen you get so agitated by another copper. What bothers you so much?'

'Aside from the fact he took my job?'

'It's more than that. There's something else going on between you and this guy.'

Phillips looked out of the passenger window and sighed. 'I guess it was bound to come out at some point.'

'What was?'

Phillips growled through her fingers. 'I cannot believe I'm saying this out loud...I may have slept with him back when we were in uniform.'

'No way.'

'Yes way.'

'How the bloody hell did that happen? The guy's a midget. I mean, he's Ewok-small.'

'Don't remind me. Every time I think about it, I get a little sick in my mouth. Probably why I've blanked it from memory.'

'But how the hell did you end up in bed with Brown?'

'You really want to know?'

'Yes, I bloody do.'

'Shit. I can't believe I'm telling you this.'

'Spit it out, for God's sake!'

'Ok, ok. Here goes. So, just after I started on the beat in

Manchester, I got very drunk at a Halloween party. Brown was there, dressed as Gene Simmons from Kiss and wearing stacked heels. He didn't look that short on the night, and was actually quite charming. He paid me a lot of attention and eventually asked if he could walk me home – which took forever in those bloody glam rock boots of his. We finally got to mine. He invited himself in for coffee, then made his move. It'd been a while, so I thought, "What the hell".'

Jones smiled broadly. 'How was it?'

'Absolutely awful. He's hung like a church mouse.' Phillips wiggled her little finger for effect.

'Brilliant!'

'Seriously, I put my hand down there and almost burst out laughing. It was like a button mushroom, not to mention the fact he'd had way too much to drink.'

'So, he couldn't perform?'

Phillips shook her head. 'Not that it would've mattered. There really wasn't anything to perform with.'

'Wow. DCI Fraser Brown. A massive prick with a tiny willy. So that's why he hates you so much?'

Phillips eyes narrowed. 'Yeah, but there's more.'

'This gets better?'

'So, after his little "performance issue", he was desperate for another date; wanted to show me what he was really capable of. Once I'd sobered up, there was no way in hell it was going to happen. He kept asking, and eventually, to let him down gently, I told him I didn't want to date coppers, that it would be messy mixing work and pleasure. Thankfully he accepted that, and everything was fine. Until, that is, he caught me snogging another copper at another party.'

'Oh dear.'

'Oh dear indeed. Especially given said copper was DCI Campbell.'

'The Silver Fox?'

'The very same.'

'Jesus, Guv. He's retired now. He must have been ancient at the time?'

Phillips punched Jones on the shoulder again, harder this time. 'You cheeky bugger. We actually got together at his fiftieth birthday party.'

'And how old were you?'

'Twenty-four. He was a really good-looking older guy and it was just a fling, nothing serious. But of course, Brown didn't see it that way. He called me a lying bitch after he saw us – said I was only with Campbell to get promoted. He later claimed Campbell was the reason I got DS before him. Nothing to do with the fact I was the better copper.'

'And he's *still* holding a grudge?'

'Yeah, fifteen years on he still believes I slept my way up to Detective Chief Inspector. It didn't help that he had to transfer to Leeds to get DCI and I managed it in Manchester. He always thought GMP was the more impressive force and would look better on his CV.'

Jones pulled the car up at a red light on the edge of Moss Side, preparing to cross the Princes Parkway towards the MRI. A moment later, they moved on.

'I know he's a bit of an idiot, but maybe you could learn something from him, Guv?'

'Like what?'

'Like how to get yourself back to DCI sooner rather than later. *You* should be running this squad, not Brown. But that's not going to happen if you keep fighting with him.'

Phillips stared out of the window. Jones was right, of course, but following his advice would be easier said than done. 'So how do I play the game then, Jonesy?'

'I'm not suggesting you pretend to be best mates. Just try and hide the fact you hate him every time you set eyes on him. It's written all over your face.'

'It's that obvious?'

'To a blind man, Guv, and it's bloody awkward to be around.'

Phillips raised her hands in mock defeat. 'All right, all right. I'll try and get along with him. For the good of the team. But I'm not making any promises. There's something about him that makes me want to punch him in the mouth every time I see him.'

The hospital came into view up ahead. Jones smiled. 'We all feel like that, Guv. He has a very punch-able face. The trick is not to let it show.'

'I'll see what I can do.'

9

Like most British hospitals, the mortuary at Manchester Royal Infirmary is in the lower basement. Phillips and Jones took the stairs to avoid the early morning rush of outpatients. After being buzzed through the heavy locked door, the familiar, overpowering stench of chemicals hit them. No matter how many times they visited, it never got any easier.

Dr Tanvi Chakrabortty waited for them inside, dressed in perfectly pressed blue scrubs, her long brown hair tied back against her head and the slightest hint of make-up accentuating her classic features. On the table next to her was Gillespie's body, eyes closed, torso and genitals covered by a green sheet.

'Morning Jane, Craig,' she said as they walked in. She was surprisingly tall up close, and moved with an elegance that seemed perfectly deferent to the lifeless bodies that required her patient, methodical inspection each day.

'Morning, Tan. What have we got?' Phillips asked.

'Considering the frenzied nature of her last moments, it's quite unusual that we found no sign of a struggle. Nothing under the fingernails, and her feet have no abrasions or lacerations. We did find bruising on her wrists and ankles from the cable ties, but nothing excessive; the killer didn't break the skin, for example. But the bruising does mean she was alive when she was tied to the chair, so it's highly likely she died in the position in which you found her.'

'Cause of death?'

'Asphyxiation. The plastic bag wasn't a prop; it's your murder weapon. I estimate she was killed between seven and nine on Tuesday evening. Her stomach was full of undigested mashed potato, pork chops and green beans, so she was killed not long after her evening meal.'

'Was she sexually assaulted?'

'No.'

'Any prints or DNA?' asked Jones

'Plenty of DNA from the victim's urine, which was all over her legs and clothes. But none from the killer. Whoever did this was extremely careful. No prints or fluids on the body or anywhere else in the house. We did find traces of latex, the kind used in medical gloves, which explains why nothing showed up. As well as large quantities of benzalkonium chloride on the bag and her cardigan, around the neck and shoulders.'

Jones looked confused. 'Benzal-what?'

'Benzalkonium chloride. It's commonly found in anti-bacterial agents, like wipes and cleaning sprays.'

'So, our boy was thorough?' said Phillips.

'Very, and I'm afraid it's impossible to tell whether the killer was a man or woman. The fact Gillespie was almost certainly suffocated in the chair gives us no indication of the killer's height or potential build.'

'So, we're no further then?'

'Not necessarily. I *can* explain why she doesn't appear to have fought off the killer and there's no signs of a struggle.'

'Go on.'

'We found large quantities of benzodiazepines, methoxyflurane and chloroform in her blood and on her face, with a particular concentration around her airways. It's a potent mix that can be delivered in liquid form. As there were no signs of bruising around her nose or mouth, it would suggest she inhaled it; probably through some kind of spray.'

'And what's the mix commonly used for?' said Jones.

'That's just it. It's not. It's probably home-made. Which means your killer likely has some knowledge of chemical compounds.'

Phillips eyed Gillespie's cold, grey face a moment. 'What level are we talking, Tan? Novice, expert?'

'Most of the basic information needed to create such a concoction is available online, but the fact that each component was well balanced in the final mix would indicate they have some knowledge that goes beyond your average man-on-the-street. Having said that, you wouldn't need a medical or chemistry degree to make it.'

Phillips summarised her thoughts. 'So, what we're saying is that Susan Gillespie had her dinner before being knocked out with a potentially home-made sedative. She was then tied to a chair and suffocated with a plastic bag between seven and nine on Tuesday evening?'

'That's about the size of it, yes.'

Jones scribbled a note in his pad before looking at Chakrabortty 'Anything else we need to know, Tan?'

'Just that she was a virgin. When I checked for signs of sexual assault, her hymen was still intact.'

'Jesus. She was the original forty-year-old virgin.'

Chakrabortty flashed a smile. 'Forty-three, to be precise.'

10

Back at Ashton House the team gathered in the incident room as they waited for Brown to emerge from his office for the debriefing. Jones and Bov chatted amongst themselves while Entwistle kept his eyes fixed on the array of screens in front of him.

Phillips allowed herself a smile of satisfaction as she watched Brown pace around the glass box, nodding subserviently into his iPhone. She guessed the Chief Super was on the other end of the call and wasn't happy. It was just a matter of time before Brown passed whatever grief he was getting straight onto her and the team.

A few minutes later, Brown ended his call and emerged from his office.

'Here we go,' Phillips muttered under her breath as Brown stomped towards them, his face almost puce.

'Right. Which one of you silly bastards has spoken to the press about this case? I've just got off a call with the Chief Super. Turns out some fucker has leaked details of the crime scene to that hack Don Townsend, who's gone and splashed it across one of the red-tops.'

Jones flashed a glance at Phillips, who did her best to hide the smile creeping into the corners of her mouth.

Brown continued. 'Not only is this murder the talk of Manchester; it's now making national headlines. Meaning we have to be seen to be giving it every possible resource – and that will royally fuck our budget. So, who was it?'

Each of the team looked at each other and then back to Brown, shaking their heads in turn.

'Who's Don Townsend?' asked Entwistle.

Brown glared at his protege, saying nothing before casting his eyes around the room, 'If I find out one of you is behind this leak, I'll have you back in uniform quicker than shit through a goose. Do you understand me?'

A unison of nodding heads was followed by a chorus of 'sir's.

Brown pulled up a chair and straddled it back to front a la David Brent from *The Office*. 'So, what have you got? I need something to placate her.'

Jones pulled out his notepad. 'Well sir, there was no sign of forced entry, so we're pretty sure Susan Gillespie either knew her killer or was comfortable enough to let them into her home at night.'

'*And?* We knew that yesterday.'

Jones paused a moment before continuing. 'The post mortem indicates she was suffocated with the plastic bag after being tied to the chair—'

'We could have guessed that when we found the body.'

Phillips jumped in. 'Correct, sir. At that point it was just a guess. Jones is now confirming our suspicions.'

Brown shot her a look. She held his gaze until he looked away. 'Carry on, Jones,' he said impatiently.

'The post mortem also confirmed she was drugged using a powerful, potentially home-made, sedative, which explains why there was no sign of a struggle. The killer

wore latex gloves similar to those used by medical professionals.'

'So, we can assume the killer has medical knowledge?'

'Chakrabortty suggests not necessarily. Perhaps just some
experience in handling chemicals. You can buy latex gloves in
any pharmacy,' said Jones.

Brown waved his hand like a Roman emperor. 'Continue.'

'Based on the bruising patterns on her wrists and ankles,
she was still alive when she was tied to the chair, which would
suggest she was suffocated in the position we found her. And
finally, before they left the house, the killer used an anti-bacterial agent to clean the outside of the bag as well as a host of
surfaces, including all the downstairs door handles, to cover
their tracks.'

'So no prints or DNA at all?'

'Other than Gillespie's, no, sir. Seems she was something of
a loner and a clean freak.'

'And what about the sex-game-gone-wrong angle?'

'Unlikely, as she was a virgin,' said Phillips. 'Her hymen was
still intact.'

Brown flinched at talk of the female anatomy. 'So, that's it?
That's the sum total of our investigation into one of the most
sadistic murders in the GMP's history? She was drugged by
someone she opened the door to, then suffocated with a plastic
bag after being sedated. How the fuck am I going to sell that
upstairs?'

Phillips ignored Brown. 'Entwistle, what did you come up
with when you tracked her mobile?'

The rookie, clearly not expecting the question, appeared
flustered as he tried to gather the data sheets from his desk
before passing copies round to each of the team.

Phillips ran her eyes over the pages in her hand. 'What are
we looking at?'

'Well, these are maps of her mobile phone's movements. I

was able to track it through the GPS data her service provider shared with me this morning. Each point represents a different location and is time-stamped. As you can see, on the day of the murder she left home at 7.30 a.m. and arrived at the family business at 7.50 a.m. She remained there until 2 p.m., and we pick her up next at the post office in Cheadle at 2.20 p.m. The dry cleaners appears at 2.30 p.m., the Co-op on Cheadle High Street at 2.40 p.m., back home for 3.10 p.m. and then St Patrick's Catholic Church at 3.45 p.m., where assume she stayed – or at least, her phone did – until 6.05 p.m., returning home at 6.10 p.m. The phone remained switched on within the house until 4.02 a.m., when we lost the signal. Digital Forensics confirmed the phone was recovered and had run out of power. They're currently going through the data on the device for anything that might help identify the killer.'

Phillips studied the map closely as the rest of the team looked through their own copies in silence.

Brown stood, pushing his chair away dramatically. 'See? That's modern policing from a modern copper.' He slapped the pages in his hand. 'We know where our victim was from the moment she got up to the moment she was killed.'

'Well, we know where her phone was, at least,' said Phillips, before catching Jones's icy stare. She knew she was supposed to be playing the game, but Brown made it so hard with his wild assumptions and desperation to please the top brass.

Brown responded sharply. 'I think it's safe to say we're not dealing with a career criminal deliberately trying to set a digital trail, Inspector. Susan Gillespie was a law-abiding spinster whose technical knowledge was more than likely limited to switching the bloody phone on and off. We're probably safe to assume her movements match her phone's.'

Phillips avoided looking at Jones. She couldn't sit quietly when Brown's sloppy policing threatened their chances of finding the killer. 'With respect, sir, it feels a bit early for assumptions. All we know for sure is what we've got back from Chakrabortty. Everything else needs further investigation.'

Brown turned to face Phillips square on. 'I couldn't agree more, Inspector. But so far – aside from Entwistle – you and your team have delivered nothing new in two days. Get me more evidence and I'll gladly listen to your theories. Until then, I'll be forced to listen to my own instincts and superior experience.'

Phillips opened her mouth to speak but thought better of it.

'Entwistle, good work, son,' Brown continued. 'The rest of you, it's time to raise your bloody game.' With that, he headed back to his office.

When the door was securely shut, Phillips turned to Jones and Bovalino. 'That was fun. Right you two, I need you to retrace Gillespie's movements at the post office, the dry cleaners and the Co-op. See if anyone remembers seeing her or anyone who may have been with her.'

'On it,' said Jones.

Bovalino nodded.

'As for you, Golden Boy—' Phillips pointed at Entwistle. '—you're coming with me to church.'

11

P hillips drove with Entwistle in the passenger seat. The journey from Ashton House to Cheadle would take twenty minutes and she wanted to use the time to think. Sadly, the new boy had other ideas.

'It's really great to be on your team, Guv,' he said enthusiastically as Phillips pulled the car onto the M60, heading south on Manchester's outer ring-road. 'You're a bit of a legend in the Force.'

'Not really,' Phillips replied in a disinterested tone, trying her best to kill the conversation.

'I mean, what you must have gone through in that house with Michaels. Not many people could survive that.'

Phillips remained silent, but he wasn't giving up.

'What was it like, Guv?'

'What was what like?

'Getting shot. What did it feel like?'

She pulled into the outside lane and accelerated rapidly, pushing her right foot down on the pedal to help stem the rush of anxiety suddenly consuming her. 'It bloody hurt.'

A long moment of silence ensued, before Entwistle pushed on. 'Did you think you were going to die?'

Phillips glanced at the speedo and realised she was pushing 95 mph. Releasing her foot, the car slowed to a more reasonable 75 mph. 'Look, Entwistle, I'd prefer it if what happened in that house stays there. People died, and I was almost killed.'

'Yeah, and you still got a result.'

'We might have got a result, but at what cost? I know the media made it out to be some kind of heroic deed, but let me tell you this: it was the single most idiotic thing I've ever done. Coppers are supposed to uphold the law, not break it; going into a murder suspect's house without backup was unthinkable. Lunacy, plain and simple. I'm lucky to be alive.'

Entwistle appeared unsure of what to say next, and they drove in silence a few minutes. As they passed the Stockport Pyramid, he shifted in his seat. 'Guv, can I ask you something else?'

'As long as it's nothing to do with the Michaels case.'

'It's not. It's about the team.'

'Go on.'

'Well, I get the impression Jones and Bovalino think I'm Brown's boy and might not trust me.'

'Quite the detective, Entwistle.'

'So, it's true, then?'

Phillips glanced at him before turning her attention back to the road as she took the exit for Cheadle. 'Look. We go back a long way, and as a team we've been through a lot. We've got one of the best conviction rates in the Force and we know how to get results together. Anyone coming in is going to find it hard to break into that.'

'And it doesn't help that Brown brought me in?'

'No, it doesn't.'

'And because I'm black they think it's a box-ticking exercise?'

Phillips shook her head. 'The colour of your skin has nothing to do with this. You've just joined the team at a difficult time. When Brown took my job, he took over *my* team and it's been a tough adjustment. You have to remember, I ran the squad for five years. Brown has totally different methods to mine and none of us are finding it easy. You coming in without warning, hand-picked by him – that's going to make it hard for the guys to accept and trust you straight off the bat.'

'What about you, Guv? Do you trust me?'

'Entwistle, trust has to be earned. You've been here a couple of days and I have no background on you. No recommendation from anyone that I know. Brown brought you in without so much as a word to the rest of us. If you prefer to follow his lead as SIO, that's up to you, but I won't change my approach and nor will Jones and Bovalino. If you want to be part of the team, you don't have to be like us or do it how we do, but you'd better not pass anything on to Brown that he could use against us.'

'Funnily enough, Bovalino said something very similar yesterday.'

'Like I said, we've been together a long time. We look out for each other on this team. Always.'

Entwistle nodded but remained silent, the only sound the noise of the tyres bumping up and down on the weather-beaten road.

Phillips began to reduce speed. 'What's the name of the street we're looking for?'

Entwistle checked the directions he had keyed into Google Maps on his phone. 'Fraser Road. It's at the end of here and then left.'

12

F ather Maguire was brushing leaves away from the front door of St Patrick's when Phillips and Entwistle arrived. After the initial introductions, he led them down the side of the sixties-built building and into the attached house. They followed him through to a small kitchen-diner, where he removed his hat, gloves and scarf, appearing to lose ten pounds and fifteen years of age in the process. Phillips placed him in his early fifties and noted his sporty physique, looking slightly incongruous covered in the black garb and white collar.

'Tea or coffee?' he asked.

'Coffee for me,' said Phillips

'Same for me, please.'

'Right, three coffees it is. I'm afraid it will have to be Instant.' Maguire switched on the kettle, then pointed to the kitchen table in the middle of the room. 'Please take a seat.'

A minute later, he placed three steaming cups of coffee on the table and took a seat beside them.

Phillips took a tentative sip from the scalding liquid. 'Father, we'd like to talk to you about the murder of Susan Gillespie.'

Maguire shook his head sombrely. 'A very sad business.'

Entwistle moved his coffee to the side, then pulled out his tablet and portable keyboard, placing them on the table in front of him. Phillips shot him a look.

'It's for taking notes, Guv. Saves typing them up later.'

She turned her attention back to Maguire. 'Father, we believe you may have been one of the last people to see Susan alive. Can you confirm the last time you saw her?'

Maguire took a sip of coffee before cradling the mug in both hands. 'Susie was here until just after six. She was in charge of the cleaning group and was the last to leave. I had to lock up the church after she'd gone, which takes a few minutes. By the time I got back here to the house, it was about quarter past.'

'Did you remember seeing anyone hanging around the church at that time?'

'No, but it was dark and we have a lot of mature trees in the grounds. At night, it's hard to see anything without a torch.'

Entwistle tapped lightly on his keyboard as Phillips continued. 'You say she was the last to leave. Who else was here that night?'

'Mrs Kelly and Mrs Higgins.'

'And what time did they leave?'

'About ten minutes before Susie. You see, Susie always liked to catch up with me at the end and go through what they'd done.'

'Do you know whether Mrs Kelly and Mrs Higgins went straight home?'

'I can only assume so. They both live locally, and at their ages I doubt they had plans to paint the town red. They're both octogenarians.'

'Do you have their addresses?'

'Of course. They both live on Sandringham Lane, but I can't be sure of the exact numbers.' Maguire stood. 'I'll go and get them from the office. Won't be a moment.'

Phillips and Entwistle sat in silence, but Phillips surveyed the room. It was furnished simply, and appeared untouched since the eighties. Definitely in need of some TLC. The cream-coloured crucifix hanging on the wall opposite looked nicotine-stained. Maguire returned a minute later, a bright yellow Post-it Note in his hand. 'They live a couple of doors down from each other, number eleven and seventeen Sandringham Lane. It's just a few minutes' walk across the green.'

Phillips thanked him and put the note in her pocket. She took another sip of her coffee, giving herself a moment to think. 'Tell us about Susan, Father. What was she like?'

'She was a wonderful woman, Inspector. A true Christian, and devoted to the church; particularly since her parents died. She was their main caregiver, you see, and when they passed, she seemed lost for a time. She had always played an active role in the congregation when they were alive, but it seemed to ramp up even more after they died, as if she was filling the void. She was here most days in some capacity, but also spent a lot of time at St Joseph's Hospice, visiting patients without family of their own. She couldn't bear to think of anyone dying alone in their final days. In fact, she was of particular help to Father Donnelly, our old parish priest who passed a few months back. Pancreatic cancer. It was mercifully quick in the end.'

'Do you know if she was romantically involved in any way?'

Father Maguire shook his head. 'She was incredibly shy and seemed quite wary of men. Social situations were off limits unless they involved the church. Strangely, she seemed to blossom inside these walls.'

Phillips changed tack. 'Do you know how business is for the Gillespie's?'

'Fine, as far as I can tell. The family business has been going for over forty years, and Noel and Susie always seemed busy.'

'No debts or finance issues?'

'None that I'm aware of.'

'And how about gambling. Did Noel or Susan gamble at all?'

Maguire smiled wryly. 'I feel confident saying that Susie would never gamble. She felt it was against God. As for her brother, outside of the confessional, Inspector, people rarely share their intimate secrets with a priest. Unlike his sister, Noel is what we would call *lapsed* when it comes to attending mass. Strictly christenings and funerals these days. In fact, the last time I saw him was at Father Donnelly's funeral with Susie a few weeks back.'

'And how did he seem?'

'Same as anyone else on the day...quiet, mournful perhaps? Difficult to say with Noel, as he always looks a little troubled. I've often wondered what haunts him so much.'

'I know what you mean. Would you know who benefits from Susan's will, Father?'

'I don't. It's not something we ever discussed. I would imagine Noel and the girls.'

'His daughters?'

'Yes, Susan's nieces, Hollie and Chloe. She loved them like her own, Inspector.'

Phillips finished her coffee and placed the cup on the table. 'One last question, Father. Can you think why anyone would want to kill Susan?'

Maguire closed his eyes a moment and took a deep breath. 'I honestly don't. If there were more people like Susie, the world would be a much better place. She really was an extraordinarily kind human being.'

Phillips stood up, extending her hand to Maguire. 'Well, thank you for your time. We should be going.'

Entwistle followed her lead, quickly packing away his tablet and shaking Maguire's hand on the way out.

'Just one thing, Inspector,' the priest called after Phillips as she stepped out into the church grounds. 'When can we expect Susan's body to be released? I'm thinking of the arrangements for the funeral, you see.'

'It really depends on the coroner's verdict. Hopefully not long.'

'Thank you. I'll wait to hear from Noel in that case.'

Out by the roadside, Phillips turned to survey the church and wondered if Susan's killer had been lying in wait in the shadows that evening. As thorough as they'd been at the house, they may not have been so considered away from the crime scene. It was worth checking out. 'Entwistle, get forensics to go through the church grounds. See if we can find anything connected to the murder.'

Entwistle pulled out his phone. 'Yes, Guv.'

'And get some intel on Susan's will. There's something about the grieving brother that's not sitting right with me. While you're at it, look into Noel's financials, see if he's in trouble. That house of Susan's must be worth close to four hundred grand. If he stands to inherit it, that could be motive enough to kill her.'

'On it.'

Phillips opened Google Maps app on her phone and typed in the address from the Post-it Note Father Maguire had given her. 'Right, let's pay a visit to Mrs. Kelly and Mrs. Higgins, they only live down the road. And let's hope one of them has some biscuits – I'm starving.'

13

D eidre McNulty poured the steaming tomato soup into a flask before placing it into her husband's rucksack, alongside a Tupperware container filled with freshly made cheese and tomato sandwiches. She liked to ensure he was well fed during his nightshift at the airport while stuck in a cold warehouse, ferrying freight for the early morning flights. She knew his decision to move to nights six months ago had been a necessary one due to their financial issues, but she really missed him in bed. Nothing sexual of course; that had subsided eighteen months ago when she had undergone chemotherapy and a mastectomy for a malignant tumour in her breast. Feeling like she'd been hit by a truck had made just getting in and out of bed an effort; anything else was impossible. That horrific period of their marriage had changed the dynamic of their relationship forever. They had never been prolific lovers, but a couple of times a month had seemed to satisfy Kevin for most of their twenty years together. Since the chemo, he appeared as content as she was with the abstinence that had become the norm, and they were more like best friends than lovers now. No. What she really missed was his big arms, wrapped tightly around her in bed. That feeling of being safe and warm. Totally protected.

'Right, love, that's me.' Kevin walked into the kitchen just before 8.30 p.m.

'You really have lost weight, haven't you?' she said, observing him in the tight-fitting jumper he wore.

He looked down at his belly, then back at Deidre. 'You think so?'

'Absolutely. All that time in the gym is paying off.' She giggled. 'I'll have to watch you and those air-hostesses at work.'

Kevin appeared embarrassed and turned away in search of his car keys.

Deidre moved towards him, arms outstretched. 'I do wish you didn't have to work nights, love'.

Kevin turned around and smiled, pulling her close. 'We've been through this, Dee-Dee. You know we need the money. And it won't be forever, I promise.'

Deidre nestled her head under his chin. 'I miss you, that's all.' At that moment, the dog padded over to join them and pressed her hindlegs against Kevin's thigh. 'And so does Cocoa. See? She doesn't want you to go either.'

'I'm being tag-teamed here, aren't I?' he joked. 'Sorry Dee-Dee, I've really got to go or I'll be late.' He kissed her on the cheek before zipping up his coat and pulling on his woolly hat.

'Are you sure you're going to be warm enough?'

'Yes, Dee-Dee. You ask me the same question every night, and my answer is always the same. I'm going to be absolutely fine. Once I get the truck warmed up, it's actually quite cosy in the cab. It's all good.' Throwing his rucksack over his shoulder, he headed for the front door.

Deidre followed him out into the narrow hallway. 'See you later. Love you, babe.'

'Love you, too.' Kevin smiled faintly as he closed the door behind him.

Deidre stood motionless as the sound of the engine filled the air. Then the headlights illuminated the glass in front of her and Kev reversed out onto the road. A moment later, he set off on the fifteen-minute journey to the airport, less than five miles away.

When the sound of engine faded in the distance, she knelt down and rubbed the dog's head. 'Just us girls again, heh Cocoa?' Then, standing up, she went back into the kitchen and started on the washing up.

It was close to nine o'clock when she'd finished. Cocoa was snuggled down in her basket. 'Time for a cuppa for me and a pee-pee for you.' She went over to the back door and let the dog out, who trotted into the garden.

The kettle boiled as she stood in front of the sink. Catching sight of her reflection in the window, she felt a sudden chill run down her spine and quickly closed the blinds. Leaving them open had never bothered her when Kevin was at home, but over the last few weeks she'd grown increasingly anxious when they were open after dark, almost as if she was being watched. Once again dismissing the idea as ridiculous, Dee-Dee made herself a sweet tea to take upstairs to bed.

At 9.05 p.m., she opened the back door and Cocoa sauntered back into the kitchen. 'Come on, you.' Grabbing her mug, she switched off the kitchen light, 'Up we go.'

Deidre's bedtime routine had never been elaborate, but since beating cancer she rarely wore make-up. She had lost interest in it, and after a quick once-over with a facecloth, followed by flossing and brushing, she was ready for bed.

Switching off the bathroom light, she tip-toed across the landing to her bedroom, a strange habit she'd had since childhood. She couldn't recall why it had started, but it had never left her. She flicked the hall light off and closed the bedroom door before climbing under the duvet, just as Cocoa jumped up onto the bed and curled up next to her feet. 'I may not have Kev, but at least I've got you, Cocoa.' She slid her feet under the big Labrador's warm body. 'Like a hot-water bottle, you are.'

As usual, she managed just one chapter of her romance novel before she began to drift into the story, half awake, half dreaming. Catching herself nodding off, she closed the book and placed it on the nightstand. 'Night night, girl.' Cocoa was already snoring loudly as she switched off the bedside lamp.

Deidre drifted off quickly, and felt as if she had been asleep for hours when she woke with a start. Instantly sitting upright, she peered into the darkened room. What on earth was that noise? It sounded like a giant rat scratching at the walls. She sensed something moving around by the door, but without her glasses she struggled to make it out. Fumbling a moment, she found the bedside lamp and flicked it on. Light flooded the room, and she screamed when she found herself almost nose to nose with Cocoa. 'Jesus you scared me.' She rubbed the dog's head. 'Why are you standing? That's not like you.'

Cocoa whined, glancing between Deidre and the bedroom door, a pained look on her face that Deidre didn't recognise.

'Are you okay, sweetheart? Did you have a bad dream?' She reached for her watch, squinting to see the numbers. 'Eleven o'clock? You're kidding me, we've only been in bed an hour and half. Come on, you, get back on here.'

Cocoa's whining grew in volume. She turned her head back to the door before padding over to it and scratching at it noisily.

'Stop it, Cocoa. You'll ruin the paintwork. Kev'll go mad.'

The dog continued scratching and whining.

'Get away from there, you daft thing.' Deidre jumped out of bed, went over to Cocoa and grabbed her collar. 'Come on now, stop being silly. There's nothing there, see?' She yanked open the door.

'Well...that's not *strictly* true.' The voice from the darkness was ice cold.

Deidre screamed in terror as she came face to face with a man wearing a surgeon's mask.

'Now, now. There's no need for that, Dee-Dee.'

Before she could react, the man lifted his arm and sprayed something into her face.

A moment later, Deidre McNulty's world went black.

14

His heart pounded as he waited for the sedative to wear off. The rush he'd felt killing Susan had taken him by surprise, but he felt better prepared for this kill. Everything was ready, and he would enjoy this even more.

Standing at the bottom of her bed, he looked with some regret at the lifeless chocolate Labrador laid out by the door. As much as he'd liked the old girl, a barking dog was too much of a risk tonight.

Finally, Deidre began to stir. He watched intently as she became aware of her position on the bed, her wrists and ankles securely tethered with a series of connecting cable-ties to the metal bedposts above and below her. The black gaffer tape across her mouth ensured any screams were stifled as her eyes met his.

'Wakey wakey, Dee-Dee.'

The terror on her face was exactly as he had fantasised so many times before. A wave of satisfaction surged through him. 'Dee-Dee. *I* am going to take the tape off your mouth, and *you* are going to stay calm and quiet. Do you understand me?'

Her eyes bulging, Deidre nodded vigorously.

He leaned over and ripped the tape off, causing her to yelp. 'There, that's better. Now we can have a proper chat.' He perched on the bed next to her, like a doctor visiting a patient. 'By the way, I'm very sorry about your dog.' He drew her attention to Cocoa's position on the floor.

'Oh my God! What did you do to her?'

'Let's just say she won't be needing to use the garden tomorrow night.'

Deidre began to sob.

His voice was almost soothing. 'Don't cry, Dee-Dee. She was very old. She can't have had more than a couple of years left at best.'

She stared at him, eyes wide. 'Wh-who are you? How do you know my name?'

'Tsk. Tsk, Dee-Dee. You really don't remember me?'

Deidre shook her head.

'I don't know whether to be offended or take that as a compliment. I'll admit, I have changed in the last twenty-eight years.'

She pulled at her restraints. 'What are you going to do to me?'

'All in good time. For now, we should concentrate on jogging that memory of yours. I can't leave here until I'm convinced that you not only remember me, but remember what was done to me all those years ago. Back when you chose to look the other way, just like Susie.'

This seemed to jog Deirdre's memory, and her face began to change in front of him. He smiled broadly. 'It's coming back to you now, isn't it? I can see it in your eyes.'

Deirdre looked him up and down. 'It can't be.'

He smiled. 'It can be, and probably is. Come on, Dee-Dee...'

'*Winnie?*'

His smile vanished at hearing the nickname that had caused him so much pain as a child. 'I do not answer to that stupid nickname anymore.' He walked over to the chest of drawers opposite the bed, his back to Deidre. Picking up the plastic bag, he pulled it taut in his hands, checking its strength. It had worked perfectly on Susan Gillespie, and he had every faith it would do likewise with Deidre.

Behind him, he heard her breath quicken. 'Are you going to kill me?'

He turned to face her. 'That very much depends on you,' he replied, revelling in the power he now wielded. How times had changed.

'Did you kill Susan?'

'Yes, I did.'

'Oh my God!'

'I did it for a good reason. Do you want to know why?'

Deirdre remained silent, clearly afraid to speak.

'I wanted information, so I asked her a few simple questions. Sadly for her, I didn't like the answers she gave me. They just weren't good enough.' He smiled. 'I'm sure you can do better, though. You can tell me what I want to know, can't you, Dee-Dee?'

She nodded.

'Good. But I must warn you, the same rules apply. I'll ask you the questions. You give me the answers I want – *or you die.* Understood?'

Deidre stared blankly at him, tears rolling down her cheeks.

'Do you understand the rules, Dee-Dee?'

'Yes, yes...I understand.'

He came over to her and she instinctively recoiled as he readied the bag.

'What's that for?'

'*I'm* asking the questions. Besides, you'll see soon enough.' His delivery changed now to mimic that of a TV game-show presenter. 'So, Deidre McNulty, your starter for ten. Do you admit to knowing what was happening to me all those years ago?'

'What do you mean?'

'Wrong answer.' In one move, he had deftly pulled the bag tightly over her head.

Panic instantly filled her eyes as the plastic relentlessly filled her mouth and nostrils. He silently counted to ten before yanking the bag away.

Deidre gasped for air as saliva poured out of her mouth and nose.

'This is how Susan played the game – pretending she didn't know what I was talking about. And look what happened to her. Is that what you want too, Dee-Dee?'

She shook her head as she sobbed. He marvelled at how similar her reactions were to Susan Gillespie's.

He held the plastic bag ready once more in his gloved hands. 'I'll ask you again. Do you admit to knowing what was happening to me all those years ago?'

'Yes. Yes, I do!'

'Good, now we're getting somewhere. So, why didn't you do anything to help me?'

'I was scared. He said I'd be next if I said anything about his special visits.'

He stared at her silently, his jaw clenched rigid as he digested her words.

'Oh Winnie, I'm so, so sorry.'

'That's not the answer I'm looking for.'

He thrust the bag over her head and gripped it tightly. Deirdre's body started to writhe as she gasped for breath, the restraints pulling noisily on the metal bed posts. He increased his grip as her mouth fought the thick plastic – in and out, in and out. Her eyes widened as she jerked her head to either side, desperately seeking oxygen. It was useless, though, and in less than two minutes she had finally stopped moving.

He maintained his grip another thirty seconds, her dead eyes staring back at him as he breathed deeply to control the adrenaline rushing through his veins. Finally, he let go and checked her pulse. It was done.

Stepping away from the bed, he retrieved a long white cable-tie, looped it around her neck and pulled it tightly, enclosing her head inside the bag. Next, he took out the gaffer tape, tore off four strips and carefully placed two Xs over Deidre's eyes. When he was happy with the way everything looked, he stood and surveyed the scene, processing what Deirdre had said.

He felt no remorse. She deserved to die, just like Susan Gillespie.

For the next hour, he painstakingly cleaned the surfaces within the room, the dog's collar, then the bannister along the stairs, and finally the backdoor handle.

When he felt confident no-one was watching, he slipped silently through the back door and into the shadows beyond.

15

P hillips was getting out of the en suite shower just before 7 a.m. when her phone rang on the nightstand next to her bed. She rushed to answer it, leaving a trail of wet footprints on the carpet. The call was brief; another murder with all the hallmarks of Susan Gillespie's killer. After Brown hung up, she immediately called Jones and Bovalino, brought them up to speed and instructed Jones to call Entwistle.

Forty-five minutes later, thanks to her wailing siren and blue lights, she pulled up to the address Brown had barked down the phone. Jones and Bovalino arrived as she got out of the car, and together they headed to the SOCO tent that had been erected outside the 1930s semi-detached house on another quiet suburban street in Cheadle. They quickly pulled on their white overalls and hairnets in the freezing cold enclosure.

'Did you get hold of Entwistle?' asked Phillips, her breath visible.

'Yep. He may already be inside. He lives in Gatley, so he's the closest.'

'Is Brown here?'

'His car is parked next to Evans's down the street, so I'm guessing the dynamic duo are already inside.'

Jones zipped up his suit. 'That's all we need; "Mr Keen" and "Mr Assumptions" trampling all over the crime scene.'

Pulling on latex gloves, Phillips readied herself. 'Right. Let's get in there and see what conclusions Brown's *superior experience* has brought him to, shall we?'

Jones and Bovalino fell in behind Phillips as she headed inside the house.

Entwistle was waiting at the top of the stairs. 'Up 'ere, Guv. This one's in the bedroom.'

The team moved cautiously, careful not to step on any evidence the killer might have left behind.

When she reached the landing, Phillips leaned in close to Entwistle, her voice a whisper. 'Brown?'

She followed his gaze and walked over to the main bedroom at the front of the house, stepping over a chocolate Labrador lying prostrate in the doorway as the body of Deidre McNulty came into view. On the floor next to the bed, two smiling faces stared at her out of a broken picture frame.

Brown stood with his back to her, watching as Evans and one of his team photographed the scene from a multitude of angles.

Hearing her, he turned. 'Inspector,' he said, as Jones and Bovalino came in.

'Sir.'

Brown turned back to the bed. 'This is Deidre McNulty. Forty-one years old, married, no children. One dog, both deceased.'

'This looks almost a carbon copy of the Gillespie crime scene,' said Jones, surveying the body. 'Do we think we're looking for the same killer?'

Brown rubbed his chin and nodded. 'Certainly looks like it. Evans, what can you tell us?'

The newly appointed senior CSI appeared nervous, and coughed slightly as his words seemed to stick in his throat. 'Er, well, consistent with the Gillespie murder, the victim was secured to the bed whilst she was still alive – the bruising and small cuts around her ankles and wrists would indicate that. As we can see, the killer used cable-ties linked together to form longer chains. Based on rigor mortis, I would estimate the time of death between 10 p.m. and midnight last night. At this stage, having done a preliminary examination of the body, there is nothing to indicate she was killed by anything other than the plastic bag over her head. Obviously, Dr Chakrabortty will be able to tell you more in the post mortem.'

Phillips pointed to the doorway. 'What about the dog?'

'I'm no vet, but it looks like a broken neck. Poor thing.'

'Jesus, that's cold,' whispered Jones.

'So is suffocating a middle-aged woman in her bed,' Brown snapped. 'Can we focus on the priority here.' Evidently, he wasn't much of an animal lover.

Phillips glanced at Jones and gave him a reassuring nod. 'So it looks like we could be looking at a serial killer, sir? Should I brief the Profiling Team?'

'He's not a serial killer until he murders three people. Let's not get ahead of ourselves by wasting budget on profiling. And besides – I can do that myself.'

'Really, sir. You can do profiling?'

'Yes, Phillips. Really.' Brown eyed each of them. 'This is a fucking PR disaster. None of this gets out to the press – not a word. Are we clear?'

The team nodded. 'Who found her?' Phillips asked.

'The husband. Came home from his night shift at 6.30 a.m. Found her when he came upstairs to get changed,' Brown replied.

'And where is he now?'

'Across the street with Deidre's best friend and a Family Liaison Officer.'

Phillips looked at Jones. 'Shall we take the husband?'

He nodded.

'Bov, take Entwistle and canvas the neighbours. See if they saw anything last night.'

Jones and Bovalino began to move out of the room, then stopped in their tracks as she spoke again. 'Sorry, sir, are you ok with that plan?' Phillips smiled with forced deference.

The question and its tone seemed to catch Brown off guard momentarily, 'Er, yes. That's fine. Right, well, I can't stand about here all day.'

Phillips nodded empathetically. 'Of course not, sir. I'm sure you'll want to get back to HQ and brief the Chief Super.' If there was one thing she didn't miss about her old job, it was dealing with the bullshit that came with managing upwards, particularly DCS Fox.

Brown surveyed the room, appearing unsure of his next move. 'Well, it looks like you have it under control, Inspector. Best I get back to Ashton House and get to work on the media plan. It's going to need some skilful handling on this one.' He moved towards the door before turning back to Phillips. 'I want to be kept across everything, Inspector, no matter how small.'

'Of course, sir.'

'Very good.' Brown headed for the stairs.

The team stood in silence for a moment, then Bov walked over to the bedroom window and looked down on the street. 'He's outside,' he said finally.

Jones turned to Phillips and laughed. 'Jesus, did you take a happy pill this morning or what? I think that's the first time you two have been in the same room and it hasn't turned into a shit fight. And how many times can you call him *sir* in one conversation?'

'Just taking your advice, Jonesy. And besides, he's out of our way now, heading back to a world of shit from the Chief Super. What's not to like?'

Bov walked over to Entwistle as he walked into the room. The big man clamped his hand on the rookie's shoulder. 'Right, Guv, I'll take Golden Boy with me and speak to the neighbours.'

'Good man.' Phillips cast her eye over to Deidre McNulty one last time before turning to leave. 'Jonesy, let's go and see what the husband has to say for himself.'

16

Claire Speight answered the door to a carbon copy 1930s semi located fifty meters down the street from Deidre McNulty's house. Inside, however, in stark contrast to her friend's home, it had been modernised to a high standard. Claire showed them into the tastefully decorated living room, where Kevin McNulty sat on a large leather sofa, cradling a glass of what looked like brandy. Phillips noted a graze and dark bruising above his right eye. Staring into the distance, he appeared not to notice them as they entered. A Family Liaison Officer – FLO – stood behind him.

'Mr McNulty. I'm Detective Inspector Phillips and this is Detective Sergeant Jones. We'd like to ask you a few questions if you're feeling up to it?'

McNulty looked up at them. He'd been crying and his eyes were puffy and bloodshot. 'I'm sorry, what did you say?'

'I'm DI Phillips and this is DS Jones. Could we talk to you about Deidre?'

McNulty placed his glass on the coffee table in front of him next to the box of tissues. He plucked one out and began dabbing his eyes as Claire Speight made her excuses and headed to the kitchen with the FLO.

'I'm sure this is very difficult for you, Kevin, but can you tell us what happened leading up to finding Deidre?'

Jones pulled out his notepad and pen.

McNulty blew his nose loudly into the hanky still in his left hand, and took a deep breath to steady himself. He appeared on the verge of tears again. 'I finished work at 6 a.m. and pretty much headed straight home.'

'And where is work?' asked Phillips

'The airport. I work in the freight team, driving one of the trucks.'

'How long have you been doing that?'

'About five years, but the last six months I've been on nights. Better money. Some of Dee-Dee's treatment was only available privately.'

'Treatment? Was she ill?'

'Breast cancer. Thankfully in remission after a mastectomy and chemo. We had to borrow money from my parents to pay for some of the medications, and I've been paying it back since I went on nights.'

'I see. So you finished at six. What happened after that?'

'I had a natter with a couple of the day-shift lads about the football this weekend, United – City. We had a little bet on who was going to win, and a bit of banter. Then I came straight home.'

'Talk us through what you saw when you entered the house. Anything unusual when you came in?'

'Not really. Everything seemed normal at first. Although Cocoa would usually start barking when she heard my key in the door. Today she was quiet as a mouse. I shouted up to Dee-Dee, who would always say hello back, but again nothing. That's when I started to panic a little. I thought she might have been sick overnight. Since the cancer, her immune system is shot to pieces. So, I rushed upstairs and into the bedroom. I was in such a rush I tripped over the dog and banged my head on the drawers as I went down.' He touched his temple. 'That was when I saw Dee-Dee lying there. I thought I was dreaming at first. It was so surreal. Everything seemed to slow down and I just couldn't process what I was seeing.'

'We know this must be very difficult. But if you could tell us what happened after that, it could really help.'

Tears streamed down McNulty's cheeks. Jones leant forwards and lifted the box of tissues closer to him. McNulty wiped his eyes and took a deep breath, clearly struggling. 'I got up and went over to her, shouting her name over and over. I was shaking her by the shoulders, trying to wake her up. I couldn't stop crying. I couldn't believe she was dead. I mean, who would do that to my Dee-Dee?'

'That's what we're going to find out.'

'And you were the one who made the call to the police?' asked Jones.

'Yes, I'm not sure when. It's all a bit of blur, but I remember fumbling for the phone, knocking a picture off the cabinet as I did, which smashed on the floor. It was of our wedding day.' His shoulders began to shake. He was clearly struggling to hold it together.

Jones scribbled in his pad. 'And did you touch anything else after you called the police?'

'Just Cocoa. I went to check if she was still breathing but she was cold, just like Deidre.' McNulty began to weep.

Phillips decided he was unlikely to give them anything else for now. 'Kevin, I'm just going to speak to Claire. I'll leave you with DS Jones for a few minutes.' Jones glared at her, clearly unhappy with the arrangement.

In the kitchen, Phillips found Claire Speight, her eyes red and puffy. She stood with her back to the sink, light flooding in from the winter sun. The FLO sat at the kitchen table opposite her while Sky News played on a small wall-mounted TV.

'Claire, could I ask you a couple of questions, please?'

'Of course, Inspector' Picking up the remote, Claire muted the TV.

'What's your relationship to Deidre and Kevin?'

'Deidre was my best friend. I was their chief bridesmaid.'

'And when did they get married?'

'I think it was 2001. I remember it was on the August Bank Holiday.'

'So, you've known them both a long time?'

'God yes, since college.' Speight smiled a moment, then her bottom lip began to tremble. 'Sorry, it's all come as such a shock.'

'Are you ok to carry on? I can come back later if you'd prefer?'

'No, no, honestly I'm fine. Please, go on.'

'All right. What was the name of college where you met?'

'South Manchester Technical College. Dee-Dee and I did a BTEC in hospitality management and Kevin did the first year of engineering. But he hated it and left. Got a job working for a bakery doing deliveries.'

Phillips was taking notes now. 'I see. Do you know Susan Gillespie?'

Claire looked at her in surprise. 'You mean, the local girl who was murdered last week?'

'That's the one.'

'Yes, but only to say hello, and only through Deidre.'

'They were friends?'

'Not really. They knew each other from school and they both went to the same church. That was about as far as it went, I think.'

'They never spent any time together?'

'Not that I was aware of. Maybe at church functions, but to

be honest, since Dee-Dee beat the cancer, she's not been out much. The mastectomy really dented her confidence. She seemed happiest at home or coming over here for a coffee and a chat.'

'I see.' Phillips paused a moment. 'Tell me, how did you hear about what happened to Deidre today?'

'Kevin called me on the mobile.'

'What time was that?'

'I'm not sure. Sometime before seven, I think.'

'Could you check for me?'

'Is it important?'

'Maybe not. It just helps to have the details.'

Speight retrieved her mobile from the counter where it was plugged in on charge. She unlocked the screen, then checked her call log. 'Says here, 6.44 a.m.'

Phillips noted it on her pad. 'One more thing, and, well, it's of a delicate nature. Do you know if Deidre and Kevin were happily married? Any issues we should know about?'

Speight appeared uncomfortable with the question. 'Nothing that I was aware of, Inspector. But if they *were* having problems, she'd have told me. We told each other everything.'

'Of course, I'm sorry. I have to ask.' Phillips affected her best smile. 'Well, I think that's everything we need for the moment. Claire, because of the sensitivity of this case, could I ask that you keep any details Kevin may have shared with you regarding the crime scene confidential?'

'Of course, Inspector.'

'Thank you for your help.' Phillips moved back into the living room. 'Jones...' was all she needed to say to get him off the sofa in a flash. She stopped to speak to McNulty one last time, who remained seated. 'Kevin, I want you to know we're doing everything we can to catch Deidre's killer. If you remember anything else that might help us, no matter how trivial, please let us know. The Family Liaison Officer can get in touch with us anytime, day or night, and she has my details if you want to speak to me directly.'

McNulty looked up at her, his eyes red. 'Th-thank you,' he mumbled.

Phillips gave him a brief nod. 'We'll be in touch when we know more.'

17

B ack at Ashton House, the team was gathered in the incident room. Brown's office was empty, the Chief Super having summoned him upstairs an hour ago.

Phillips turned to Jones and Bovalino. 'How far did you get on retracing Gillespie's movements on the day she was killed?'

Bovalino leaned forwards in his chair. 'She went where her phone log says. Nobody saw anything suspicious and everyone said she seemed happy enough. Nothing untoward.'

'We got the same from the priest and her cleaning partners. A couple of lovely old dears in their eighties. Both short-sighted and stone deaf, so neither saw or heard anything on their way home. What about you Entwistle?'

Entwistle stood and handed out copies of Gillespie's digital activity in the weeks leading up to her death.

Phillips scanned it for a moment. 'Okay, talk us through it.'

'Yeah, come on, Golden Bollocks,' said Bovalino.

Entwistle shot him a look.

Jones laughed. 'I think you've upset *her*, Bov.'

Phillips smiled. 'Ignore them, Entwistle. They're just jealous because they're still using index cards.' She turned her attention to Jones and Bovalino now. 'And pack it in, you two. If Brown comes in and hears you pissing about, he'll go off his head.'

'Got his period again, has he?' joked Bovalino. Jones laughed – until he saw Phillips's face.

'You do remember I'm a woman, don't you?'

Jones looked sheepish. 'Sometimes, Guv.'

Phillips produced a fake smile. 'Funny, aren't you? Don't let HR catch you two talking like that or you're in big trouble.'

Jones smirked. 'We won't, Guv.'

'Let 'em catch us,' added Bovalino.

Phillips glared at them both. 'Are you quite finished?'

Looking like a couple of chastised schoolboys, Jones and Bovalino replied in unison, 'Yes, Guv. Sorry.'

Phillips turned to Entwistle. 'Back to you.'

'Ok, so I've given you copies of all the social media relating to Susan Gillespie over the last six weeks. Either her own accounts or places where she's been mentioned. As you'll see, she really only used Facebook and, occasionally, Instagram. She was on Twitter, but only to follow the family business page and the St Patrick's community page.'

'A church on Twitter?' said Jones.

Phillips drummed her fingers on the desk. 'Pretty progressive, our Father Maguire, heh?'

'Certainly seems that way compared to other parishes within the diocese,' said Entwistle.

Bovalino appeared confused. 'What's a diocese?'

'It's like a region of the church,' Entwistle explained. 'An area that includes a number of churches under one bishop.'

'As an Italian Catholic, shouldn't you know that, you big lump?' Jones mocked Bovalino.

Phillips slammed her hand on the desk. 'What's got into

you two today? Can we please concentrate on Gillespie?' She turned back to Entwistle again.

'There's not much to go on, really,' the young officer continued. 'She certainly wasn't prolific on social media. Most of her posts were church-related...coffee mornings, pound-sales, fund-raising events and special services. The rest were work-related, reminding people of new tax regulations and upcoming deadlines.'

Phillips leafed through the pages. She stopped to examine one – an old-looking photo of a group of kids with a couple of adults in the background. She showed the page to Entwistle. 'What's this photo?'

Finding the same page, he scanned the image in more detail. 'That was posted on the day of Father Donnelly's funeral. I put it in because Father Maguire mentioned Susan had helped him a lot in the last month of his life.'

'Who was he and what happened to him?' asked Jones

'He was the parish priest before Maguire. Pancreatic cancer. This post stood out for me as the others were current. It's one of the few that gives an insight into Gillespie when she was younger.'

Bovalino read out the title under the post. 'A church trip to Lourdes. Where's that?'

Phillips opened her mouth, but Entwistle beat her to it. 'It's in southern France. A holy place of pilgrimage considered to have healing powers for the sick. It's claimed that during the late eighteen-hundreds, the Virgin Mary appeared to a young girl called Bernadette almost twenty times. She told the girl to dig into the ground until she found a spring of water. It's said that people started drinking from that spring and were miraculously cured of all manner of illness and disease. These days, over five million Catholics make the pilgrimage to Lourdes each year.'

Jones was impressed. 'Bloody hell, Entwistle – where did that come from?'

'A childhood of mass every Sunday, plus I went to *Our Lady of Lourdes* Catholic School. We were well-versed on the miracle of Lourdes and St Bernadette.'

Bovalino looked a bit confused. 'So how come you went to a Catholic school if you're black. I thought you'd be into the gospel church.'

'That's a bit presumptuous, Bov,' said Phillips.

'It's fine, Guv, I'm used to people making assumptions because of how I look.' Entwistle turned his attention back to Bovalino. 'My parents were both Catholic, and I'm mixed-race, actually. Mum's from Trinidad and my dad's from Dublin. They've been in England since the fifties.'

This seemed to satisfy Bovalino, who nodded.

'Well, as fascinating as Entwistle's heritage is, can we focus on the matter in hand, please?' said Phillips. 'So, do we think this picture was taken on a pilgrimage?'

'More than likely, Guv.'

Phillips examined it closely. 'So what's its significance to Gillespie?'

'Nothing jumps out other than she posted it on the day of Father Donnelly's funeral. She mentions him in the post. As you can see, there's a priest in the picture. I'm guessing it could be Father Donnelly.'

Phillips looked at the row of faces, all in a line and staring back at her, with the slight fuzziness that came from pre-digital images. 'Ok. So, who are the kids in the photo?' She smiled wryly. 'Judging by the looks on their faces, it doesn't appear like they were enjoying the trip. Is there a date on the photo?'

Entwistle checked his notes on the tablet in his hand. 'No date, but I've googled the branding on some of the kids' clothing, and it's coming back as popular in the early-to-mid nineties.'

Phillips pointed to one of the adults. 'And what about this older lady? Any idea who she is?'

'Dunno, Guv, but it can't be that hard to find out.'

Phillips gazed at the photo for a long moment, her eyes fixed on the image. Was it significant? It was hard to know. She closed the document and focused on Entwistle again. 'All right, what else?'

'Both victims went to the same school, but one year apart. Gillespie left St Mary's Catholic College, Cheadle in 1993, and McNulty in 1994.'

'Anything else?'

Entwistle pulled out his tablet and appeared excited by what he was about to show them. 'There is one more thing, Guv. The husband of victim two called in sick last night. I checked with his boss.'

Jones sat forwards. 'He did what?'

'He called in sick...didn't turn up for work. Well, strictly speaking, *he* didn't call in. According to the night manager, his wife did.'

'Are you sure?'

Entwistle looked triumphant. 'One hundred per cent. I spoke to his boss in person.'

Phillips's brow furrowed. 'The grieving widower told me he was at work all night.'

'Not to mention the fact the lying bastard had fresh bruises on his head,' Jones added.

Phillips felt her pulse quicken. The case was about to open up. She pointed to Jones and Bovalino. 'You two, get over there and find out what else our Kevin's being lying about. Entwistle, dig into his background and see if you can find anything to link him to Gillespie – besides his wife. In the meantime, it's time I paid Chakrabortty a visit. Let's see what she has to say about Deirdre McNulty's death.'

Gathering their notes, all four stood up from the table and

filed out of the incident room. As Phillips walked back to her desk, she considered Brown's words from Gillespie's bedside earlier. The man they were looking for wasn't a serial killer, not yet. Not until he had killed at least three people. But she had a terrible sense of foreboding that that was exactly what he was going to do.

18

When Jones rang the bell at the McNulty house for the fourth time without answer, Bovalino wandered around the back, looking for any indication of life inside. A few minutes later, he returned. 'Place looks empty. Do you think he's done a runner?'

'I bloody hope not or we're in deep shit.'

Bovalino stood back and looked up at the upstairs windows, hoping to see a nose peek out from behind the curtains. 'You think he's in bed?'

'Nah, I've been ringing that bell for five minutes. He'd have heard it by now.'

'What about the wife's mate. He could be there'

'Worth a try. It's just down the street.'

The pair headed over to Claire Speight's house. On the way, Jones's phone rang. It was Entwistle. He hit the green icon. 'Hello?'

Jones listened intently for a minute, then ended the call.

Bovalino looked intrigued. 'What's up?'

'According to Entwistle, Kevin McNulty went to school with both victims. He was four years older than them, but with only five hundred pupils in the school, there's a chance he's known Susan Gillespie for over thirty years.'

Jones raised an eyebrow. 'That's good to know. Entwistle's certainly keen to impress, I'll say that for him.'

'Yeah, but who's he trying to impress – *us* or *Brown*?'

They reached Claire Speight's house and Jones rang the bell. After a few moments, a tall, muscular man wearing a designer T-shirt and jeans answered. For a moment, Jones thought he had the wrong house. He flashed his credentials. 'DS Jones and DC Bovalino, Greater Manchester Police. Can we speak with Claire Speight?'

'Of course. Claire's upstairs in her office.' His accent was almost certainly public-school. He opened the door wider. 'Please, come in and I'll get her. I'm Malcolm by the way, Claire's husband.' He stretched out his hand.

The two shook it, then followed him inside. At the bottom of the stairs, Malcom craned his neck and called out, 'Darling. It's the police.'

A moment later, Claire Speight appeared on the landing looking nervous. 'Can I help you officers?'

'Sorry to bother you again, Mrs Speight, but we're looking for Kevin McNulty. He's not answering his door.'

'Kev?' Malcolm said. 'You should have said. He's out the back in the conservatory. It's this way. Don't worry, darling, I'll show them through.'

Jones and Bovalino fell in behind Malcolm as he guided them through the kitchen-diner and into a large conservatory that overlooked the long narrow garden at the back of the property.

Kevin McNulty sat in a wicker chair, facing out into the garden. He turned, looking surprised to see them.

'Mr McNulty, this is my colleague, Detective Constable Bovalino. We'd like to ask a few more questions, if we may?'

McNulty shot Malcolm a glance, who immediately excused himself.

'Do you mind if we sit down?' asked Jones.

'Er, no, not at all, Inspector.'

'It's *Sergeant* actually. I'm not that important, I'm afraid.' He took one of the cushioned wicker chairs next to McNulty, while Bovalino dragged over another.

McNulty was the first to speak. 'What can I help you with?'

It was Bovalino's turn to pull out his notepad, with Jones taking the lead on questioning.

'Can you tell us again where you were the night of your wife's murder?'

McNulty looked startled. 'Why – am I a suspect?'

'It's purely routine. I just want to make sure I got all the details correct last time we spoke.'

McNulty shifted in his seat before answering. 'Like I said, I was working at the airport.'

'And what time did you leave your house?

'Same as usual. Eight-thirty on the dot. It's not far and I start at nine. It gives me enough time to park up and put my sandwiches in my locker.'

Jones's eyes locked on McNulty. 'I see. And if we check the ANPR cameras, your car will pop up at the airport at that time, will it?'

McNulty didn't reply, but looked increasingly uncomfortable.

'Where were you on the night of your wife's murder, Mr McNulty?' asked Bovalino.

'I told you, I was at work.'

Jones continued to stare at McNulty. 'Then how come your manager, Gordon Stevens, reckons your wife called to say you were sick and wouldn't be in for your shift? It's in the log.'

McNulty closed his eyes and clenched his fists.

'If you come clean, we can help you. Keep lying to us and you're in a world of shit.'

McNulty opened his mouth to speak, then appeared to think better of it.

Jones spoke in a low, assured voice. 'Let me explain something to you, Kevin. To get a conviction for murder, we need to prove to a jury beyond a reasonable doubt that a suspect killed the victim, right?'

McNulty nodded nervously.

'To do that, we offer DNA evidence. You know, traces of sweat, blood, tears, stuff like that. We also put forward physical evidence, like cuts and bruises on the suspect's body, sustained during a struggle with the victim. And then there's the credibility of the suspect. Did they lie to us? Did they say they were in one place when, really, they were somewhere else? Are you following me?'

'I-I guess so.'

'Let me tell you, Kevin, from where we're sitting, it doesn't look good for you. Your DNA will be all over that room. Whether it found its way there on the night of the murder or not, that'll show up on lab tests. You admitted to touching your wife's body when you found her. You're sporting fresh cuts and bruises and, to top it all, you're lying about where you were the night Deidre was killed.' Jones leaned in close. 'As you can see, the picture I'm painting looks bad to any jury. So, unless you can provide an alibi, and sharpish, I'm about thirty seconds away from arresting you on suspicion of your wife's murder.'

'Oh God,' McNulty sobbed.

Jones had seen it all before when questioning suspects and was in no mood to relent. 'Where were you on the night of your wife's murder, Kevin?'

McNulty dropped his head to his chest. 'I knew it would come out one day.'

'What would?'

'Jesus, where do I start?'

'Try the beginning,' said Bovalino flatly.

McNulty took a deep breath, closed his eyes for a long moment before exhaling loudly. 'When Dee-Dee got cancer, it hit us both hard. She went through hell with the chemo, then the mastectomy...well, that really broke her. Even though she made a full recovery, she wasn't the same woman after treatment. Intimacy became a real problem. I never pushed her because it didn't feel right after what she'd been through. And, to be honest, I was scared how *I* would react to her body after the surgery. She seemed to sense that and, after coming out of hospital, she never let me see her naked, insisting on getting changed in the bathroom. I still loved her dearly, but over time I began to crave physical contact. You know – *sex*.' McNulty blushed.

'Go on.'

'I'm not proud of it...'

'Of what, Kevin?'

'I started using prostitutes.'

'Were you with a prostitute the night your wife died?

McNulty nodded.

'Can you tell us her name? I'm assuming it was a woman.'

'I don't know her name. I picked her up in my car in Cheetham Hill.'

'And where did you have sex?' Jones pressed.

'In my car.'

It was Bovalino's turn now. 'Can you describe her? Was she white, black? Tall? Blonde?

McNulty raised a finger to his mouth a moment, as if scanning through his memory of the night. 'She was white, average height. Very blonde – but it could've been a wig.'

'Any distinguishing marks – you know, tattoos, scars?' asked Bovalino.

'Nothing that stands out. To be honest, having sex in a car is quite tricky, so I was concentrating on that as opposed to her.'

'Where did you pick her up?' asked Jones.

'On the corner of Sherborne and Great Ducie.'

'Is that where you normally pick up women for sex?'

'It varies. The idea is to keep it random, to avoid *you* lot.'

Jones looked puzzled. 'You do know The Purple Door is only ten minutes from there, don't you? It's practically legal. Why not just go there and reduce your chances of getting pinched?'

'I can't afford that place on my wages. Plus, I don't get paid if I'm off sick, so I can't afford to lose a night's money, then spend a couple of hundred quid on a hooker. Pick 'em up off the street and you can get full sex for twenty-five quid.'

Jones sat back in his chair and thought for a moment while Bovalino scribbled in his notepad. 'So, let me get this straight. You're telling us that your alibi for the night of the murder is a streetwalker whose name you don't know, who's white, of average height and build, with blonde hair – which may have been a wig.'

McNulty laughed nervously. 'When you put it like, it doesn't sound great, does it?'

'No, it doesn't.' Jones frowned. 'So how do you explain the fact your wife called in sick?'

'The girl pretended to be Dee-Dee. I gave her an extra tenner for it.'

'Of course you did, and why wouldn't you?' Jones's tone was sarcastic.

Bovalino looked up from his notes. 'How long were you with the girl?'

'About an hour all in, I guess.'

'That takes you to about 10 p.m. What did you do after that?'

'I drove around for a bit, then came back to Cheadle and pulled the car up round the corner and went to sleep.'

'And that's where you stayed all night, is it?'

'Yes. I'm not proud of it.'

Jones pulled his mobile from his jacket and unlocked the screen. 'Would you mind if I get a picture of you, Kevin?'

'What for?'

Jones's camera clicked. 'We're going to have to track down your alibi. Hopefully this will help jog a few memories.'

McNulty's voice was a whisper now. 'Please, you won't tell Claire and Malcolm about this, will you?'

'Your secret's safe with us for now,' Jones replied. 'But until this alibi checks out, make sure you don't go anywhere. Understood?'

'Yes. You have to believe me, Sergeant, I loved my wife. I could never hurt her.'

'I really hope that's the case, Kevin. For your sake.'

Bov sat forwards. 'Did you know Susan Gillespie?'

'Who?'

'Susan Gillespie. She was murdered a few days ago.'

McNulty thought a moment before answering. 'I can't recall her.'

'Are you sure?'

'Yes, I'm sure.'

Bovalino laughed, 'Really? You went to the same school and she's friendly with your wife. Strange that you wouldn't remember her.'

'School was a long time ago.'

Bovalino made a note in his pad as Jones rose from his chair. 'We have no more questions for now,' he said. 'Don't worry, we'll see ourselves out.' Bovalino stood next and the two men walked out of the conservatory.

Malcolm Speight stood waiting in the hallway as they

headed for the front door. 'Get everything you needed, Sergeant?'

'For now.' Jones pulled the door open, before stopping in his tracks. 'Out of interest, Mr Speight—'

'Malcolm, please.'

'Malcolm. Where were you on the night of Deidre McNulty's murder?'

Speight looked taken aback. 'I was in Denmark on business. I'm out there the first week of every month.' He pointed towards the kitchen behind him. 'I can show you my passport stamps if you like?'

'That won't be necessary, Malcolm. Thank you all the same.' Jones paused a moment. 'Keep an eye on Kevin, will you? He's going through a lot at the moment. If you notice anything unusual, let us know.'

'Of course, Sergeant. Like I say, happy to help.'

'Good man.'

Jones stepped out onto the front path. Behind him, Bovalino shook Speight's hand and moved in close. 'Mind how you go, sir.'

Jones and Bovalino walked back towards the car, which was still parked outside the McNulty house. When they were a safe distance from the Speight's house, the big man was the first to speak, 'I don't trust him, Jonesy.'

'Me neither. I mean, how can he not remember what the girl looked like? He only had sex with her a couple of nights ago.'

'He's lying about something, Jonesy. I can feel it.'

'Yeah, and I'm not sure he's smart enough to keep whatever it is hidden for long. So whatever he's up to, we'll find out. I'm sure of that.'

19

Since her husband's death two years ago, Betty Clarke liked to shop at the local supermarket each night, rather than one weekly visit. It broke up the monotony of each evening, and if she arrived after 9 p.m., she could pick up fresh produce and bread that had been reduced to clear. Tonight, she found some organic bananas, a custard tart and a milk loaf for half their original price. As she wandered up and down the aisles, she smiled at the regular workers she had come to recognise over the last few years. Her last stop was always the wines and spirits section, where she would pick out a small bottle of something dry and white to enjoy when she got home. After losing Harry, she found it harder to sleep these days, and a little night-cap helped her on her way.

She never used the self-service checkout, always opting for one of the manned tills, making the most of a little chit-chat as she bagged up her groceries. Her server tonight was Angela, who was looking forward to a day-off tomorrow with her kids and planned on taking them to the park. Betty smiled as Angela shared her itinerary for the school holidays, remembering her own children running around Bruntwood Park when they were little. She missed those days but felt blessed to have grandkids to take to the same place their parents had loved; although their visits were limited to once or twice a year now. Both her son and daughter had moved away with their work, to Glasgow and Kent respectively.

Pushing her trolley filled with a couple of bags of shopping, Betty smiled as she passed the usual security guard on her way out of the store. She wished him a pleasant evening as she pulled her hood up against the cold February night before stepping out into the darkness.

One of the things she liked most about shopping late in the evening was how the empty carpark made it easy to locate her car, parked alone in a bay far away from any of the other shoppers. She wasn't the world's best parker, and preferred to leave her car in a space where no-one was likely to pull up next to her. Arthritis had taken hold in her hips and she needed to push the door fully open, taking her time getting in and out.

When she approached the car, she fished in her bag for the keys, then clicked the central-locking activation on the fob. The indicators flashed once as she pulled the trolley up to the back of the car and pressed the automatic boot release. To her surprise, it remained closed. *Is it one light or two to open?* She couldn't remember. Practically new, the car had been recently sourced by her son from one of his friends in the trade, and she was still coming to terms with how it all worked. In truth, she didn't even know the make or model was – just that it was silver – her only stipulation to Liam when buying it. She pressed the key fob again and the indicators flashed twice this time, the audible sound of the locks releasing echoing around her. 'That's it,' she muttered to herself. Opening the hatchback boot, she placed her bags inside the pristine space.

After returning her trolley, she slipped gently into the front seat and buckled herself up, switching on the heater and letting the window de-mist for a few minutes. As she sat in the darkness, she thought about Liam and the kids, and Kerry and her two boys. She really missed having them around, especially since losing her husband. Both had offered to move her closer to them, but Manchester was her home and all her friends were here. It would be lovely to see the grandkids regularly, but at seventy-two she didn't relish the thought of having to make a whole new set of friends, and she had no desire to live either in Scotland or down south. No, she was better off in Manchester, and besides, with video-calling on the mobile phone Kerry had bought for her, she at least got to see them on screen every Sunday.

Feeling like a chat, Betty decided to call Kerry on the way home, and used the hands-free function to ring her. The call connected just as she pulled out of the carpark onto the main road, and for the next ten minutes Kerry brought her up to date on everything that had been happening with the family that week on the South Coast. It was the school holidays, and Kerry wasted no time telling her mum how busy she was, planning each day to keep the kids occupied and her own sanity intact. Smiling, Betty wondered if being a parent was harder these days or whether modern parents simply weren't as resilient as those of her own generation. In her day, you just got on with it; complaining wasn't an option.

As she pulled into the drive, she said goodnight to her daughter, who promised to Skype with the boys on Sunday, then activated the automatic garage door Liam had fitted for her when she got the new car. He had been adamant it should never be left outside in a 'crime-riddled city like Manchester', as he so eloquently put it. Also, that a woman her age should not be lifting heavy metal doors anymore. She loved her boy with all her heart, but couldn't help thinking he was a bit over-protective – and a doom-monger at times. She'd lived in the same house since she married Harry almost fifty-years ago, and they'd never been burgled or witnessed any kind of vandalism. It was a lovely area.

Bringing the car gently to a stop by the breeze-block wall at the end of the garage, she pulled on the handbrake and switched off the engine as the electric door rumbled closed behind her. 'Home sweet home,' she said, unbuckling her seatbelt.

The voice from the back seat was muffled and deep. 'Hello Betty.'

Jumping out of her skin, she turned to face the man staring at her, a surgeon's mask tied across his face. 'Goodnight Betty,' he said softly, and pumped the spray dispenser in his hand.

A moment later, she slumped sideways against the driver's door, her head thudding loudly against the glass.

20

Once again, Phillips found herself stuck in the morning rush-hour traffic on the notoriously busy M60 motorway, heading from her home in Chorlton to Ashton House. It was 8.45 a.m. and she was late, *again*. Since her demotion, she was finding it harder to care about the little things that used to mean so much to her, like time-keeping, and another night of wine and sleeping on the sofa until the early hours had made it impossible for her to drag herself out of bed when her alarm triggered at 7 a.m. After hitting the snooze button several times, she'd eventually switched it off without realising it. Waking with a fright an hour later, she had dressed quickly without showering and jumped in the car.

For a moment, she contemplated activating the siren and lights to expedite her journey, but thought better of it. Instead, she people-watched, idly scanning the cars around her for inspiration on the case. Working through the information in her mind, she found herself coming back to the same two people: Noel Gillespie, for no other reason than a gut-feeling about him, and Kevin McNulty, because he'd lied about his whereabouts on the night his wife died. Hardly enough to warrant an arrest, though, and they didn't have enough for the Crown Prosecution Service to charge Gillespie either.

Traffic began to move, bringing her attention back to the road. She inched the car forwards. 'What am I not seeing?' she mused to herself.

After crawling along for another twenty minutes without any inspiration, she finally reached the Stockport exit. Mercifully, traffic began to flow again, and at 9.35 a.m. she rolled into her spot in the Ashton House overflow car park.

Checking herself in the rearview mirror, she adjusted her ponytail. Then, crunching on a mint, she stepped out of the car, put on her overcoat and scarf and walked briskly over to the main building in the sub-zero temperature.

To her relief, she noted that Brown's space – her former spot as DCI – was empty. Marvelling once again at the gleaming metal sign he had had maintenance attach on his very first day, *Detective Inspector Fraser Brown,* she couldn't help but say what she was thinking: 'Prick!'

A uniformed officer walking out of the revolving door at that moment stared at her. She blushed. 'Sorry, I didn't mean *you.*'

Inside, she activated the security gates and moved swiftly to the elevators.

By the time she reached the office, it was 9.45 a.m. To her surprise, the incident room was empty. Taking full advantage, she quickly removed her winter layers, fired up her laptop, and breathed a small sigh of relief when the screen burst into life; she'd gotten away with it, but this had to be the last time she was late.

Busying herself, she scanned through all the information on the Gillespie murder and took notes on anything that stood out about Noel and Kevin. After half an hour, she headed to the ladies, and returned just as the phone on her desk began to ring.

She rushed to pick it up. 'Inspector Jane Phillips.'

Jones sounded agitated at the other end of the line. 'Guv, where've you been?'

'The toilet, if you really must know.'

'For the last *two hours*?'

'What are you talking about, Jonesy?'

'I've been ringing your mobile since half-past eight.'

'You can't have.' Phillips fished her phone out of her pocket. It was dead. 'Shit, I must've forgotten to charge it last night. See, I—'

'Guv!' Jones broke in. 'There's been another murder in Cheadle. Looks like it could be the same guy.'

'Jesus. Where?'

Jones relayed the address and Phillips promised to be there as quickly as possible.

Charging out of the incident room, she ran into one of the uniformed support team assigned to support the murder squad.

'Where are you going in such a rush, Guv?'

'There's been another murder, Lisa. Can't stop now. I'll update you later when I know more.' Phillips continued at speed down the corridor.

'Where should I tell DCI Brown you're going?' Lisa called out after her.

'Wherever you like,' Phillips shouted back before heading down the stairs to the car park.

21

E ntwistle was standing in the doorway of the integrated garage that fed straight off the kitchen as Phillips entered Betty Clarke's kitchen in her SOCO suit. He gestured her over. 'In here, Guv.'

She stepped inside to see a silver Ford Focus with its doors open. Stooping, she peered into the vehicle to find Betty Clarke sitting upright in the driver seat with her hands on the steering wheel, the now familiar plastic bag over her head, black Xs over her eyes.

'Her name is Betty Clarke, age seventy-two,' Entwistle informed her. 'She's been cable-tied to the steering wheel by her wrists. He used one to seal the bag around her neck, then fed it through the headrest. Hence why she's sat to attention.'

'Jesus.'

Andy Evans's camera flashed, illuminating the grey walls around them.

Phillips caught his eye. 'Same guy, Andy?'

'Appears to be. Like the other victims, bruising around the wrists suggests she was alive when she was tied up. I estimate time of death between 10 p.m. and midnight last night. We'll know for sure when she's—'

'On the slab, I know.'

Evans continued about his business, his team of investigators buzzing around the body. Phillips turned her attention back to Entwistle. 'Who found her?'

'The cleaning lady, Jennie Sinclair, who arrived shortly before eight this morning. She comes in every second Wednesday and has her own key. She assumed Betty was out, so she started on the house.'

'So when did she find her?'

'Not until 9 a.m. when she came into the garage to get the vacuum cleaner. The car's interior light was on and caught her eye. She went to have a closer look and found the victim.'

'Poor cow. Where is she now?'

'In the living room. Talking to Bov and Jones.'

'Ok, let's go and see where they're at.'

Phillips led the way with Entwistle following behind. 'Is DCI Brown not coming, Guv?'

'Doesn't look that way.'

'I expect he's in with the Chief-Super.'

Phillips didn't turn around. 'I expect so.'

Jennie Sinclair sat on the sofa in the lounge room, with Jones and Bovalino perched to either side of her. They appeared to be wrapping up the interview as Phillips entered.

'If you can think of anything else, please give me a call.' Jones handed Jennie his card.

She wiped her eyes with a tissue. 'Betty was such a lovely woman. Who would do this to her?'

Spotting Phillips, Bovalino jumped to his feet. 'Guv.'

'Can I have a word, Bov?' Phillips nodded towards the hallway.

Bovalino followed her out of the room. 'Is she genuine?' Phillips whispered once they were out of earshot.

The big man nodded. 'I'd say so, Guv. She seems pretty shaken up.'

'Did she have anything useful to share?'

'Nothing, I'm afraid. She comes in every two weeks. Usually has a cuppa and a chat with the victim before she starts on the house. There was no sign of Betty Clarke this morning, so she assumed she was out and got straight on with the cleaning.'

'Isn't eight a bit early for a cleaner?'

'Apparently Betty was an early riser and liked it done first thing so she could get on with her day.'

'Entwistle told me she was here for an hour before she found her.'

'Yep. Can you imagine that? Happily cleaning the crapper upstairs, not knowing there's a dead body in the garage below. I'm surprised she didn't have a heart attack when she found Betty. She must be in her sixties.'

Phillips frowned. 'This pours cold water on school being the connection between the victims.'

'Agreed, Guv. This old dear was in her seventies. She's the same age as my mother, for God's sake.'

'I really thought we had something with that.'

'Me too.'

'Maybe she was a teacher?'

''fraid not. Jennie Sinclair has known her for years. She said Clarke was a stay-at-home mum her whole life. Her husband, Harry, was a solicitor, so she didn't need to work.'

'Could she have been a dinner lady?'

'Living in a house like this? I doubt it, Guv.'

'Damn it, Bov. That was our best lead. I...' She broke off as Jones appeared, followed by Jennie Sinclair, who smiled awkwardly as she passed them.

Jones handed her over to a uniformed officer at the front door, then joined Phillips and Bovalino. 'Seriously, what the fuck is going on?' he said. 'I've never seen anything like it.'

Bovalino leant against the wall. 'It's as if the killer is determined to rid the world of caring, vulnerable women. You talk to people that knew the victims and he may as well be killing Bambi, over and over again.'

Phillips stared past the big man. Her eyes widened into a thousand-yard stare.

'Jonesy, she's got that look again,' Bovalino warned. 'What you thinking, Guv?'

Phillips didn't answer. It took several seconds before she turned her focus back to the room, 'You might be on to something, Bov. What if he is deliberately targeting vulnerable women who are on their own? Gillespie was a spinster, McNulty lived like a single woman whilst her husband was out working – or up to no good. And Betty Clarke lived alone. Each one was killed late at night, their bodies not found until the following morning. Assuming the killer is a man, our guy attacks them when they're alone and at their most vulnerable. He suffocates them when the neighbours are likely to be asleep, allowing himself plenty of time to clean up the crime scene. By the time anyone knows what's going on, he's long gone. That could be the pattern, right there.'

Jones slipped his notepad into his suit-jacket pocket. 'Add in the nature of the murders, the staging of the bodies, and we've got ourselves a very effective killer. He's put a lot of thought into these attacks to ensure the victims are alone when he makes his move. He has complete control of the scene and how it's left – without the need to rush his work. He's methodical and cautious.'

Bovalino chimed in. 'Chances are he's been watching them and knew their routines.'

'That would make sense why no one has seen anything,' said Phillips. 'If he knows their routines, it's quite likely he knows the neighbours' too, and works around them.'

Jones nodded. 'What I don't get it is the different locations?

They're all at home, but each one is in a different part of the house. The lounge, the bedroom, and now the garage.'

'If he's as meticulous as he appears, maybe it's no accident?' Bovalino mused.

'Maybe not.' Phillips's eyes narrowed. 'But aside from how and when they were killed, what's the link between the victims?'

Bovalino shrugged. 'Dunno, Guv. Like we said, our seventy-two-year-old victim seems to kill off the school connection. No pun intended.'

Phillips paused before speaking. 'I was with Chakrabortty yesterday afternoon. She told me Deidre McNulty's injures were consistent with those suffered by Gillespie. The same sedative was used to knock her out.'

'So, no doubt this must be the same guy?' asked Jones.

'Not in my mind.'

At that moment, Entwistle reappeared. In his gloved hand, he held a framed photo of a couple drinking cocktails at a beach bar. He passed it to Phillips. 'Hold that will you, Guv?'

'What am I looking at, Entwistle?'

'I just spotted it on the kitchen wall. I'm pretty sure it's a holiday snap of the victim and her husband, Harry. He died a couple of years ago but, judging by her hair and glasses, plus the graininess of the image, I'd say it was taken in the late eighties or early nineties.'

Jones appeared unimpressed. 'And?'

'*And*, when I saw that photo in the kitchen, I recognised the woman.'

Bovalino scoffed, 'Well, you've been looking at her body for the last half an hour.'

'Yes, Bov, but the body in the garage is seventy-two.' Entwistle pointed to the image. 'This woman is twenty to thirty years younger. I recognise her from somewhere...' He pulled out his iPhone, scrolled through a list of photographs, then opened one. 'See?'

All three peered at the digital image Entwistle presented to them.

Phillips glanced at the frame in her hands, then back at the screen. 'I'm looking at the same women in both photos.'

Entwistle smiled triumphantly. 'Exactly.'

'So, where have I seen that image before? I recognise it too.'

'It's one I've already shown you, Guv, from Susan Gillespie's Facebook account. She posted it the day of Father Donnelly's funeral, remember?' He pointed at the phone screen. 'It's the trip to Lourdes. That kid there looks like Susan Gillespie, the girl next to her could easily be Deidre McNulty. And that older lady...is *Betty Clarke.*'

Jones suddenly got it. 'Bloody hell; the victims *are* all connected.'

Phillips continued glancing between both images. 'It's certainly a possibility.' She grabbed Entwistle's phone and pointed at the man in the image. 'So, if we're assuming this guy here is Father Donnelly, how can we confirm that's Gillespie and McNulty? And who are these two boys?' she asked, pointing to the two other figures in the photograph.

'We could ask Noel Gillespie,' said Bovalino.

Phillips thought for a moment. 'I don't fully trust him, but it's worth a shot.'

Jones pointed to himself and Bovalino. 'We'll go.'

'Thanks, guys. Entwistle, do me favour and dig into Father Donnelly's post mortem results. Make sure he died of what they say he did. You never know, he might just have been our first victim.'

'Got it, Guv.'

22

When Jones and Bovalino arrived at Noel Gillespie's house, his wife directed them to the family business located on Cheadle High Street, no more than a five-minute car journey from the house. Gillespie and Son Ltd was nestled between a trendy estate agent on one side and a Boots pharmacy on the other, and looked like any other high street accountancy firm from the outside. Inside was unremarkable too; magnolia walls and grey carpet tiles, with a few professional certificates dotted in frames around the space. A fresh-faced receptionist greeted them, her name badge identifying her as Jodie.

She smiled broadly, revealing a set of straight, sparkling white teeth. 'How can I help you?'

'We're here to see Mr Gillespie,' said Jones.

'Do you have an appointment?'

Bovalino flashed his ID. 'No, but we do have these.'

Jodie's smile disappeared. 'One moment please.' Stepping up from her chair, she disappeared through a door directly behind the reception area.

A few moments passed before it re-opened and Jodie

returned, followed by Noel Gillespie, who held the door open. Despite being clean-shaven and dressed in a suit and tie, he still managed to look dishevelled. 'Officers, please come through.'

Jones and Bovalino followed him past a small kitchen area and into a conference room, marked Private, that contained a large walnut table and matching chairs that looked dated by modern standards.

Gillespie pulled out a chair, and Jones and Bovalino followed his lead. 'What can I do for you officers?' Gillespie asked once they had all sat down.

Up close, Jones noted the dark circles under his bloodshot eyes. 'Back to work so soon?'

'We're short-handed without Susie, and besides, sitting around the house wasn't helping. This place helps take my mind off things.'

'I understand.' Jones pulled out his phone and opened up the screenshot of Susan Gillespie's Facebook post. 'Do you recognise this photo, Noel?'

Gillespie pulled out his glasses from his shirt pocket. Taking the phone, he examined it a moment. 'Bloody hell, that's Susie. She looks so young.'

'Have you seen this photo before?'

'I don't think so. It doesn't look familiar.'

'Are you sure? It's taken from your sister's Facebook feed.' said Bovalino.

Gillespie shrugged. 'Social media is more my daughter's thing. I still have an ancient handset – doesn't even have a camera.' He moved to pass the phone back.

Jones stopped him. 'Do you recognise anyone else in the photo?'

Gillespie took another look.

'It was taken on a trip to Lourdes in Southern France, if that helps,' Bovalino told him.

'Oh wow, Lourdes. I remember Susie going on that trip. She was so excited in the lead up to it. She'd never been abroad until then.' Gillespie's voice cracked, his eyes fixed on the screen.

'Do you remember when that was?' asked Jones.

Gillespie looked up. 'God, now you're testing me. I left school that year, so I think it was the summer of 1992.'

Bovalino made a note of the date in his pad. 'And do you remember who went on the trip with her?'

Gillespie placed the phone down on the table in front of him, then swivelled it so Jones could see the screen. 'This guy here is Father Donnelly – he used to be our parish priest. He died a few weeks back: cancer. Susie spent a lot of time with him at the hospice in his final month. He was a cranky old sod and had no family to speak of. She felt sorry for him and didn't want him to die alone. We both went to his funeral, actually.'

Jones raised his eyebrows. '*You* went? Father Maguire said you're not much of a church-goer these days.'

'True. I wasn't planning on going, but Susie insisted. She said Mum and Dad would have wanted us to pay our respects. He married them and did both our baptisms. It was local, so it wasn't much of a hardship, plus I didn't bother going to the crematorium. Susie did, but I came straight back to the office.'

Jones pointed to the image again. 'I see. And do you recognise these two?'

'Sure. The older lady is Betty Clarke. She was a volunteer at the church. Used to chaperone the kids on trips away. And that slip of a thing is Deidre McNulty.'

'Are you aware that both those women were killed in the last week?'

Gillespie looked at him in shock. 'Jesus, no. What happened?'

'They were both suffocated, like Susie.' Jones scrutinised Gillespie's face.

'My God. Do you think it's the same guy?'

Bovalino looked up from his notes. 'What makes you think the killer was a *man*?'

Gillespie stuttered, 'W-well...er, I just assumed it. You don't see many female murderers, do you?'

Jones's eyes remained fixed on Gillespie. 'At this stage, we're keeping an open mind.' Jones tapped the screen. 'Do you know these two boys in the photo with Susie?'.

Gillespie pulled the phone towards him and studied it again. 'It's been a long time, but I remember they both used to play at our house in the summer holidays. If my memory serves me right, that skinny kid is Matt Logan and the other one is Thomas Dempsey.'

'Are they still living in the area?' asked Bovalino.

'Wouldn't have a clue.'

Bovalino continued, 'Do you remember what they were like back then?'

'Like I say, it was a long time ago, but from what I can recall, Logan was highly strung. Happy one minute and running off home crying the next. Dempsey was a quiet kid. Never really said much. Well, not to me, at least.'

Jones had kept a close eye on every movement of Gillespie's face as he'd been speaking. There was nothing to indicate he was lying, but something didn't sit right with this guy. 'Do you know why anyone would want to kill Susie, Deidre and Betty?'

Gillespie took a deep breath, then exhaled loudly. 'No, I don't. I've lost touch with Dee-Dee and Betty—'

'Dee-Dee?' Jones queried.

'I'm sorry?' Gillespie appeared confused.

'You called her Dee-Dee. That was what her husband and close friends called her.'

'Is it? Well, it's what she went by as a kid. That's how I knew her when she played with Susie.'

Jones quickly changed tack, attempting to catch Gillespie off guard. 'How's business?'

'Er, ok, I guess. Could be better, could be worse.'

He changed tack again. 'Do you know if Susie made a will?'

'Knowing Susie, I'm sure she did.'

'She didn't talk to you about that sort of thing?'

'No, Sergeant, she didn't. What's the old adage – a builder's house is always the one that needs fixing? Well, it's the same in finance. When you talk about money all day every day, it's not something to chat about on the weekend.'

Jones nodded. 'We're just wondering if anyone in particular would benefit financially from her death.'

'Your guess is as good as mine.' Gillespie looked at his watch, appearing flustered. 'Look, I'm very sorry, but I have an appointment in five minutes. I'm going to have to go.'

'Of course. Don't let us keep you,' said Jones.

Gillespie placed both hands on the table as he stood. They were large and calloused, more like a labourers' than an accountant's. 'If you head back the way you came, just press the green button on the wall to open the door back into the main office. Jodie will see you out.' He smiled weakly, then left the room and made his way noisily up the staircase just outside the conference room.

A few minutes later, Jones and Bovalino were back on Cheadle High Street, walking through the freezing rain towards their car.

'What do you think Jonesy?'

'Dodgy as fuck, Bov. I mean, did you see his mood change when we started talking about money?'

'Yeah. Couldn't get us out of there quick enough.'

'And how does he *not* know about the McNulty and Clarke murders? Their names have been released to the press already. He may not use social media, but he's got a huge telly in his lounge. His sister was murdered a week ago; he must be watching the bloody news, surely?'

'It does seem odd. But he has a cast-iron alibi. He was at home with his wife and kids'

Jones thought for a moment. 'I know, but money can turn even the most normal people into cheats and liars. I don't quite know what it is, but I'm sure he's involved in this case somewhere.'

They reached the car and climbed inside out of the rain. As usual, Bovalino was driving as they began the journey back to Ashton House. Both men said nothing for a few minutes before Bovalino spoke. 'Ok, say Gillespie is involved. I can understand why he could be tempted to kill Susan; for the inheritance. But then why kill McNulty and Clarke?'

'To throw us off the scent?'

'One more murder, *maybe*, and it's a big maybe – but two? That's a lot of risk to distract an investigation, Jonesy'.

'I know. It's just there's something about him I don't like. And did you see the size of his hands?'

'Can't say I did.'

'Bloody enormous things, like a construction worker's; he's an accountant, for Christ's sake.'

'Maybe he does a lot of home improvement?'

Jones laughed. 'That house of his hasn't been touched since the day it was built. Nah, there's something dodgy about this guy. Let's have a look and see if Gillespie was financially involved with McNulty and Clarke. If he was managing their assets, their deaths may also benefit him, along with his sister's will.'

'Time to do some digging.'

'Yeah. And I have a feeling the more we dig, Bov, the more shit we're going to find.'

23

D CI Brown seemed unusually chirpy as he sat opposite Phillips. Having called her into his office as soon as she arrived at the incident room, he had asked how she and the team were doing, almost managing to sound genuine in doing so. Something was afoot.

'So, Jane, how are you getting on with the Cheadle murders?'

Jane? He never called her Jane.

'We now believe the victims were all connected, sir.'

'Really? How so?'

Phillips pulled out her iPhone and passed it across the desk. 'This picture includes all three victims – Susan Gillespie, Deidre McNulty and Betty Clarke. It was taken on a Catholic pilgrimage to Lourdes in 1992 or thereabouts.'

'And who are the others? The two boys and the priest?'

'Father Donnelly – he died about two months ago from pancreatic cancer. Entwistle is looking into his medical records to double-check that's what killed him.'

The fact Entwistle was being useful to the team seemed to please Brown. 'You think he may have been murdered too?'

'Impossible to say, sir. Just checking every angle.'

'What about the two kids?'

'According to victim one's brother, the skinny one is Matt Logan and the other is Thomas Dempsey. He doesn't know much about them these days, so Entwistle has been looking into their whereabouts. I'm expecting an update this morning.'

'Any suspects yet?'

'Two potentials at the moment, sir.'

Brown sat forwards attentively. '*Two*? Really? That's great. Who are you looking at?'

Phillips could feel herself being drawn down a rabbit hole she would struggle to get out of. Brown was notorious for taking the quick and easy option. If he saw either Noel Gillespie or Kevin McNulty as potential suspects, she knew he'd be upstairs sharing their names with the Chief Super within the hour. Going forward, it would be almost impossible to present any other theories after that. She decided to dial down their importance. 'Well, I say two suspects – more like two people of interest.'

Brown's face betrayed his disappointment. 'So, who are these people *of interest*?' His tone was closer to his usual disdain.

'Noel Gillespie – that's Susan's brother – and Deidre McNulty's husband, Kevin. Kevin initially lied about his whereabouts on the night of his wife's murder, and Noel could potentially inherit his sister's estate.'

'That's all we've got on them?'

'Well, McNulty also presented with bruising to his temple, and we found his fingerprints on the bag that was used to suffocate Deirdre as well as on the dog collar.'

'A good lawyer will explain away the fingerprints in no time. It's a natural reaction of anyone to try and release a loved one from such a situation, and to check if the dog was still alive. The bruising is interesting, but nothing more.'

'As I say, I'm hoping to get more info from the team this morning.'

Brown's return to his normal agitated state was complete. 'Fucking hell, Phillips. The first murder is a week old and this is all we've got? A dodgy alibi and some looming inheritance. The Chief Super won't be happy. In fact, the mood she's in today, she's likely to chew me a new arsehole.'

Phillips did her best to keep her face straight, but the image of such a scenario playing in her mind's eye made her want to burst out laughing.

'Look, Phillips, I don't know if you've heard, but Collins is retiring next month. That means there'll be a Superintendent spot coming free...and it's got my name on it.'

He needed her help to get a promotion. Of course, it was so obvious.

'A quick result on the Cheadle murders would almost guarantee it for me. This PR disaster could actually turn into an open goal. Now, we have three murders that appear to be linked, the press are hungry for information, and the Chief Super wants me to hold a press conference this afternoon. If I'm going to turn this situation to my favour, I need something to give them. So, you and the team need to double your efforts. You got it?'

The thought of Brown going even higher and having more influence in the Force made Phillips's blood run cold. Conversely, Collins's squad had nothing to do with the murder team. Brown moving out of their way was an attractive prospect. The greater good versus the needs of her team? A tough one, but she knew where her loyalties lay.

'I understand, sir. Like I say, we're about to debrief, and I'm sure the guys will have more to share. Why don't you join us?'

'Now?'

'Yes sir.'

Brown looked at his watch. 'I'm due upstairs in half an hour to plan the press conference, but I can give you twenty minutes.'

'Very good, sir.' Phillips did her best to sound deferent.

'Right. No time to waste. Let's get on with it.'

JONES, Bovalino and Entwistle were all busy at their desks exploring various lines of enquiry when Phillips and Brown walked into the incident room.

'Heads up, guys. DCI Brown is joining us for the debriefing.'

Jones and Bovalino's faces gave away their disappointment, though Entwistle seemed as enthusiastic as only a rookie could.

Phillips took a seat at her desk as Brown adopted his favoured position – to her right, straddling a chair turned backwards.

'So, Entwistle, did forensics find anything in the church grounds that might help?' asked Phillips.

''fraid not, Guv. Nothing at all.'

'Ok, and what about Donnelly's death. Anything?'

'I went through his records with Dr Chakrabortty. She'd never seen them before, as his care came through Wythenshawe and then the hospice, but she was confident pancreatic cancer was what killed him. Although it was probably a combination of that and liver failure in the end. He was a big drinker, which is quite common amongst older priests.'

'Says who?' asked Brown.

'Well...er...just my personal experience, sir. I was brought up a Catholic, you see. As a kid, it was well known that priests liked a smoke and a drink. A lot of our teachers at school were priests. Back then, they could smoke in the staffroom. Up close they reeked of it, with yellowing fingers and sometimes browning facial hair. Not to mention bulbous, ruddy noses from the drink.'

Brown nodded. 'Inside knowledge, I like it. Good observation, Entwistle.'

Phillips caught Jones rolling his eyes at Brown's comments. She felt the same, but ploughed on. 'And what about Gillespie's estate? Anything on who benefits from her death, Bov?'

'Yes, Guv.' Bovalino handed her a photocopied file. 'As you can see from this copy of her will, Noel Gillespie gets seventy per cent of her assets, with ten per cent going to her each of two nieces, Chloe and Hollie. The remaining ten per cent goes to the church.'

Phillips scanned the document quickly and found what she was looking for. 'It says here that the executor for the estate is Noel Gillespie. So he must have known he was a beneficiary?'

'Another one that's lied to us, Guv,' said Jones.

'When did he lie to you?' asked Brown.

'Yesterday, sir. When we pushed him on who benefitted from Susan's will. He said he had no idea.'

'Then there could be something in this inheritance link after all?'

Jones nodded. 'Potentially, sir. The business is also in trouble. Seems Noel was investigated by the HMRC last year and owes them a lot of money.'

'How much?' asked Phillips.

Jones handed over a thick file containing copies of documents from the HMRC and Companies House. 'Almost half a million in back-taxes and penalties for his role in tax avoidance schemes, dating back ten years. Looking at their accounts, the business turned over £400,000 last year, with dividends for Noel and Susan of over 40k each. Based on those numbers alone, Noel Gillespie cannot pay his tax debt and is potentially looking at a custodial sentence.'

Brown sounded excited now. 'That's a clear enough motive for me.'

Phillips did her best not to react and let out a long, silent breath. 'He's certainly putting himself into the frame, sir, but I'm also keen to know more about the boys in the Lourdes photo. Entwistle, did you find out anything on Matt Logan and Thomas Dempsey?'

Entwistle pinned enlarged copies of Logan's and Dempsey's driving licenses to the incident board. 'I'll start with Dempsey first, as he seems the most straightforward. Born and bred in Cheadle but, unlike Gillespie and McNulty, he went to the grammar school on a scholarship; a bright student by all accounts. He was educated to A-level standard and then went to work as an apprentice at DR Smith Engineering Ltd. He stayed with them for twelve months, but was released and ended up working as a postman, which he still does. He's forty-three and lives alone in a former council house in Fallowfield, which he has a small mortgage on.'

Brown appeared to be losing interest and began checking his watch. Phillips urged Entwistle to continue.

'Logan, on the other hand, is quite a colourful character. He went to the same school as Gillespie and McNulty, but left before taking his GCSEs. He then took a job at Hexagon Paints in Stockport. He was with them for a couple of years, but was sacked when he was arrested for burglary in 2012. He's been in and out of prison for the last seven years. His most recent stint was three years in 2016, this time for drug possession and breaking and entering. He served eighteen months. Since then, he's drifted between the streets and various shelters and hostels across Manchester. He's well known to the city centre division for begging to fund his drug habit.'

'Sounds like a prize ratbag. Could he be our guy?' said Brown.

Phillips sensed where Brown was leading them: the easy win. 'Well, sir, it's certainly a possibility. *But* – we should also consider that both Dempsey and Logan could be in danger themselves. If the killer is working his way through the group in the photo, then either one of them could be our next victim.'

'Or the killer, Guv.' said Jones.

Phillips agreed. 'Again, it's possible.'

Looking incensed, Brown rose from his seat. 'Let me get this straight. I'm due on live TV this afternoon to share our progress, and my crack team of detectives is telling me that both our current suspects could also be our next *victims*. How the fuck am I supposed to sell that upstairs? *"Yes, ma'am, we have a couple of suspects who fit the profile, but they could also be our next murder victims."'* He threw his pen across the room petulantly. 'How the hell did I end up with you lot in my team?'

Phillips opened her mouth to speak, but Brown cut her off by pointing a finger at her. 'You're in charge of this sorry lot, Phillips, and you're going to be sat right next to me at that press conference this afternoon – I'm not about to let you lot fuck up my chances of making Superintendent.' Without waiting for a response, he stomped out of the incident room, muttering under his breath.

The team sat in silence for a moment until they could see Brown was out of sight and earshot. Phillips was still shaking her head at his tantrum.

'There was one more thing, Guv,' said Entwistle quietly.

'Go on.'

'Logan made a claim of sexual abuse against an unnamed Catholic priest in the early nineties. I found it in the local police logs. But it didn't go anywhere.'

Phillips said nothing for a moment, instead tapping her index finger against her lips. Then she stood. 'Right. It seems Logan is someone we need to talk to. Jones, Bov, go pick him up. Entwistle, keep digging into his background. Find out if he ever handled chemicals when he worked at the paint factory. In the meantime, I'd better see if I can get myself out of this bloody press conference.'

24

For the remainder of the morning, Phillips tried in vain to find an excuse to get out of the press conference. She'd hoped to conjure up a strong enough lead that needed her urgent attention, to play on Brown's desire to close the case quickly. Sadly, all avenues appeared very general at this stage of the investigation. She knew damn well he wouldn't go for any of them.

She had never relished speaking in public, but after the trauma of being shot and almost killed, her anxiety levels had increased exponentially. The pressure she felt walking into the Media Room at Ashton House almost pushed her into the floor. Her heart raced, her breathing was shallow, and she just hoped to God she wouldn't have to speak.

She took the seat next to Brown, behind a long table that had been placed in front of a GMP-branded media wall. A row of microphones emblazoned with various newspaper, radio station and TV network logos sat in front of them. The Force's Director of PR, Rupert Dudley, stood to one side facing the room full of journalists and TV crews, a permanent and well-practiced smile locked on his face. When the last of the attendees had taken their seats, he introduced himself to the audience and handed over to Brown, who placed his scripted statement on the table in front of him.

A cacophony of automatic camera flashes erupted as the 'presser' went live.

'Good afternoon, everyone. My name is Detective Chief Inspector Fraser Brown, the lead investigator in this series of murders. To my left is Detective Inspector Jane Phillips, who is assisting me in the investigation.'

Phillips looked out at the sea of faces as nausea washed over her.

Brown glanced down at his statement, then up to the cameras again, and proceeded with a steady delivery. 'As you may be aware, in the last two weeks a number of residents from the Cheadle area have been found dead in their homes, in what can only be described as suspicious circumstances. I can now share the names of all three victims. The first was Susan Gillespie, aged forty-three from Brunswick Street in Cheadle. Her body was discovered on the morning of Tuesday the twenty-ninth of January, and we believe she died between the hours of 10 p.m. and midnight the night before. Three nights later, the second victim, Deidre McNulty, aged forty-two from Lawther Avenue, Cheadle was killed; again, somewhere between the hours of 10 p.m. and midnight. Her body was discovered the following morning. Lastly, Betty Clarke, aged seventy-two and of Blackmoor Gardens, Gatley, was found dead in her home on Tuesday the fifth of February. Evidence suggests that she too had been unlawfully killed the night before.'

Evidence suggests? The understatement of the century. Phillips mind filled with images of Clarke bagged and tied to the steering wheel of her car.

Brown continued. 'Due to the ongoing nature of this investigation, at this stage I cannot offer any further details on how the victims died. But I would like to reassure the people of

Cheadle, and Manchester as a whole, that we have dedicated significant resources to finding the killer and bringing them to justice quickly. I would urge any members of the public who may have information that could help the investigation, to contact the incident room on 0800 541-3372. All calls will be treated in the strictest of confidence. I'd like to remind the public to remain vigilant when out late at night, and to ensure that someone knows where they are going at all times. Also, it is advisable to lock all doors and windows until the killer is in custody. I'm pleased to say that DI Phillips and her team have presented me with a number of people of interest who we are currently investigating. Thanks to their work, I am confident it's a case of *if*, as opposed to *when*, we catch the killer.'

Shit. Brown had just thrown her under the bus on live TV. If they failed to make any arrests, she would be the one in the firing line, not him. Sneaky bastard.

'That completes my statement.' Brown folded his script slowly, before placing it in his inside pocket.

Dudley stepped forwards now, the smile back on his face. 'Thank you very much, everyone. Any further questions should be directed to my team via email. For those of you that don't already have it, please take one of the PR-team contact cards on your way out.'

Next to her, Brown stood up from the table, nodded to a few people in the room and hurried out through a side door, keen to avoid any renegade reporters.

She followed hot on his heels. As he reached the adjacent room, she grabbed him by the shoulder, forcing him to turn and face her. 'What was that all about?'

'What was *what* about, Inspector?'

'Throwing me under the bus out there.'

'I don't know what you're talking about.'

'Oh yes, you do. "I'm pleased to say that DI Phillips and her team have presented me with a number of people of interest who we are investigating." You know damn well they'll blame me if we don't get a result on this.'

Brown smiled. 'Can I help it if your previous heroics have given you a high profile with the press-pack?'

'No, but you can bloody use it your advantage, can't you? Catch the guy and *you're* the hero. Don't, and you can blame me and my team for your lack of success.'

Brown glanced left and right, then stepped closer to her. When he spoke, his voice was a conspiratorial whisper. 'It's nothing personal, Phillips, it's just business. I want to be Superintendent and you're going to help me, one way or the other. We both know we can't work together long-term. So why not make it easy on yourself, and your boys, and help me get that promotion?'

It took all her resolve not to smash her fist into Brown's jaw as she stared down at the pathetic excuse of a man in front of her. A lopsided grin spread across his face, his hand shaking the change in his trouser pocket.

Phillips stepped in even closer, and mirrored his tone. 'I'm going to catch this guy, but let's be crystal clear: I'm not doing it to save my arse or help get rid of *yours*. I'm doing it because three innocent women and their families deserve justice. I happen to believe that honouring their memories matters. That's why I do this job.'

Brown took a step back. 'Admirable, Phillips, admirable. Send me a postcard from the cheap seats when you get a moment, will you?' With that, he turned around and walked out of the room.

25

Matt Logan looked like he hadn't had a hot bath in a very long time. He smelled that way too. Jones had warned Phillips of his current condition after he and Bov tracked him down to a homeless hostel in Cheetham Hill. Still, she wasn't quite prepared for the stench that greeted her as she followed Jones into interview room three: a mixture of body odour, cigarette smoke and stale alcohol. He looked frail, like a malnourished animal, vulnerable and unsure of himself.

Taking a seat at the plain wooden table opposite Logan, Phillips passed him a plastic cup of water and introduced herself as Jones took the seat beside her. She explained that their conversation was being recorded by a video-camera on the wall behind them, as well as a separate digital interview recorder – DIR – positioned against the far wall on the other side of the room. Logan nodded without conviction. After the long and unnecessarily loud tone indicating the start of the DIR, Phillips began the interview.

'Do you know why you're here, Matt?'

'I can't really remember. His mate...' Logan pointed at Jones, his accent a thick Mancunian drawl. 'The big lad told me, but I've forgotten.'

'Do you know Susan Gillespie, Deidre McNulty or Betty Clarke?'

Hearing their names had a physical effect on Logan. His body straightened, and he paused for a long moment before replying. 'I went to school with a Susan Gillespie and Deidre McNulty, but that was a long time ago.'

'And Betty Clarke?'

Logan shook his head.

Phillips produced a printed copy of the Lourdes group shot. 'That's Betty Clarke there.' She placed her finger on the photograph.

'Oh, you mean *Mrs* Clarke? I didn't know she was called Betty.'

'So, you *do* know her?'

'Yeah, she used to take us on church trips when we were kids.'

'Do you recognise anyone else in this photo, Matt?'

Logan studied it closely, sipping his water as he did. He pointed to the print, his fingernails black with grime. 'That's Susie, that's Dee-Dee. Wow, fucking hell, that's me.' He chuckled.

'And who is this boy next to you?'

'Been a long time, but I think his name was Tom.'

'Do you remember his last name?'

'Er, it began with a D...' He squinted at the image. 'Den... Denny... No...Dempsey. That's it, Dempsey.'

'What about this man?' Phillips pointed to Father Donnelly.

Logan instantly stiffened. 'I-I can't say.'

'You can't say, or won't say?'

'I don't want anything to do with that man.'

Phillips watched Logan's physical reactions. She recognised

the sudden onset of anxiety, so similar to hers. 'What's the matter, Matt. Are you afraid of him?'

'Is this why I'm here? Because of the allegations?'

'What allegations are you talking about?'

Logan's eyes darted between Phillips and Jones. 'Has he made a complaint against me? If he has, you can tell him he's a fucking liar. Whatever he says I did, I didn't do, right?'

'Matt,' Jones cut in, 'can you confirm Father Donnelly is the man in this picture?'

Logan nodded reluctantly. 'Why?' he asked in almost a whisper.

'He died a couple of months ago.' Phillips allowed this information to land as Logan's upper body appeared to soften. 'Matt, why would Father Donnelly want to make a complaint about you?'

'Because he's a lying, abusive bastard who would say anything to save his own skin. That's why.'

Recalling Entwistle's info on the allegations of abuse, Phillips changed tack. 'Around the time this photo was taken, you made allegations of abuse against a priest, didn't you? Was Donnelly that priest?'

'I don't want to talk about it.'

'Matt, it's okay,' she said softly. 'He can't hurt you anymore. Please, tell us what he did to you.'

Logan took a long drink of water, as if hiding behind the cup.

'You're safe here. You can tell us.'

Logan said nothing for a while before finally responding. 'I'll talk to *you,* but *he* has to go.' He pointed at Jones. 'I'm not having him taking the piss out of me.'

Phillips nodded and Jones stood quickly, leaving the room to watch on a monitor in another room farther up the hall.

'It's just you and me now, so please, tell me about your relationship with Father Donnelly.'

'It wasn't a relationship. It was abuse.'

'Okay. Can you tell me about the abuse? Maybe I can help you.'

'How can *you* help me? Can you make it all go away inside here?' Logan tapped his temple with another filthy finger. 'Can you get me off the streets and off the shit? Can you take away my criminal record?'

Phillips shook her head. 'I can't imagine how frightened you must have been as a young boy.'

'You have no fucking idea!'

'So please, help me understand.'

'You can never understand, *no one can*. Not unless you've had a predator manipulating your every thought until you don't know your own mind anymore.'

Phillips could sense Logan was close to cracking, so continued gently, using his name over and over to personalise the conversation.

'What did Donnelly do, Matt? Tell me.'

'Look, forget I said anything. Let's just drop it.'

'I'm a police officer. I'm sworn to protect people. I can't drop an allegation of abuse, Matt.'

'It was almost thirty years ago – and you've just said he's dead. So what's the point in dragging up shit from the past?'

'Because I want to give you justice, Matt. I want the church to admit what happened to you.'

Logan scoffed. 'Justice. You're having a laugh, aren't you? They covered it up once before. What makes you think they'll tell the truth now he's dead?'

'The truth about what? What did Donnelly do to you? Tell me.'

Logan finally lost control and slammed his fists down on the printed picture on the table. 'I'll tell you what that bastard did, shall I? He raped me, over and over again!' Tears began to roll down his cheeks. 'He raped me. You happy now?'

Phillips reached up and passed Logan a box of tissues from the top of a nearby cabinet. She felt a sudden pang of guilt that she'd elicited such painful memories from him in a soulless room like this. People like Logan deserved better treatment. Still, catching the killer was her main priority. She had to keep pushing. 'I can only imagine what you went through, Matt, and I'm sorry to keep asking such difficult questions, I really am, but I need to know something. Did Father Donnelly abuse you on the trip to Lourdes?'

Logan's whole body was shaking now. He began to sob, 'Yes.'

'How long did it go on for?'

There was a long pause before Logan answered, clearly fighting to control his emotions. 'Two years.'

'And you told someone what he was doing to you, didn't you?'

'Yes.'

'Who did you tell? Who was it, Matt?'

Another long pause followed. 'My parents.'

'And what did they do about it?'

'They didn't believe me at first, but eventually they talked to the local police. The coppers wanted nothing to do with it, though. They advised them to speak to the church directly.'

'And did your parents speak to the church?'

'Yes, stupidly, they went direct to Donnelly, who of course denied it. He told them that I was making it up because he'd caught me masturbating on the Lourdes trip. He said I was trying to shift the focus onto him, away from my own sinful behaviour.'

'And they believed *him* over you?'

Logan snarled, his contempt for his parents etched across his gaunt face. 'Of course they did. His lies were much easier to accept than the truth – that their parish priest had raped their own son'

'Did you ever think about harming Father Donnelly, Matt? Revenge for what he did?'

'Sure, I thought about it. Watching him prancing around, up by the altar every Sunday like he was God Himself, pretending to the world to be pious and holy when all the time he was abusing young kids. I used to sit and fantasise about staring into his eyes as I took his last breath.'

'And did you ever fantasise about suffocating him?'

Logan shrugged. 'Sometimes. Other times I wanted to stab him or beat him over the head with a crucifix. That was my favourite. Didn't matter, though. All I really wanted was to see his face full of fear, like mine was whenever he came for me.'

'Did he ever abuse Susan or Deidre?'

Logan looked at the photograph again. 'I don't know. After Mum and Dad didn't believe me, I never spoke about it again.'

'Did Susan and Deidre know you were being abused?'

'We talked about it once, but as far as I know they never told anyone else.'

'When did the abuse finally stop, Matt?'

Logan thought for a moment. 'I guess when I was about fourteen or fifteen.'

'What changed?'

Logan leaned back in his chair and folded his arms tightly across his chest. Phillips could see the early signs of drug withdrawal filtering into his movements. He let out a mirthless chuckle. '*I* did. He liked them young – and I grew up.'

Phillips watched Logan in silence, studying his face, trying to look for any signs he was telling the truth. He was nervy and twitchy, as she'd expect from someone in need of his next hit, but still, he appeared genuine enough. However, she knew from experience that someone capable of murdering three women so methodically was also capable of concocting and delivering a powerful cover story.

'Matt, can you tell me where you were on the nights of

Monday the twentieth-eighth of January, Thursday the thirty-first, and Tuesday the fifth of February?'

Logan blew his nose on a tissue, then looked up at Phillips. 'What's today?'

'Friday the eighth of February.'

Logan thought for a moment. 'So Tuesday was three nights ago?'

'Yes.'

'In that case, I was with Mitchy under the arches at Castlefield. We scored there before crashing at his sister's in Levenshulme.'

'Do you know what time that was?'

'What was?'

'What time you were under the arches, and what time you got to Mitchy's sister's?'

'Nighttime.'

'Can you be more specific?'

'I live between hits; that's the only time I use.'

'Ok. Where does Mitchy's sister live?'

'Like I said, Levenshulme.'

'You don't know the address?'

'No. Those terraced houses all look the same to me.'

'So where can we find Mitchy?'

Logan began rocking lightly in his seat. 'You can try the hostel where you picked me up, or just go where the beggars go. That's how he makes his money. Like me.'

'And what about the other dates I mentioned: Monday the twentieth-eighth, Thursday the thirty-first of January?'

Logan looked at her blankly. 'I have no idea.'

'You don't remember where you were on those days?'

'No.'

Phillips studied him a moment, then closed her file. 'Right. I think that's all I need for now. Thank you, Matt. You've been very helpful. For the purpose of the tape, I am drawing this interview to a close.' She shut off the tape and stopped the video.

'Can I go now?'

'Soon, Matt.'

'Can I have a fag, then?' Logan's face was pained, almost desperate.

Phillips stood and walked over to the door. 'I'll get one of the officers to escort you to the smoking area.'

Stepping out into the corridor, Jones was waiting for her, his eyes wide and expectant. 'What do you think, Guv?'

They began walking down the corridor back to the incident room. 'Either he's a bloody good actor or he's not our guy. I know he's got form, but I can't imagine him cleaning a crime scene of every single trace of evidence when he can barely clean himself.'

'So what now?'

'Let him go but keep an eye on him. See where he lands. He may still be connected to this somehow.'

'Got it.'

'And you and Bov should head over to see Thomas Dempsey. See if he has anything he can share on Logan and the victims.'

'What about Entwistle?'

'Tell him to keep digging on Noel Gillespie and Kevin McNulty – see what else he can find on Logan. Plus ask him to find out if the city division have anything on this guy Mitchy. We need to talk to him, or his sister, to verify Logan's alibi; preferably both. In the meantime, I'm off to see Father Maguire again and find out more about Donnelly. Call me if you come up with anything, okay?'

'Will do, Guv,' Jones replied as they went their separate ways.

26

T homas Dempsey opened the front door of the end-of-terrace house and peered out tentatively. Jones was immediately struck by his heavy black-framed glasses, curly brown hair and thickset beard. 'Can I help you?'

'I'm Detective Sergeant Jones and this is Detective Constable Bovalino.' Both men presented their credentials. 'May we come in?'

Dempsey stared at Jones, frowning. 'Is there something wrong, officer?'

'We'd like to talk to you about Matt Logan, if we may? We believe you were friends.'

'Matty? Wow, I've not spoken to him in over twenty years.'

Jones glanced up at the sky. 'Can we talk inside, Mr Dempsey? It's starting to rain.'

'Oh God, where are my manners? Please...come in.' Dempsey opened the door wide. 'Go straight through to the lounge on the right.'

Jones and Bovalino followed his instructions and found themselves in a rather dated, sparsely decorated living room where an ancient net curtain covered the front window overlooking the street. A small two-seater couch and an armchair pointed towards an old tube TV, with a small glass coffee table between them.

'Please, take a seat.' Dempsey pointed towards the couch.

As they sat, Bovalino pulled out his notepad.

'Is Matt okay? Has something happened to him?' There was a concerned look on Dempsey's face.

Jones forced a smile. 'He's fine.'

'I just wondered, you know, with his drug problem and everything.'

Never one for small talk, Jones pressed on. 'Can I ask how you know Matt Logan?'

Dempsey produced a warm smile. 'We met at primary school when we were just five years old. St Patrick's – it's attached to the church in Cheadle. We became good friends. We'd play out on the weekends and see each other at church every Sunday.'

'And when did you last speak to him?'

'Like I said, I've not spoken to him in over twenty years, but I have seen him a couple of times in the last twelve months; begging in the city centre by Piccadilly Station. It's so sad to see him like that.'

'You still recognised him after all that time?'

'He's always been very distinctive looking. That thin face and wiry frame haven't changed much. He's just got older and even thinner – if that's possible.'

'And you never spoke to him on any of those occasions at Piccadilly?' asked Bovalino.

'Not really, just to say hello. I always give him some money, but he doesn't seem to recognise me. He's usually in a bit of a state, to be honest. I presume it's the drugs.'

'You mentioned that earlier. If you've not seen him for twenty years, how do you know about his issue with drugs?'

Dempsey glanced at Jones and Bovalino in turn and let out

a nervous chuckle. 'Well, it doesn't take a genius to spot a junkie, does it?'

Jones paused a moment before asking his next question. 'Can you tell us what he was like as a kid?'

'Sure. Matty was a bright, fun-loving kid. Very smart and academic. We went to different schools, but *his* mum was always telling *my* mum, at church, how well he was doing. I think it's because I went to the grammar school on a scholarship. She seemed determined to let Mum know Matt was just as bright as I was. Competitive parents and all that.'

'You say he was academic. Did he ever show any interest in chemistry?'

'Funnily enough, he did. He was never any good at sport, so he focused most of his energies on learning new stuff. It's fair to say he was more interested in science than soccer.'

'And what sort of stuff did he like learning about?'

'Well, my lasting memory is of this amazing chemistry kit his dad brought back from a business trip to the States. I'd never seen anything like it at the time. His shed looked like Frankenstein's lab.'

'And what was in this chemistry kit?'

'Oh God, all sorts. Must have cost a fortune. It had white coats, goggles, real glass test-tubes, a Bunsen burner with a refillable gas bottle. It even came with dry ice.' Dempsey smiled. 'Can you imagine that nowadays? Propane gas and dry ice for kids? They were different times back then, for sure.'

Bovalino scribbled the elements in his notepad as Jones continued. 'Did Logan ever talk to you about being abused?'

Dempsey's demeanour grew serious. He appeared uncomfortable with the question. 'Yes, I'm afraid he did.'

'How old were you when he told you?'

Dempsey thought for a moment. 'It was after a trip to France. Not straight after, though. It was probably a couple of months later when he mentioned it to me.'

Jones produced a printed copy of the Lourdes photo and handed it to him. 'Was this the trip?'

Dempsey studied the image. 'Wow, Lourdes. Look at the state of me with my bowl-cut hair. That seems like a lifetime ago now. Yeah, that was the trip.'

'And what did he tell you about his abuse?'

'Well, he said it started on that trip.'

'Did he say who was abusing him?'

'Not at first. He just asked me if it was ok for an adult to touch you, you know, *down there*? I said no, and that was the end of that. Then a couple of weeks later he came to me and asked me if Father Donnelly had ever offered me "special attention"? I asked him what he meant, and he told me that Father Donnelly had kissed him on his genitals.'

'And what did you say?'

'I said no. I'd never let anyone do that to me. That made him cry and he got really upset. I told him he had to tell someone about it – that it wasn't right. Eventually he agreed and said he was going to speak to his parents.'

'And did he?'

'Yes. The next day.'

'What did they say?'

'I don't know. I saw him a week later at church and when I asked him about it, he clammed up, told me to be quiet and said it didn't matter. That it had all been a misunderstanding. We never spoke about it again.'

'And do you think it was a misunderstanding?'

'I really don't know. I never saw anything happen, but you do wonder why Matt would make something up like that? Plus, Donnelly did have a bit of a funny way about him.'

'What do you mean by *funny*?'

Dempsey bit his bottom lip. 'I feel bad saying this about an old priest, but he was always a bit creepy, if I'm honest. He kind of made me nervous. I never actually saw him do anything to

Matt or any of the other kids, but when we were away on church trips, he'd regularly come into the boy's bedrooms when we were getting dressed or ready for bed. It sometimes felt like his eyes would linger on us in our underwear for longer than was necessary. Do you know what I mean, Sergeant?'

Jones nodded. 'So, in your opinion, was Father Donnelly abusing Matt as he claims?'

'I can't be certain, but I'm pretty sure something went on in France.'

'And do you think the abuse continued after your conversation?'

Dempsey sighed. 'I'm afraid so.'

'What makes you think that?'

'Just the way Matty changed. We used to have such a laugh after mass each week. After Lourdes, he seemed to go into himself, did everything he could to avoid church outings. He stopped hanging out after mass to play anymore and always went straight home. I'm ashamed to say it, considering what was probably happening to him, but after a while I lost interest and found new friends.'

'Do you recognise anyone else in the photo?' asked Bovalino.

Dempsey glanced down at the Lourdes image again, his face grave. 'Mrs Clarke, Dee-Dee and Susie. So unbelievably sad.'

Bovalino took the lead now. 'So you're aware they were all killed recently?'

'Yes, I saw them named on the news last night. I couldn't believe it.'

'Did you have contact with any of them lately?'

Dempsey shook his head. 'Not since our late teens. Once I was old enough, I stopped going to the church group altogether. In fact, I think all of us did bar Susie, and we just drifted apart. It's hard to keep friendships going once you get to a certain age.'

'And how about Father Donnelly. Have you had any contact with him? Did you continue to go to church?'

'Me? No way. My mum made me go whilst I was living at home, but once I moved out, I never went back. I had better things to do on a Sunday morning.'

'Did you go to Father Donnelly's funeral?'

'Father Donnelly? I didn't even know he was dead. When did that happen?'

'A couple of months back. Pancreatic cancer,' said Bovalino.

It was Jones's turn to lead the questions again, 'Can I ask where you were each evening, on Monday the twentieth-eighth of January, Thursday the thirty-first and Tuesday the fifth of February?'

Dempsey frowned. 'Why do you want to know?'

'Those are the dates the three women were killed.'

'Am I suspect, Sergeant?'

'It's procedure. We're ruling out all possibilities.'

Dempsey pulled out his phone. 'The twenty-eighth?' He scrolled through a few screens as he searched for something. 'Let me see...I was at the casino.'

'Which one?' asked Bovalino

'Parrs Wood.'

Bovalino tapped his notepad with his pen. 'Wouldn't Great Northern be closer to you?'

'It's six and two-threes, really. Plus, I like vibe in Parrs Wood. It's less intense.'

'And the other dates?' asked Jones.

'Same.'

'Really?'

'Some people go to the pub every night; I play poker. You can check the logs at the casino if you like. They use a swipe card system to get in and out.'

'Are you any good?' asked Bovalino.

Dempsey chuckled. 'I'm up overall. That's the main thing.'

'As a postman, I thought you'd have to be up early?' said Jones.

'I do; that's why I get the last bus home. To be honest, I'm not a great sleeper. I'm lucky if I get four hours a night and a bit of a disco nap in the afternoon.'

Jones nodded. 'Have you noticed anyone hanging around the house lately?'

'This house?' Dempsey sounded surprised.

'Yeah, anyone on the street you don't know when you've come home from the casino?'

'I can't say I have. But then I've not really been looking. Besides, this is Fallowfield. I barely know my next-door neighbours. Why do you ask?'

'The three women killed were all from the same church group, a group you used to be part of. We're just being cautious.'

'What, you think I could be next?'

'I'm not saying that, but it doesn't hurt to be careful.'

Dempsey laughed. 'Come on, seriously. Why would anyone want to kill me, Sergeant? I'm just a postie.'

'What about Clarke, Gillespie and McNulty?'

'What about them?'

'Can you think why anyone would want to kill *them*?'

Dempsey shook his head. 'No, but then I've not seen them for a long time. A lot can happen in life, I suppose.'

'True enough,' said Jones.

'Maybe they were killed by a Vatican hitman,' said Dempsey jovially.

'What makes you say that?' asked Bovalino, frowning.

Dempsey raised his hands as if defending himself. 'It was a joke. Bloody hell, I didn't mean it.'

Jones wasn't amused either. He rose to his feet. 'Looks like we have everything we need,' he said icily. 'No need to take up anymore of your time.'

'I do hope I've been of use, although I'm not sure I have, Sergeant.'

'It all helps, Mr Dempsey.'

Dempsey showed them to the front door and opened it. 'Do you have any ideas when the funerals will be taking place?' he asked as the two men stepped outside.

'We're not sure at this stage,' Bovalino replied. 'If you contact Father Maguire at St Patrick's, I believe all the families have instructed him to look after arrangements. He can update you when it's all sorted.'

'I'll do that. I would happily break my church ban to say goodbye to the girls. Wonderful human beings, each one of them.'

Jones handed Dempsey his card. 'If you see anything suspicious, anything at all, call this number.'

Dempsey smiled and tapped the card on the door. 'I will, Sergeant. You can be sure of that.'

Jones sensed he still wasn't taking the threat seriously. 'Right, well, I appreciate your help, sir.'

Dempsey gently closed the door. 'Anytime, Sergeant. Anytime.'

27

A n icy wind was blowing strong enough to release a chunk of Phillips's hair from the bobble that kept it tied neatly in place as she walked up to St Patrick's. Pulling it back from her face, she tucked it behind her ear. When she reached the church entrance, she noticed the door was open. Stepping inside, she found it empty and stood for a moment, taking in the deafening silence. It was surprisingly warm inside, a welcome relief from the winter weather; and she felt her cheeks starting to flush almost immediately.

A door in need of oil creaked loudly to her right and she spotted Father Maguire stepping out of a small wooden box. She recognised it as what the Catholic Church referred to as a confessional; two small rooms with an adjoining screen where parishioners confessed their sins and ask for God's forgiveness.

'Good afternoon, Inspector.' His cheery voice echoed around the vast space as he approached.

'Sorry to bother you, Father, but I wonder if you might be able to spare me five minutes?'

'Of course. Please, follow me. We can nip to the house through the vestry.'

Following him, Phillips could have been forgiven for thinking the priest was just a regular guy from behind. Aside from the usual black garb, he carried himself with confidence, his walk almost a swagger. She couldn't imagine there were many priests who commanded such a physical presence.

Maguire stepped through the vast oak door to one side of the sanctuary and into a large room with ornate chairs and a wall of mahogany closets. 'This is where we get dressed and ready for action.'

Phillips smiled politely, but there was something about the space that gave her an uneasy feeling in the pit of her stomach, as if it was the domain of ghosts of a past she was yet to uncover.

Maguire opened the door at the far side of the room and Phillips recognised the kitchen up ahead.

'Coffee?' he asked brightly as they entered the room.

'Yes please.'

Phillips took a seat at the table, but this time sat where Maguire had positioned himself the previous time. It was an old trick that allowed her to get a different perspective on her surroundings. She liked to challenge herself to always look at situations from every possible angle. One thing remained the same, though; the chair, like the one she had used during her last visit, was almost impossibly hard and uncomfortable. The old, loosely tied cushion had long lost its usefulness.

A short time later, Maguire placed a cafetière of steaming coffee on the table.

'Come into some money, have you?' Phillips pointed to the filter coffee.

The priest laughed. 'Hardly. We had a pound sale in the church hall the other day and I spotted this. Thought I'd give it a go instead of the instant. You know, a change is as good as a rest, as they say. You're my first guinea pig.' He poured the rich black liquid into Phillips's cup. 'So, how can I help, Inspector?'

Phillips added milk to her cup, stirred the mixture and took a sip before speaking. 'I need to ask you about some historical claims of abuse.'

'Abuse, by whom?'

'A Catholic priest from this parish. I have reason to suspect it could have been Father Donnelly.'

Maguire looked surprised. 'Father Donnelly? Really?'

'I'm afraid so.'

'Well, I'm not sure I can be of much help, Inspector. This is the first I've heard of it.'

Phillips took out her mobile phone, found what she was looking for and placed it on the table in front of Maguire. 'Have you seen this photo before?'

Maguire inspected it. 'Yes, that looks like one of the church's trips to Lourdes.'

'Do you recognise anyone in the photo?'

Maguire stared at the screen again. 'Yes. That's Father Donnelly, Betty Clarke on the right, Susan Gillespie and Deidre McNulty.'

'Do you recognise the two boys?'

'I'm afraid I don't.' This time Maguire didn't look at the screen.

'Are you sure?'

'Quite sure.'

Phillips kept her eyes locked on the priest. 'Have you ever heard of Matt Logan or Thomas Dempsey?'

Maguire appeared deep in thought as he repeated the names quietly to himself. 'I think they may have been part of the church group around the time I was here as a seminarian, but I can't place them.'

'They are the two boys in the photo.'

Maguire glanced down at the phone again. 'Oh yes, I think I do remember them. Not well, though.'

Phillips pointed to the image. 'This chap here is Matt

Logan. As we understand it, he made a claim of sexual abuse against Father Donnelly not long after this photo was taken. In fact, we have reason to believe the abuse actually started on this trip to Lourdes.'

Maguire looked appalled. 'Oh dear God, really? I knew nothing about that.'

'Not many people did. In fact, Logan reported the abuse to his parents, who took the claim direct to Donnelly.'

'And what happened?'

'He dismissed it. Said the boy was a fantasist who made up the claim to avoid getting into trouble for an indiscretion that took place on the Lourdes trip.'

'An indiscretion? I'm not following you.'

'Father Donnelly allegedly caught Logan masturbating in France and threatened to tell his parents. The claims were supposedly Logan's way of getting in first to discredit him.'

Maguire pursed his lips. 'Well, I have to say, in spite of the teachings, it's not uncommon for young men to experiment sexually. It sounds a plausible explanation.'

'True, but claiming a priest had molested you to stop your parents finding out seems a bit extreme, doesn't it?'

A wry smile crossed Maguire's face. 'You're not a Catholic are you, Inspector?'

'No, agnostic.'

'Thought as much. Well, in the world of Catholicism, there are varying degrees of...how can I put it? *Intensity.* Some families come to church once a week, say their prayers and go about their business under the wider umbrella of Catholic doctrine. Others, however, take it a whole lot more seriously. In many of those cases, it's feasible to believe a young boy would pretty much do anything rather than admit to his parents he was masturbating.'

Phillips took another swig of coffee. 'I understand. Still, I think it's a big claim to make in order to avoid being chastised.'

'Inspector, a lot of the older generation in our community come from rural Ireland, where punishment was delivered indiscriminately with a belt. That behaviour travelled with them, and we're not talking a couple of strokes of the leather either; more like the buckle across the back repeatedly. Nowadays it would be classed as child abuse. Maybe that's what Logan was trying to avoid by making the claims against Father Donnelly? Maybe his parents were the *real* abusers in this case?'

Phillips took a moment to process Maguire's theory before returning to the image on her phone. 'Father, do you know why anyone would want to kill the three women in this photo?'

Maguire shook his head. 'It's a question I've prayed on a lot this last week, but I'm afraid I don't have an answer.'

'Could it be something to do with the trip itself?'

'Perhaps, but I can't think what that could be.' Maguire drained his cup. 'I wish I could tell you more, but I wasn't there. Sorry I can't be much more help.' He glanced at the plastic clock on the wall above the crucifix. 'Look at the time! I'm due to start confession in five minutes. Would you excuse me, Inspector?'

'Of course.'

The two stood. 'And I'm sorry to ask, but would you mind going out through the side door. I'm worried what the old dears might think if I walk out of the vestry with a woman in tow.' Maguire smiled. 'They'll be calling the Bishop's hotline within the hour.'

Despite never having been religious, Phillips knew gossip was a key currency in all church communities. She returned his smile. 'I understand. I should be getting back anyway.'

'Thank you, Inspector,' Maguire said warmly as he turned and walked back towards the main church.

Phillips called after him. 'Father, there is just one thing...'

Maguire stopped and turned to face her, a quizzical look on his face.

'If anything does come back to you about Logan's claims, or the trip to Lourdes, please get in touch, won't you?'

Maguire nodded. 'Of course, but I really don't think there's anything else to tell you. Goodbye, Inspector.'

Phillips watched him walk away until he disappeared into the vestry and closed the door behind him. With one last look around the kitchen, she made her way out through the side door and headed back to her car.

28

P hillips had already paid the taxi driver via the Uber app by the time the car stopped. Jumping out of the cab, she rushed to Thomas Dempsey's front door in the pouring rain, chastising herself for forgetting her umbrella. Earlier that evening, she had fallen asleep on the couch again after another bottle of Pinot, waking only when Jones called her mobile. He'd relayed the details of the panicked conversation he'd just had with Dempsey, who believed he'd been followed home from the casino by the Cheadle murderer. His Fallowfield address no more than ten minutes from her home, she'd agreed to deal with it rather than have Jones come all the way from the other side of the city. He'd covered for her on many an occasion over the last six months, and she was happy to return the favour. Besides, she was keen to hear exactly what Dempsey had seen.

She rang the bell and sheltered from the rain under the tiny porch. A moment later, she heard the deadbolt release before the front door opened on its chain. Dempsey peered out.

'Hello, Mr Dempsey, I'm Detective Inspector Jane Phillips.'

She held up her ID close enough for him to read it. 'DS Jones sent me. May I come in?'

Dempsey scrutinised it closely a moment, then closed the door. He released the chain and opened it fully to let her in. When she stepped inside, he closed it and secured the dead-bolts once more.

'I'm having a brandy to settle my nerves,' he said, bringing her into the kitchen at the rear of the house. 'Do you want one?'

Phillips was sorely tempted. 'Better not. I'm on duty.'

She took a seat at the small breakfast table in the middle of the room while Dempsey poured himself a large tumbler of a brandy, then placed the supermarket-labelled bottle on the table in front of him, next to a large carving knife.

'How are you feeling, Mr Dempsey?' she asked, staring at the knife.

'Please, call me Tom.'

Phillips smiled briefly. 'Tom.'

Dempsey ran a hand through his hair. 'I've got to be honest, I'm a little shaken up. After what happened to the girls in Cheadle, I seriously thought I was next.'

'I can imagine. Look, I know you've already explained this to DS Jones, but it'd really help to hear what happened directly from you. Especially now you've had time to process it.'

'Of course. Where do I start...?' Dempsey took a mouthful of brandy, pausing a moment to reflect. 'Well, I went to the casino again tonight.'

'DS Jones said you go quite a lot.'

'Three or four times a week, depending on work shifts. I tend to avoid the weekends, as it's full of stag-dos and hen-parties. It's much quieter during the week.'

'Ok, so what happened at the casino?'

'Nothing, the casino was absolutely fine. I had a good night, actually. I walked out two hundred quid up. It was after that. I was planning on using some of my winnings to get a taxi home, but managed to catch the last bus back into town. I get free travel on my post office pass, you see. So, I jumped on at Parrs Wood Interchange and headed back here.'

'What time was that?'

'It was the last bus, so it would have been just before midnight.'

'Then what happened?'

'It's only a short journey, around ten minutes. I was back in Fallowfield before I knew it. I jumped off at the stop there by Victoria Road and began walking home.'

'Did anyone else get off at that stop?'

'Nope, just me.'

'And did you see anyone around when you got off?'

'That's just it. There was literally no one around. Not a soul. I've rarely seen it like that round here.'

'So, when did you notice you were being followed?'

'It was just as I was coming up to the junction between Victoria and Wellington Road. I stopped to make sure there was no traffic coming before I crossed, and heard footsteps behind me. I paid no attention to them at first, but then I started to think about the girls and what happened to them, and what Sergeant Jones had said about being careful, and I panicked. I wasn't far from home, so I hurried as fast as I could – almost running at the end. I was petrified he was coming for me.'

'And you're sure it was a man?'

'I think so. To be honest, it was hard to tell from that distance and whoever it was was wearing a thick coat with the hood up.'

'So you managed to get inside. Then what happened?'

'The house was in darkness and I sat for a moment behind the door. I needed to get my heart rate down before I dared look through the security spy-hole. When I did finally pluck up the courage, there was no-one there. I checked the back door was locked, as well as all the windows downstairs. I stood in the dark for about five minutes, peering out from behind the net curtains at the front and then the back. I couldn't see anything, so I grabbed that knife and headed up to bed. I was in the bathroom brushing my teeth when I heard an almighty bang in the alley behind. God, I almost shat myself.'

'Did you recognise the noise?'

'Not really. Maybe it was bins falling over or something like that.'

'So what did you do?'

'Nothing initially. Like I say, I was terrified, unable to do anything. Eventually I got a hold of myself and turned out the bathroom light and went through to the bedroom. I looked out the window onto the yard and the alley beyond, but there's a broken streetlight, so I couldn't see anything to begin with. And then, when my eyes finally adjusted to the dark, I saw him.'

'The same man from earlier?'

Dempsey took another swig of brandy. 'I'm almost certain it was him. He was stood in the shadows and seemed to be watching the house downstairs, peering through the metal gate at the back. Thankfully it's locked with a huge padlock from this side, so he couldn't get in.'

'He was trying to get through the gate?'

'He held two of the bars in his hands like this...' Dempsey imitated the action. 'Pulled it back and forth for a while. I could hear it rattling on its hinges.'

'What happened next?'

'I was stood, virtually holding my breath, peering out through the side of the curtain by the window frame, when he looked up and *straight* at me. Honest to God, my heart almost stopped right there and then. I swear he could hear it beating out there in the alley.'

'Did he see you looking at him?'

'I can't be certain, but I think so.'

'What about his face. Did you get a look at it?'

'No, like I said, he was wearing a hood and it was silhou-etted in the shadows. And then all of a sudden, there was another noise in the alley which caught his attention. I remember he jerked his head towards where it had come from, and rushed off in the direction of the main road.'

'Did something startle him?'

'Maybe. I definitely heard something, but I couldn't see anything, or anybody else in the alley.'

'Was that the last you saw of him?'

Dempsey appeared to shudder. 'Yes, thank God.'

'And how long was it before you called DS Jones?'

'Right then, from the back bedroom. Well, as soon as I could speak. I was in shock, petrified he was going to come back.'

'I can imagine.' Phillips paused a moment. 'Look Tom, I think it might be best if you take tomorrow off work, just until we can have a look around the back of the house and see if he left anything behind.'

Dempsey nodded enthusiastically. 'Whatever you say, Inspector. Until you catch this guy, I'm staying at home with the doors locked and the curtains drawn.'

'Sounds like a sensible plan. Staying inside is the safest option right now. I'll organise for a patrol unit to keep an eye on the place and arrange for uniform to call in each night to check on you. Just to make sure you're ok. You good with that?'

Dempsey looked visibly relieved and smiled for the first time since Phillips had entered the house. 'God, yeah, that'd be brilliant. When will they come?'

'Probably early evening. If he *is* hanging around, the pres-ence of a squad car will let him know we're protecting you and watching the house.'

'That's amazing. Thank you so much, Inspector.' He

drained the remainder of his glass and poured himself another large measure before holding the bottle up to Phillips. 'You sure I can't tempt you, Inspector?'

A stiff brandy was exactly what she wanted right now, but she steeled herself. She was on duty, she reminded herself. 'No thank you, but before I head off, is there anything else you can recall that might be of help?'

Dempsey appeared deep in thought for a long moment before turning his attention back to Phillips. 'No. I'm sure that's everything.'

Phillips pulled out her phone to order her taxi home. Luckily there was a car dropping off just a couple of streets away. She glanced up to see Dempsey staring at her, his mouth open as if trying to find the right words.

'Inspector. maybe I shouldn't be asking this, but considering what happened tonight, I'd like to know.'

'You'd like to know what?'

'Do you think it was Matt Logan – you know – out in the alley tonight?'

Phillips paused a moment before answering. 'Probably best not to speculate at this stage. But whoever was out there, we will get them. It's just a matter of time. For now, stay inside and keep all the doors locked. In fact, better still, is there anywhere you could go for a few days – any friends who could put you up?'

A fleeting sadness seemed to cross Dempsey's face. 'Not really. I don't have many friends, to be honest.'

'Well, in that case it's even more important that you stay in touch with us and let us know immediately if you see or hear anything that worries you, okay?' She passed him her card. 'You can contact me day or night.'

'Thank you, Inspector.'

Her phone pinged, signalling that her car was outside.

'Look after yourself, Tom, and stay safe. I'll keep in touch.' She moved towards the front door as Dempsey unlocked it.

'I will. I really appreciate you coming here so quickly.'

Phillips stepped out under the tiny porch, which was struggling against the torrent of rain. 'No worries. It's what we're here for.' With a brief smile, she ran out to the waiting car.

29

P hillips planned to use the journey to Matt Logan's parent's home to bring Jones up to speed on last night's visit to Dempsey's. She was about to debrief him when her phone pinged, signalling she'd received a text message. She took a moment to read it before sighing loudly and tapping her response. When she was finished, she turned her attention to Jones, waiting patiently.

'Everything ok, Guv?'

'Fine, Jonesy.'

'Really? You sounded a bit annoyed by that message.'

She exhaled loudly. 'It was just Marty.'

'Marty Michaels?'

'Yep.'

'Are you guys still in contact, then?'

'On and off. He sometimes comes round for a drink after he's finished recording his show.'

Jones looked at her sideways. *'Just a drink?'*

Phillips looked aghast. 'God yes. He's not my type.'

'What, not a midget with a small willy like Brown?' teased Jones, making Phillips laugh.

'I knew I shouldn't have told you about that.'

'Sorry, Guv, I couldn't resist. So what's Marty done now?'

She shrugged. 'It's nothing really. He promised to take me to see a play at the Lowry on the weekend, but he's double-booked himself with Rebecca and can't go. I was really looking forward to it, that's all.'

'His ex-wife Rebecca?'

'Yes.'

'Well, can't you take someone else?'

'Sure, and if I'm honest it's not really the fact he can't go. It just pisses me off that it's me that gets dumped instead of his *precious* Rebecca.'

Jones stared at her. 'Are you sure you don't have feelings for him, Guv?'

'Yes, yes, I'm sure. It's just my ego. No-one likes to be second choice, do they? Look, in the grand scheme of things it's really not important right now. I'll get over it. Enough about my rubbish social life. Let me tell you about last night.'

As they continued to Cheadle, Phillips relayed her conversation with Dempsey and shared her views on whether Logan was, or wasn't, the man he had seen at the back of his house. If truth be told, she couldn't be sure either way. Entwistle and Bovalino had been despatched earlier that morning to try and track him down and check his whereabouts the previous night. Easier said than done considering his nomadic lifestyle, and she was waiting to hear back from them.

A short time later, they arrived at the Logan family home, situated on a leafy street on the edge of the suburb; a detached four-bedroom house with large gardens front and back. Two cars sat in the drive, both Volvos.

Phillips had called ahead to make an appointment, and Mr Logan let them in. He was a tall imposing man with a heavy brow and an austere appearance. He showed them through to the conservatory, where his wife, Denise, sat on a wicker chair reading a copy of the *Daily Mail*. She looked up as they entered. She looked frail and wiry, and it was obvious Matt had inherited his mother's genes.

Mr Logan – Peter – made the introductions and all four sat. Jones took out his notepad in preparation.

After the usual pleasantries, Phillips brought the conversation round to their son. 'When was the last time you saw Matt?'

'Matthew,' Denise corrected her.

'Sorry, Matthew.'

The Logans glanced at each other before Peter took the lead. 'It's been a few years. After his last prison sentence, we decided it would be best to try and let him go.'

'Why did you decide that?'

Denise let out a sad sigh. 'Because he's broken our hearts too many times. We really tried to help him, welcoming him back into the family home whenever he was released, but it was no use. He just kept going back to the drugs; stealing from us, from his grandmother. Sometimes even the neighbours. I felt so ashamed.'

'He was a good boy as a child, but once he hit puberty, he became a different person. Moody, withdrawn, secretive. Always angry about something,' said Peter.

'Was that around the time of this trip to Lourdes?' Phillips handed him her phone.

Peter stared down at the image for a moment. He nodded without saying anything, and handed the phone to his wife. She immediately started to cry. 'My little Matthew.' She was barely audible.

Phillips needed to tread carefully. 'I know this will be difficult for you, but can you tell us about the accusations of abuse Matthew made against Father Donnelly?'

The Logans looked at each other, as if each was checking the other's reaction.

Peter responded. 'It was a misunderstanding. Long forgotten.'

Denise remained silent, her eyes fixed on her husband.

'Matthew doesn't think so,' said Jones.

Denise's gaze turned to Jones. 'How do *you* know that?'

'We spoke to him earlier this week. He came in to talk to us.'

Denise appeared incredulous. 'About what?'

'He's helping us with our enquiries.'

Peter took Phillips's phone from his wife's hand and scrutinised the image again. 'Is that Betty Clarke?'

'Yes,' said Phillips.

'Is that what Matthew has been helping you with, her murder inquiry?'

'Yes.'

Denise put her hand to her mouth. 'Oh my God. You don't think Matthew had anything to do with it, do you?'

'As DS Jones said, he is helping us with our enquiries at the moment.'

Peter's tone was suddenly confrontational. 'Is he under arrest?' he asked, staring at Phillips hard.

'No, he merely came into the station a couple of days ago to answer a few questions. He went home the same day,' said Jones.

Denise seemed surprised. 'Home? Is he off the streets?'

'A hostel in Cheetham Hill.' Phillips attempted to steer the conversation back to Logan's abuse. 'Matthew told us he was repeatedly raped by Father Donnelly.'

Peter's agitation continued to build. 'Nonsense. Like I said, it was all a misunderstanding. We spoke to Father Donnelly at the time and he explained everything.'

'Which was?'

'That he had caught Matthew...well...fondling himself on the trip to France. When he told him he was going to inform us, Mathew made the allegations about Father Donnelly.'

'And you believed him?'

It was Denise's turn to get agitated now. 'Of course we did. He was a man of God.'

'I don't mean to be rude, but I take it you're both aware of the sheer volume of historical abuse being levelled at members of the Catholic Church now?' said Jones.

Peter remained defiant. 'Father Donnelly was a good man. A kind, warm and caring priest. He married us and baptised Matthew, as well as oversaw his first communion and confirmation. He was practically part of the family. There is no way he would molest Matthew, or anyone else, for that matter.'

'Then can you explain why, almost thirty years on, Matthew still believes he was raped by him?' said Phillips.

Peter's fists clenched in time with his jaw. 'Matthew was always a little highly strung. As a teenager he went off the rails, he started hanging around with the wrong crowd and got into drugs. He's been lying every day since. I have no reason to believe anything has changed, Inspector. There was no abuse, no rape and no injustice. We did everything we could for Matthew. It's the drugs that changed him. Nothing else.'

Phillips glanced at Jones, whose expression backed up her own thoughts: this conversation had gone as far it could. She gently nodded, which action her partner mimicked.

'Thank you for your time, Mr and Mrs Logan,' she said. 'If Matthew does contact you or you can think of anything else we should know, please do get in touch.'

Peter Logan said nothing as he showed them to the front door, audibly muttering 'Good day' as he closed it behind them.

Back on the road, they stopped to debrief.

'What do you make of that then, Guv?'

'No wonder Matt Logan is so fucked up. Their own kid was potentially raped by the family priest and they won't hear a word of it. They're in no doubt at all it was Matt who was lying, not the priest.'

'Like I said in there, the number of historical claims is climbing by the day, worldwide. How can they still be so sure it didn't happen in *their* parish to *their* son?'

'Denial is a powerful thing. I mean, you saw them. It's the fear of shame. What will the neighbours say? Can you imagine if it had come out that Logan *was* raped? Rather than it be about their son, it would've been about protecting their own reputation.'

'It's a fucking disgrace, Guv. A young child looks to his mum and dad to protect him, and what do they do? Call him a liar and then make him face his abuser every Sunday.'

'Yeah, *a child* who may have been driven to murder.'

'Are you leaning back towards Logan then?'

Phillips kicked the garden wall in front of her in frustration. 'I don't know, Jonesy. I mean, he's clearly unstable. I could understand him wanting to kill Donnelly, but why the others? It doesn't make sense. Plus, our guy is methodical. Logan is a meth-head.'

Jones laughed. 'He certainly doesn't look like your usual serial killer, does he?'

'No, but then these days, who does?'

30

Ricky Murray stopped for coffee despite running thirty minutes late. However, having worked late last night designing one of his client's websites for a relaunch, he figured he was owed a couple of minutes.

Margot, the barista at his favoured coffee shop, smiled as he walked through the door. She began to prepare his usual without asking: a skinny latte with a double shot of espresso.

'Can I get a large Frappuccino as well please, Margot, and a couple of those double chocolate muffins too.' Ricky's flamboyant delivery matched the brightly coloured outfit grabbing at his short, plump frame.

While he waited for his order, he chatted to Margot's business partner and girlfriend, Christina. 'Anything planned for tonight, Ricky?'

He giggled. 'Do Marks and Spencer do a Valentines meal for one?'

'No one special for you today?'

'Just me, Christina, just me. Truth be told, I don't think there's a man that can handle this candy.' Ricky ran his hand across the side of his head for effect. In truth, despite his crippling loneliness, he had major trust issues and was terrified of intimacy. For Ricky, it was far easier to be alone than risk getting hurt. 'What about you and Margot?'

'A cosy night in with a bottle of wine and a good movie. After a full day in here, we never have the energy to go out.'

Margot passed him his order before landing a kiss on Christina's cheek. 'And why would we? We have everything we need right here.'

'Ooh, you make me sick the pair of you.' He smiled, picking up the two coffees. 'Have fun and don't do anything I wouldn't do. Which to be fair, doesn't leave much!' He winked, then headed out the door.

As he stepped out of the lift on the twelfth floor of the Blue Tower in Media City, he was greeted by the beaming smile of Charlie, Media Mogul's receptionist and Ricky's BFF.

'One fresh Frappuccino from *Margot's*, and, because it's Valentines and neither of us have anyone to spoil, a naughty double chocolate muffin for you, and one for *moi*!'

Charlie grabbed the muffin and lifted it to her nose. 'Mmm, you shouldn't have – but I'm so glad you did.' She laughed. 'Anyway, what's all this about you not having someone to spoil? If that's the case, who sent you that beautifully wrapped gift on your desk?'

Ricky looked momentarily shocked. 'A gift on my desk? Are you sure it's for me?'

'Has your name on it.'

Struggling to contain his excitement, Ricky ran to his desk, placing the coffee and muffin down before picking up the parcel and whisking it back to show Charlie.

'Are you gonna open it, then?'

Ricky moved the box around in his hands, marvelling at the luxurious red paper, then opened the tiny envelope tucked inside a silver satin bow.

He read the message aloud. '"To my very secret Valentine,

with eyes and lips that shine, Can't wait to see you naked – and know you're mine, all mine." Cheeky.'

'Any ideas who it's from?'

'Not a bloody clue. It's probably just Gary or Jamie having a laugh at my expense. They know how long I've been looking for Mr Right.'

'What's in the box?'

Rick stared at it. 'It's so beautifully wrapped, it's a shame to open it.' A split-second later, he was ripping the paper off like a kid on Christmas morning. 'Oh wow, four luxury dark chocolate truffles – my absolute favourites. Whoever sent them, they really won't want to see me naked after eating them.'

Charlie giggled.

He offered her the box. 'D'ya want one?'

'No thanks, honey. They're supposed to be for you. A romantic gift on Valentines. Don't you be sharing them now.'

Ricky couldn't contain his joy. 'You're right. I'm gonna save them for tonight when I'm watching *The Notebook* for the hundredth time.'

'Good for you.'

Ricky gathered up the discarded wrapping paper and chucked it in the bin. 'Is Belinda in yet?' he asked, referring to his boss.

'Yep, came in at eight. She's been in her office with the door shut since.'

'Right. I'd better go and show my face and apologise for being late or she'll be murder for the rest of the day.' He expertly picked out a truffle and popped it in his mouth. 'Well... it'd be rude not to have *at least* one this morning!' he mumbled through chocolate-stained teeth.

Laughing, Charlie waved him off as she turned her attention back to the switchboard and picked up a waiting call. 'Good morning, Media Mogul, Charlie speaking. How can I direct your call today?'

After a slightly fractious ten-minute catch-up with Belinda, Ricky returned to his desk. Plonking down in his seat, he locked his phone into the cradle and switched on his powerful iMac. His biggest client to date had just launched their new site a few days ago, and each morning he found himself with a list of bugs that needed ironing out. This morning was no different.

When he finally looked up from his desk, he realised it was almost lunchtime. Having already devoured the muffin and all *four* of the truffles (they were just too *more*-ish to resist), he wasn't hungry. Nonetheless, he decided to go for a walk with Charlie when she asked at half twelve.

As they strolled along Salford Quays, the winter wind blowing off the water cut through to the bone and, though it was a sunny day and ten degrees, it felt more like two or three with the wind-chill. By the time they returned to the heat of the office an hour later, Ricky's skin felt hot and flushed. He checked his reflection in the compact mirror he kept in his desk drawer and was surprised to see his skin looked almost beet-root red.

Tackling the latest feedback email from his client, he flipped from feeling too hot to suddenly freezing cold, so much so that he began to shiver as one of the web developers walked past his desk 'Is there a window open, Jon?'

'I don't think so Ricky,' his colleague replied.

Unable to concentrate and feeling a little sorry for himself, he wandered over to see Charlie, leaning over the reception desk theatrically. 'Feel my head. Have I got a temperature?'

Charlie put a hand up to his forehead. 'Bit clammy but no temperature. Mind you, you don't look too good.'

'Thanks a bunch.' Ricky made off again before suddenly stopping in his tracks. He stood motionless, staring at the floor.

'Are you ok, Ricky?'

'I've got to go to the toilet.' Luckily the Gents was just to the left of reception. Rushing through the door, he burst into the nearest cubicle and vomited noisily. Thankfully the rest of the stalls were empty as his stomach heaved and hot acidic liquid poured out of his mouth. Eventually, when he was sure there was nothing left, he took his time cleaning himself up and made his way back to Charlie.

'What happened?' she asked, looking at him in concern.

'You don't want to know, but I think I've got that gastro flu that's going round.'

'Oh God, no. That's knocking everyone out. You should go home. You don't want to spread it around.'

Ricky nodded weakly. 'Will you let Belinda know? Tell her I'll call her in the morning if I'm still bad.' He headed back to his desk to collect his coat and bag.

Ten minutes later, Ricky's heart lifted when he saw the tram waiting at the Media City stop. It was due to leave in just a few minutes, which mercifully meant he'd be home soon enough.

As the tram wobbled down the line, he closed his eyes and breathed slowly, trying to control his nausea. When the tram rolled to a stop at East Didsbury, he was already by the doors as they opened. He rushed along the platform and up onto Didsbury Road before hurrying left onto Burnage Lane.

Seconds later, his front door came into view. Shoving his key in the lock, he tried to think of anything but his watering palate, but as he opened the door, he was struck by a sudden urgency in his bowels. He virtually threw himself upstairs and into the bathroom. Dropping onto his hands and knees, vomit spewed from his mouth into the basin. At the other end, his bowels gave way as he soiled himself. Hanging on to the toilet for dear life, the hot liquid continued to pour from his mouth and backside. Finally, after what seemed an age, it all stopped and he slumped to the floor, crying pitifully.

After a few moments of lying in his own faeces on the cold tiles, he summoned up the courage to lift himself up and carefully removed his trousers and underwear. The foul stench of the diarrhoea on his clothes and hands caused him to gag, and for a moment he thought it was about to begin again. Mercifully he held his breath a moment and it eventually passed.

He didn't have the stomach to wash the soiled clothing, so instead packed them into the bathroom waste-bin. Next, he stripped naked, ready to shower. He had recently bought the house at auction, and it was in dire need of renovation. He hated the fact he had to use a low-pressured shower over a bath, requiring the intricate balancing of the hot and cold mixer taps. It always seemed to take forever to get the temperature right – usually it was either freezing cold or scalding hot. All he wanted in this moment was to get under a hot power shower like the one he'd left behind in his old rented flat in the city.

When he pulled back the plastic shower curtain, the sight that greeted him caused him to jump back in terror. A man stood in the bath, his black, manic eyes staring at him above a surgeon's mask.

'Poor, sick little Ricky,' the man said softly.

Ricky tried to scream, but was instantly silenced as the man sprayed something directly into his open mouth. A moment later he tumbled to the floor, unconscious.

31

After hauling Ricky's naked body into the bath, he washed the filth off with the shower-head extension. Then he filled the tub with fresh water and, placing him flat on his back, cable-tied his wrists to the mixer taps.

Everything he needed was laid out on the floor in front of him. He sat on the toilet seat adjacent to Ricky's hands and head, waiting for him to wake from the sedative. He passed the time by checking his phone – in particular, the local Manchester news channels and GMP's twitter account – for updates on the so-called 'Cheadle Murders'. He smiled at the thought of the journalists having to find a new name for them now he had moved his hunting grounds to East Didsbury. After a thorough search of all channels, he concluded there was nothing new to report. That would soon change.

His attention was drawn back to Ricky as he began to stir, slowly at first as he opened his eyes, followed by frantic movement as he realised his predicament. He bolted upright, splashing water everywhere, and yanked at his hands, trying to free them from the cable-ties.

'It's no use, Ricky, they don't come off. I can assure you of that.' His voice was calm.

Ricky instinctively shrunk away, but the plastic ties limited his movements.

After three kills, he had grown more confident and begun to appreciate his own flair for the dramatic. He could, after all, have killed each of his victims by merely using a heavier dose of the sedative, but he had wanted them to suffer as he had. And now, with his fourth victim about to be consigned to the same fate as the previous three, he had decided to spice things up a little to keep it interesting. This time he hadn't removed the surgeon's mask, a sinister image for anyone to wake to, let alone Ricky Murray in his current predicament.

'Do you know who I am?'

Ricky shook his head vigorously.

'Do you know why I'm here?'

Ricky began to cry. 'Are you going to kill me?'

He nodded firmly. 'Do you know why I'm going to kill you, Ricky?'

'No!' Ricky wailed.

'What? Even after seeing what happened to Susan, Dee-Dee and Mrs Clarke? Come on. Surely you must have some idea?'

Ricky managed to compose himself for a moment. 'I don't know what you're talking about.'

'Oh, come on Ricky. You may not recognise me, but I sure as hell know you. I also know that you and Dee-Dee McNulty were besties when you were little. You told each other everything. *Everything!*'

Ricky's eyes widened.

'So, let's not end our relationship with even more lies.' He slowly removed the mask and smiled broadly.

Ricky stared at him, confusion filling his face.

'You still don't recognise me?'

'No,' he whimpered.

'Do you know, Ricky, each one of the others had the exact same reaction as you. They had no idea who I was at first. Have I really changed that much?' He leaned forwards and picked up the thick plastic bag. 'Do you know what I use this for?'

Ricky shook his head vigorously.

'It's my magic 'truth bag'. See, when I introduce this to the conversation, I find I'm suddenly told the truth. The truth, from people who had lied their entire lives about what happened to me.'

Ricky stared at the bag. 'I-I'll tell you whatever you want to know. You don't need to use that.'

'Really? So you'd be willing to tell me your deepest, darkest secrets in return for me sparing your life?'

'Yes. Yes. I would!'

'Well, Ricky, this is a new one for me, I must say, but I'm willing to give it a go if you are. Shall we try it your way then?'

'Yes, whatever you want to know. I'll tell you *anything*.'

He leaned in closer, just inches from Ricky's face, affecting his gameshow-host voice once more. 'Ok, first question... Who am I?'

'*I don't know.*'

He let out a loud noise imitating a gameshow buzzer, then stood and grabbed the bag tight in both hands. 'Wrong answer, Ricky. It's bag time.'

Ricky reeled backwards as far as the restraints would allow, the sudden movement causing water to slop over the side of the bathtub again. 'Wait. I'll remember, I'll remember! Just give me a second.'

He smiled and sat back down. 'Ok, and because I'm feeling generous, I'll even give you a clue.'

'Thank you, thank you.'

'Pyjamas.'

'*Pyjamas?*'

'Tick-tock tick-tock! Ricky, time's running out.'

Ricky studied his captor's face. 'Pyjamas...'

'I need your final answer, Ricky.' The bag tightened in his hands. 'What's it going to be?'

'Er...er...pyjamas? I don't understand...?'

'Come on, Ricky, you know this one. Think about it. When you were little, which kid was famous for his pyjamas?'

Ricky's eyes widened as it started to come back to him.

'You remember me now, don't you?'

Ricky looked incredulous. '*Winnie?*'

'We have a winner.' He laughed maniacally, then punched Ricky hard in the nose. A sickening crack followed by a thick rush of blood indicated it was broken. 'I hate that fucking nickname.'

Ricky was crying again, his blood catching in his lips. 'You forced me to say it.'

'Only because that's how you all knew me. None of you ever bothered to call me by my real name.' Blood continued to pour from Ricky's nose, which had already begun to swell. 'Well, you've avoided the bag *so far*. Let's see how you get on with a harder question...if you still want to play, that is?'

Ricky nodded as blood dripped into the bathwater, turning it pink.

'Ricky Murray...did you know that *he* was abusing me all those years?'

'Who?'

He thrust the plastic bag under Ricky's nose. 'Do you *want* me to use this? If you dare make me say his name, I promise you, you'll regret it. I'll ask you one more time and *once only* – did you know that evil bastard was abusing me all those years?'

Ricky nodded quickly. 'Yes, I did.' Desperate sobs followed.

'So why didn't you say anything?'

Tears streamed down Ricky's face. He closed his eyes as his whole body began to shake in the water.

'Why, Ricky? Tell me *why*? If you knew what he was doing, why didn't you say anything? You could have stopped him. You could've saved me from almost thirty years of living hell.'

Blood and snot bubbled from Ricky's nose as he spoke. 'I couldn't say anything. He wouldn't let me.'

'Bullshit. You could've said something, *anything*. Why, Ricky? Tell me why?'

Ricky was crying like a baby now. 'Because he raped me before you! He had been abusing me for years before he started on you.'

He hadn't expected that response, and for a long moment was lost for words. 'What? *When*?'

'Every Sunday after mass, in the vestry. I was an altar boy and he would make me stay behind, so he could have sex with me.'

'How old were you?'

'*Ten*. Ten years old. I knew it wasn't right, but he told me it was God's way of punishing my mother for her sins – for divorcing my dad. I was atoning for her weaknesses as a Christian. That he would turn his attention to my little brother if I wasn't willing to do what he wanted. He said if I told my mum, we would both be struck down by God and Aaron would have to go into care. I was ten years old. What the fuck was I supposed to think?'

'Jesus. I thought it was just me,' he whispered.

'When he started on you, he began to leave me alone, until eventually he stopped. I'm ashamed of myself, but that's the real reason I didn't say anything. As long as he had you, he wasn't interested in me.'

Leaning back on the toilet seat, he dropped the plastic bag to the floor and stared in silence at the black gaffer tape by his feet. 'I'm sorry, Ricky. I had no idea you went through that.'

Ricky looked at him desperately. 'Please, let me go. You

don't have to kill me. I won't say anything. I can keep a secret, I promise.'

He nodded. 'I know. You've been doing it for long enough. But you know who I really am, and I've just admitted that I killed the others.'

'I don't care about the others. *They* weren't abused. They didn't suffer like we did. They deserved what happened to them. They knew what he was doing to us and they never said a word. We owe them nothing. As far as I'm concerned, this never happened tonight. I promise you. Just please, let me go.'

For the first time since his abuser had robbed him of his innocence almost three decades ago, he felt a sense of shared pain, of empathy, for the plump little man in front of him, naked, sloshing around in the bloody bath water, battered and bruised. Superficial wounds compared to those inflicted all those years ago in the sanctuary of the church.

Could Ricky be trusted? *Could* he let him live? Having heard his story, he no longer felt the unbridled rage he had directed at him over the last twenty years. Would he really *not* go to the police? He wanted to believe him, but it had been a long time since he had trusted anyone.

'I need a drink. Do you have any?'

'My bedside cabinet. A hipflask of brandy – for when the nightmares come.'

He stood up and left the bathroom, located the cabinet next to Ricky's bed in the main bedroom. When he opened the drawer, he spotted a brushed-metal flask behind a couple of paperback books and a box of tissues. As he pulled it free, one of the books fell forwards on the floor. Photographs spilled from the pages, catching his attention. He bent down to examine them.

His face darkened. Standing up, he strode back to the bathroom and threw the flask at Ricky, who yelped as it hit him in the chest.

He thrust the photos in front of him. 'What are these, you sick fuck?'

Ricky eyes widened. 'I-It's not what it looks like.'

'Really? Because it looks like to me like pictures of small boys in a swimming pool.' He stared furiously at Ricky. 'Are you a fucking paedo too?'

Ricky began to sob. 'No, no. It's not what it looks like. I help out with a kids' group at church and took some pictures for the parents. I just haven't had time to hand them over, that's all.'

'Parents want you taking pictures of their kids in trunks? What a load of crap. You're getting off on them, aren't you? There's a box of tissues with them, for fuck's sake.'

'It's not like that,' Ricky protested. 'I have nightmares and wake up in tears when I remember what he did to me. That's why I have tissues. You have to believe me, the pictures aren't sexual – I've never touched any kids – I swear it.'

He felt the hatred pour out of him again. 'You may not have touched them yet, but *oh you fucking will*! The urge is too strong for your kind.'

He grabbed the plastic bag and thrust it over Ricky's head, wrapping his hands around his neck. Ricky frantically writhed against the bag, kicking his legs and sloshing water over the top of the bath in waves. His hands gripped tighter and tighter as Ricky's gasps became more frantic as the bag filled his nose and mouth. His head lurched backwards and forwards, left and right, until, finally, there was no more splashing water, no more movement. Nothing but the deadly silence.

Breathless and exhausted from the sudden rush of adrenaline, he slumped to the floor, leaning against the toilet, his eyes fixed on the face staring back at him through the bag. A whirlwind of emotions flooded his mind: hatred, anger, sorrow, regret. He knew what Ricky had endured since the age of ten had been a living hell – *just like his own* – but even that could never justify him taking the innocence of another child. The abuse stopped with them.

Looking around the messy room, he felt a sudden urge to get away from Ricky Murray. Tonight had not gone according to plan, and he cursed himself for getting sloppy. If he was going to finish this, he had to stick to the plan. *Always stick to the plan.*

It was time to clean up and get away.

32

'Watch out. Brown's not a happy bunny,' murmured Jones. He stood next to Phillips in the incident room as they surveyed photographs taken earlier that day of Ricky Murray's bathroom.

'No, he's fucking not.' The acerbic tones of the Scotsman filled the room from behind them.

Phillips and Jones turned in unison to see their DCI walking towards them, his angry, red face accentuated by his white shirt. 'Sir,' they said together.

'Jesus Christ! When is this going to stop?'

Phillips stepped forwards. 'Looks like it could be the same guy, sir.'

'I can see that for myself.'

'Although we could be looking at a copycat, sir,' said Jones.

'Copycat? What are you talking about?'

Jones pointed to the map of South Manchester on the wall. 'While the cable ties and plastic bag are similar to the other murders, this time he's moved out of his usual hunting ground. The time of the attack is different, too. Plus, there's no black tape over the eyes.'

'Maybe he's getting sloppy or was in a rush.'

Phillips folded her arms. 'Doesn't fit with our guy's MO. He's meticulous and methodical. Plans everything to nth degree. This one looks almost identical to the rest, but there's something different about it.'

'How could it be a copycat? We haven't released the details of the other murders.'

'Stuff leaks all the time, sir.'

Brown glowered at her. 'Not in *my* squad, Inspector.'

Phillips bit her tongue. This was not the time to go to war with the 'wee man'.

'So, tell me what we know so far?'

Jones produced his notepad. 'Well, sir, the victim is Richard Murray, known on all his social media channels as Ricky, according to Entwistle. He was forty-one, single and a web designer for a company called Media Mogul, based in the Blue Tower of Media City. Evans estimates he was killed yesterday afternoon, around four or five o'clock.' Jones tapped his pen against one of the crime scene photos. 'You can see from the rigor mortis and the saggy skin, he'd been in the water a long time.'

'Who found him?'

'His mother. She got a call from one of his work colleagues, a girl called Charlie who had been trying to get hold of him all morning. *She* says he left early yesterday after a serious case of vomiting, and didn't show this morning. She tried calling and texting, but he didn't reply, which was unusual – apparently Ricky was permanently attached to his phone. When it got to lunchtime and she'd still not heard from him, she called the emergency contact on file – his mum – to see if he'd been in contact with her. He hadn't, but she lives just a few doors down, so she went to check on him. She let herself in with her key and found him like that.'

'Jesus Christ… Poor woman,' whispered Brown.

Phillips nodded. 'She's devastated, as you can imagine. We have an FLO at her house, and we've called her youngest son, Aaron, who's on his way down from Carlisle as we speak.'

Brown stroked his jaw. 'This is getting out of hand. We need to stop this guy – and fast. Four unsolved murders is not a thing to share with the media.'

'With respect, sir, the media shouldn't be our main concern right now,' said Phillips.

'They may not be yours, Inspector, but they *are* mine. This is modern policing, and the media have a huge part to play in how we manage the reputation of the Greater Manchester Police.'

'You mean *your* reputation, don't you?' Phillips said, unable to stop herself.

Brown stepped closer to her, his face even redder. 'I know you don't like me Phillips…'

'How perceptive, sir.'

'…And I'm sure you'd love to see me fall on my sword for this one so you can get your old job back. Well, let me tell you something. Fraser Brown does not fail, and I will not let you fuck up my career the same way you fucked up your own.'

Brown turned to Jones next, pointing his finger at his face. 'And as for you, sonny, and that Neanderthal Bovalino, be careful which horse you two back. Unless, of course, you want *your* careers to go the same way as hers.' He moved his gaze between them. 'Get this into your thick skulls, the pair of you: we are going to solve these murders quickly – and I am going to be the next Superintendent in the GMP, whether you like it or not. I want every available body on this, and I want a head in the noose, fast. You can start by getting your "people of interest" in and sweating them until one of them cracks. Do I make myself clear, *Inspector* Phillips and *Sergeant* Jones?'

Jones nodded. 'Yes sir.'

'Crystal,' said Phillips.

Brown checked his watch. 'It's almost four o'clock. I want the three suspects in for questioning immediately. I don't care where they are or what you lot have planned tonight. Bring them in *now*.'

33

K evin McNulty sat opposite Jones and Bovalino in Interview Room 1, dressed in jeans and a hooded tracksuit.

'Shouldn't I have a lawyer?' he asked nervously.

'Do you think you need one?' said Bovalino.

'I've got nothing to hide.'

'That's good, because we'd like to ask you a few more questions about the night your wife was killed,' said Jones.

McNulty looked at each man in turn. 'But I've told you everything I know.'

Bovalino looked him dead in the eye. 'Everything except where you were that night.'

McNulty appeared exasperated. 'I told you, I was in Cheetham Hill with a prostitute. I'm not proud of the fact, but I'm sorry to say it's true.'

Jones leaned over the desk. 'What time did you leave home that night? You know, when you pretended to go to work?'

'The usual, just after eight-thirty.'

'And you went straight to Cheetham Hill?'

'Well, not quite. I stopped at the garage on the Parkway to get some petrol, and went on from there.'

Jones passed him a map of Manchester. 'Show me your route, please?'

McNulty peered down at the large plastic sheet in front of him while Jones marked an X on it with a black marker pen. 'This is your house here.'

McNulty placed his finger on the map and began to narrate the route. 'So I left Cheadle, went along the A34, onto the M60 for one junction, and then down onto the Parkway, heading straight for the city. I stopped here for petrol and then carried on, along and up onto the Mancunian Way before going right onto Trinity Way, up by the Arena, then turned left on Park Street and right onto Pimblett Street.'

'And what time did you meet up with the prostitute?'

'I dunno. About nine, nine-fifteen maybe. I wasn't paying attention, to be honest.'

Jones folded the map slowly for effect and set it down to one side. Bov continued to stare at McNulty, who shifted in his seat.

Jones continued. 'Do you know how many ANPR cameras there are on that route, Kevin?'

'I don't even know what that is.'

'Bov, why don't you enlighten Kevin here.'

'Delighted to, Jonesy. ANPR stands for "automatic number plate recognition". It basically means a camera that takes a photo of your number plate as you pass. It registers your details and flags if there are any issues with say, unpaid road-tax, driving suspensions, or if the car's been reported stolen.'

'Right. And what does this have to do with me?' McNulty looked puzzled.

'Here's the thing, Kevin. It also tells us what time the car passed and, in some cases, we can even see who's driving,' said Jones. A muscle in McNulty's face twitched as Jones continued.

'So, we know, having looked at *all* the cameras along your route, plus the surrounding roads leading to Cheetham Hill, that your car's number plate was never once captured in that area on the night of your wife's murder.'

McNulty shot a glance at first Jones, then Bovalino. The big Italian leered at him as their eyes locked. 'Stop fucking about, Kevin, and tell us the truth. Where were you on the night Deidre was killed?'

BROWN CHOSE to interview Matt Logan without Phillips, instead enlisting the help of Entwistle. He wanted the rookie to see some proper police interrogation in action. Before heading into Interview Room 3, he'd made it clear to Entwistle that he would do *all* the talking, and ask *all* the questions – without exception. He also explained that his tactic would be to soften Logan up before pulling him apart.

As Brown and Entwistle sat down opposite a dishevelled Logan, Brown passed him a vending-machine sandwich, which he greedily devoured.

'You hungry?' said Brown.

Logan grunted, then took another mouthful of the ham sandwich, chewing loudly.

Brown explained the various protocols of the interview before starting the DIR and beginning his questioning. 'Where were you yesterday afternoon, Matt?'

Logan shrugged his shoulders. 'Dunno. Town, I s'pose.'

'What time were you in town?'

Another shrug.

'Can you tell me *where* you were in town?'

Logan chewed loudly with his mouth open. 'By the town hall.'

'And were you with anyone, Matt?'

'On and off.'

Brown was already beginning to lose patience, and Logan's disgusting table manners were getting on his last nerve. He decided to wait until he had finished the sandwich before continuing.

'Can I have some more?'

Brown forced a smile. 'In a while. I need you to answer some questions first.'

'Can I go for a fag then?'

'Not at the moment'.

Logan looked nonplussed by this news.

'I need you to think back to where you were yesterday, from the morning to the evening. Can you do that, Matt?'

'I guess so.'

'Well?'

'Well what?'

Brown finally lost his patience and banged his fist on the table. 'Are you deliberately, trying to piss me off, sonny?'

Logan raised his arms in defence. 'No, I'm just not following you. I'm a bit confused. I don't know what you want me to say.'

'I want the truth! And if I don't get it, I'm going to charge you with obstruction and send you back to Hawk Green for the next six months.'

'All right, take it easy, man.' Logan had the air of a sulky teenager. 'I'll tell you what you want to know. Just say it slowly, will yer, I can't understand your weird accent. Is it Irish or something?'

'Scottish,' growled Brown through clenched teeth, before taking a moment to calm himself. As Entwistle's mentor, he needed to set a proper example.

'Right. Let's start again, shall we?' Brown passed Logan a notepad and biro. 'Can you write down where you were yesterday, between nine and twelve, twelve and four, four and nine, and then 9 p.m. onwards?'

Logan screwed up his face, clearly deep in thought. After a while, he scribbled for a few minutes before passing the pad back to Brown, who turned it around and attempted to decipher the scrawl on the page.

'My God, look at that. Did you actually go to school?'

'Not much in the end.'

'Missed the handwriting lessons, I'm guessing?' Brown narrowed his eyes as he read down page. 'Ok, so if I'm reading this correctly, you were at the hostel in Cheetham Hill from nine to twelve. And between 12 and 4 p.m., you were begging in St Peter's Square...'

Logan nodded along.

'From 4 to 8 p.m., you were begging by Piccadilly Station, and after nine you were in the hostel.'

'Yeah, that's it.'

'Can anyone verify any of this?'

'The hostel people can, cos they seen me leaving at lunchtime and coming in after nine. In between, it's just the other lads from the street.'

Brown opened a Manila folder and pulled out a transcript of Logan's first interview with Phillips. 'I see from your last interview that one of your alibis for the murder of Susan Gillespie is a David Mitchell, also known as Mitchy, vouched for the fact you were with him when she was killed on the night of Monday the twentieth-eighth of January.'

'Did he?'

'Are you surprised by that?'

Logan smiled. 'Only because his memory's worse than mine. Too many years on the gear. But his sister Dannielle can vouch for me too. We ended up at her house.'

'I see. And I supposed they'll both vouch for you yesterday, will they?'

'Mitchy will...for a bit of it anyway. We were together in the afternoon by the town hall, but I went up to Piccadilly on my own afterwards. He'd picked up enough to score, so went off early to see his bird. I decided to do a few more hours at the station when the commuters were going home; always a good time. I got my gear and then went back to the hostel to do it in peace.'

'You're allowed to take drugs in the hostel?'

'Not really, but they have different volunteers on duty all the time and there's a couple of new ones at the mo. They don't know how to stop us. They get nervous 'cos of the needles and HIV 'n' that.'

'Ok, so you were in Albert Square between midday and four with your mate Mitchy? If we check the CCTV cameras, you'll both show up, will you?'

'You tell me. If there's cameras there, we will.'

'Well, I hope you're right, because what we have here—' Brown placed his left hand on Entwistle's right shoulder. '—is one of the finest digital detectives in the country. Hand-picked by *me*. He's just about to go and find out if you're telling me a load of porkies, aren't you, sonny?' He smiled at Entwistle.

'Er, yes sir.' Entwistle got up to leave.

As the door closed behind him, Brown moved on to phase two of his plan for the interview.

'So, Matt, why don't you tell me about your time at working at Hexagon Paints.'

NOEL GILLESPIE LOOKED MORE haggard than normal today. Wearing a tatty grey cardigan over his work shirt, he sat with his large, gnarly hands flat on the table in Interview Room 6 at Ashton House.

Phillips's voice was warm. 'How are you coping, Noel?'

'Good days and bad, Inspector.'

'Look, I'm sorry my officers had to drag you in here this

evening, but there's been another murder similar to Susan's. I could really do with your help to catch the bastard who's doing this.'

Gillespie sat forwards in his chair, immediately interested. 'How can I help?'

'Do you know a chap named Ricky Murray?'

Gillespie looked disappointed. He shook his head. 'I'm afraid I don't.'

'Did Susan ever mention anyone called Ricky?'

'Not that I remember. Is he a suspect?'

'I'm afraid I can't say at this stage, but he's a big part of our investigation. It'd help to know a little more about him.'

'Sorry, I really don't know that name.'

Phillips opened a Manila folder and pulled out a document with the word COPY watermarked at an angle across the A4 pages. She turned it around to face Gillespie and pushed it towards him. 'Do you recognise this?'

Gillespie pulled on his reading glasses. Resting them on the tip of his nose, he examined the document briefly, then pushed it back towards Phillips. 'It's Susie's will.'

'Are you aware who inherits your sister's estate?' Gillespie hesitated, so Phillips continued. 'I'll tell you, shall I? Your daughters, Hollie and Chloe, and the church.' Gillespie seemed uneasy hearing this information. 'They each get ten per cent of her estate, with everything else going to *you*.' Phillips pulled another sheet from the folder. 'You get seventy per cent of the value of the house – that's your parent's house, I understand, which she alone inherited when your father died. Is that correct?'

'Yes.'

'That must have been tough to take as the older brother. Did it upset you, missing out on the house like that?'

'Not at all. Susie deserved it. She looked after Mum and Dad, after all.'

'That's very admirable, Noel. I'm not sure I'd be so under-standing if it was my little brother who got my mum and dad's house, but then he is a bit spoiled, being the youngest, and a lawyer, so he doesn't need the money. Was that the same with Susie? Was she the favourite?'

'No, I wouldn't say that was the case at all. Mum and Dad loved us both equally, but after what she did for them, I was happy she got the house.'

Phillips continued reading from the list. 'Then there's her savings, which stand at thirty-thousand pounds, along with ten grand in shares and five grand in premium bonds. Plus her private pension, which stands at close to one-hundred thousand. A tidy sum, wouldn't you agree?'

'Money can't bring my sister back, Inspector.'

Phillips retrieved yet another document. 'No, not at all, but it does look like your business could do with the money. Specifically *you*, Noel. This tax bill looks like a prison sentence in waiting.' She passed him the HMRC penalty notice. 'Half a million quid. That's a lot of money for a business posting just ninety grand in dividends last year.'

Gillespie stared down at the penalty notice, remaining silent.

Phillips continued. 'I'd like you to look at the second-to-last page of Susan's will, under executors. Can you read out the two names listed there for me, please?'

Gillespie flicked through the pages. 'Harrington and Moore Associates Ltd...' He stopped.

'Harrington and Moore Associates Ltd, and one Noel F. Gillespie, who, according to my notes, claimed to know nothing about his sister's will when interviewed by my detectives just a few days ago. Tell me, Noel, is that your signature under your name?' said Phillips.

'Yes.'

'So why lie to the police about your sister's will?'

'The truth is, I panicked. I knew it could look bad, with my debt and Susie's money. I didn't want you to think I had anything to do with her death.'

Phillips pulled all the documents together and laid them out slowly in front of him. 'Do you know what this looks like to me, Noel?'

Fear was etched across Gillespie's features.

'It looks like a compelling motive to murder your sister. And do you know what else I think? I think you got spooked when we came to see you and you decided to kill again, to throw us off the scent. I think you knew Kevin McNulty was on nights and Deidre would be a sitting duck. Then you figured one more wouldn't hurt in distancing you from it all, so you killed Betty Clarke. Three weak and vulnerable women. *Killed by you*.'

'No – that's not true!' Gillespie shouted. 'I never killed anyone. I *loved* Susie. She was my little sister. I could never hurt her.' He lifted his hands to his face and began to weep.

Phillips was in no mood to stop. 'Where were you yesterday between 3 and 9 p.m.?'

Gillespie pulled his hands away. 'What?' he asked, appearing confused.

Was he play-acting? She couldn't be sure. 'I want to know your movements yesterday. Where were you between 3 and 9 p.m.?'

'Er, I was at work.'

'Until nine?'

'Yes. I was working late, trying to catch up.'

'Can anyone vouch for you?'

'My receptionist, Jodie. She stayed late with me.'

'Until nine?'

'No, she was there until about seven-thirty, then I sent her home.'

'Why would you need a receptionist at that time of night?'

'She was doing some filing for me. It was overtime.'

Phillips made a note in her file. 'So, if she left at seven-thirty, that means you were alone at the office until nine?'

'Yes.'

'Can anyone verify that?'

Gillespie shook his head and his mind appeared elsewhere.

Phillips watched him in silence.

'The alarm,' he suddenly blurted.

'What about the alarm?'

'It's digitally logged. You can see who comes in and out, based on their swipe key. I can show you the logs and prove I set it on the way home at nine.'

Phillips eyed him suspiciously as Gillespie stared at her, his face full of hope.

A knock on the door broke the tension and Entwistle entered the room. 'Sorry, Guv, but DCI Brown wants to see us in the incident room ASAP.'

'On my way. This interview is suspended at 9.15 p.m.' She pressed stop on the recorder before gathering up the various documents and placed them back in the folder. 'I'll get one of the duty officers to bring you something to eat and a drink. I'll be back as soon as I can.'

Gillespie watched wordlessly as she stood up and followed Entwistle out of the room.

Brown, Jones and Bovalino were waiting in silence as Phillips and Entwistle entered the incident room. The tension was palpable. Brown stood with his hand in his trouser pocket, nervously shaking his change in front of the incident board, which was now covered with images of all four victims – in life and in death. 'So, what have you got?' he asked, staring at the team.

'Shall we go first, Guv?' said Jones.

Phillips nodded.

'Ok. McNulty's alibi is that he was with a sex-worker in Cheetham Hill at the time of his wife's murder. But when we ran McNulty's car through the ANPR database on the night Deidre was killed, it was nowhere near there. We mapped all the possible routes he could take from Cheadle to Cheetham Hill, and nothing came up. Not just at the time of the murder, but from 6 p.m. to 6 a.m. Nothing.'

'So, he's lying.'

'Yes, sir, but he now has a fresh alibi.'

Phillips scoffed. 'Of course he does. Who is it this time?'

'Have a guess, Guv.'

Brown was in no mood to play along. 'This is no time for games, Jones,' he snapped. 'Just get to the fucking point, will you?'

Jones looked slightly put out. 'Claire Speight.'

Phillips took a moment to process the name. 'Deidre's best mate?'

'Yes, Guv.'

'What was he doing with her?' asked Phillips.

'Shagging, Guv,' said Bovalino flatly.

'What?'

Jones cut back in. 'Yes, Guv. According to McNulty, he and Mrs Speight have been having an affair for two years.'

Phillips paused. 'Two years? That means they were together when Deidre had the chemo and mastectomy, doesn't it?'

'Yes, Guv.'

Phillips was disgusted. 'Jesus. Your wife, and your best mate, is fighting for her life – and you two are shagging behind her back. What is wrong with these people?'

'And have you verified this alibi?' asked Brown.

'No sir. Not yet.'

'Well, get that done ASAP.'

'Yes sir.'

'Anything else from McNulty?'

'No sir.'

Brown turned his attention to Phillips, perched on the edge of her desk. 'Ok, what about Gillespie?'

She unfolded her arms, placing her hands on the desk either side of her. 'Well, if only Susan had been murdered, he'd be a prime suspect, but he's not our guy.'

'What makes you so sure?'

'He has an alibi for Ricky Murray's murder, for a start. He was working late with his receptionist Jodie.'

Bovalino laughed. 'Doing the same as McNulty and Speight, more like.'

'What makes you say that?' asked Phillips.

'Cos she's seriously hot, and there was definitely something between them when we called in. She seemed very protective of her boss when we asked to see him, didn't she, Jonesy?'

'Yeah, she did. And it certainly could explain why he's being so shifty. Worried if we dig too deep into his life, we'll discover his little secret. Hard to believe, though; he looks like a melted candle most of the time.'

Brown interjected. 'This is all supposition at this stage. Any other reason you *don't* like him for this?'

Phillips shrugged her shoulders. 'Just motive, really. With his sister's death, he's in the clear of his money troubles, so I could see him in the frame for that. But I cannot see any reason why he'd torture and kill three more people. Sure, we could argue he was creating a false trail away from himself, but I don't see that at all. He hasn't got it in him. We'll look into the alibi, but I'm pretty sure it'll check out. I really don't think he's our man, sir.'

Brown looked happy for once. 'Well, I have to say, I think Logan is. Entwistle, pass around those printouts.'

Entwistle handed each of them a series of CCTV stills.

Brown's chest seemed to expand as he began sharing his

theory. 'Logan claims he was in the city centre yesterday, begging in St Peter's Square, at the time of Murray's death. Brown pointed to the printed image in his hand. 'As we can see here, there are two men positioned at two cash machines on either side of the square. Both are wearing dark hoodies, which matches the description Thomas Dempsey gave of the man who followed him and tried to gain access to his property. The film is time-stamped, so we can see that at three o'clock, the guy on the library side of the square leaves his position and joins the man on the opposite side by the War Memorial for about ten minutes. He then leaves and gets on a tram heading to East Didsbury, where he eventually alights and the cameras lose him. Now, Logan claims that David Mitchell left early and that it was actually *Logan* who changed his location to Piccadilly Station. He insists he stayed there from 4 to 8 p.m. Looking at the image on page three, we can see one of the men sat by the main entrance during that time, *but* importantly, he has his hood up throughout his stay, meaning we never see his face. I think Logan knew Mitchell would go to Piccadilly at the end of the day, so dressed the same as him so he could create his alibi.'

'It's certainly possible, sir,' said Jones.

'I detect a 'but', Sergeant?'

'No, not really. It's just Logan rarely knows what day it is. It's hard to see him as a calculated killer, that's all.'

'Really? What about his experience working with chemical compounds at Hexagon Paints?'

'He loaded the wagons, didn't he? I'm not sure that makes him an expert on creating sedatives,' said Phillips.

Brown's face had turned almost beetroot again. 'I don't get you lot, I really don't. We have a suspect sat down *that* corridor. A man who has done serious time for breaking and entering, was known to all the victims, has no *real* alibi for any of the murders, and has experience in handling chemicals. And none of you like him for these murders. Why? Because the killer is smart and methodical. Did it ever occur to you that if he's so smart, he may even be hiding in plain sight, *pretending* to be a junkie?'

Phillips was first to respond. 'When you say it like that, I'll admit it's compelling, sir. But the CPS won't charge on those facts alone. We need hard evidence: DNA, fingerprints, witnesses.'

'Well, do your fucking job and find them. Logan is our man. I want him arrested on suspicion of murder immediately, so we can hold him for at least twenty-four hours, by which time you'd better have found what we need to charge him. Got it?'

A reluctant chorus of 'Yes sir's' echoed around the room before Brown dismissed them and headed for his office.

The team milled around their desks until the door to Brown's office closed. Phillips turned her back to him and tried to her best to appear casual, in case he was watching. She kept her voice low as she spoke. 'Should we be worried that Murray doesn't feature in Susan Gillespie's Lourdes photo? Have we been following a red herring?'

'Maybe it's just that particular photo he wasn't in?' said Bovalino.

'Maybe. But neither Gillespie nor McNulty knew him.' Phillips turned to Entwistle. 'Brown said Logan was known to all the victims. What did he have to say about Murray?'

'Dunno, Guv. He sent me out to get the CCTV footage before he got on that.'

'So, we don't actually know if he talked to him about Murray?'

'No, Guv. Not without looking at the tape.'

A determined look came over Phillips's face. 'That seals it for me. We're doing this *our* way. Brown can think we're doing what he wants, but you lot follow my orders, got it?'

All three officers nodded enthusiastically.

'Here's what we do. I'll pay another visit to Maguire in the morning and see if he can shed any light on Murray for us. While I'm doing that, Jones, you check out McNulty's alibi.'

'Got it, Guv.'

'Bov, you go and see Gillespie's secretary and check the alarm logs.'

The big man nodded.

'Entwistle, see if you can find any CCTV of the surrounding streets, to see where our mystery man went after he got off the tram.'

'Will do, Guv.'

'And remember, Brown has already decided it's Logan, so unless we find something that can change his mind, he doesn't need to know we're doing any of this. Right, it's late. Let's get out of here.'

Jones and Bovalino stood and began packing up to leave.

Entwistle stared at Phillips tentatively. 'Guv...there's one more thing.'

'God, what now?'

'How about Logan. Don't we need to arrest him?'

'Oh, shit. Well remembered.' She stood up and patted him on the shoulder. 'And well-*volunteered*, Entwistle – I'll leave that to you. Jonesy, Bov, can you let Gillespie and McNulty know they can go. They'll need transport from uniform. And then let's all go home. I don't know about you guys, but I've had more than enough "expert" policing for one day.'

34

Claire Speight answered the door when Jones called just after 9 a.m. She was dressed in a smart suit with her hair tied back and, unlike last time, wearing make-up. She looked surprised to see him.

'Sergeant Jones?'

'Can I come in, Mrs Speight?'

'It's not really convenient. I'm due to leave for a client meeting in twenty minutes.'

'I see. In that case, maybe you can come down to the station after your meeting and we can talk there?'

Speight's lip curled at the edge, then she opened the door wider. 'Let's do this now.' Jones stepped inside and followed her through to the kitchen, where she sat at the table and folded her arms. 'So, what I can do for you?'

Jones took the seat opposite her. 'Is your husband in?'

'No, he's away in Denmark again this week. Why do you ask?'

'Have you spoken to Kevin McNulty since last night?'

Speight flinched. 'No. I've not seen Kevin in about a week. Why, is something wrong?'

Jones didn't answer, instead taking a moment to look around the room. He noted the framed photos on the walls. One of Claire Speight lying on a beach alone; another of her standing in what looked like a paddy-field in Asia – alone. There was one of her standing in front of the Grand Canyon with her arms outstretched – once again solo. And a solitary photo of her and her husband Malcolm together, wearing swimwear and shorts, holding hands over a dinner table on a sun-drenched beach.

'Do you holiday alone a lot?' he asked.

'Yes, and if that's the extent of your questions, then I really must be getting off.' Speight made a move to stand up.

Jones didn't react. 'Where you were on the night Deidre was killed?'

Speight stopped in her tracks before slowly sitting back down. Her face appeared tense as she forced a smile. 'Why, Sergeant? Am *I* a suspect?'

'No, but we've been given certain information about a certain suspect's movements that we need to verify. Part of that includes your own whereabouts on the night Deidre died.'

'Me? Well, I was here all night watching TV and then went to bed early.'

Jones already knew the answer, but he wanted to see her reaction when he asked the question. 'Was your husband with you?'

'No, Malcolm was in Denmark that week. He came back on the Friday night.'

'So you were alone?'

Speight paused before answering. 'Yes, I was.'

Jones didn't respond, and deliberately stared at Speight for a long moment. He wanted her to hear the silence, to feel uneasy; an old interrogation technique that still came in handy. Eventually he spoke. 'I'll ask you again, Claire, and I want you to think very carefully before you answer. Were you alone on the night Deidre McNulty died?'

Speight took a moment before finally shaking her head.

'Who were you with?'

Another pause. 'Kevin.'

'McNulty?'

'Yes'.

'And was that here, or were you elsewhere?'

Tears began to form in Speight's eyes. 'No, it was here.'

Jones took out his notepad and pen. 'When did he arrive and what time did he leave?'

Speight was clearly struggling to hold back the tears. 'He arrived at about eight-forty, and left just after six-fifteen the next morning.'

'So he spent the night?'

'Yes.'

'Kevin claims you've been having an affair for the last two years. Is that true?'

Speight grabbed a tissue from a box on the kitchen bench, dabbing it into her eyes as she sat back down. 'Yes, it is.'

'I take it your husband doesn't know?'

'No, and I doubt he would believe it. Malcolm always sees the best in people. Sergeant, I know you must think we're monsters, but honestly, we never intended for it to happen.'

'Really, it's none of my business.'

'Please, Sergeant, I want you to know what really happened.'

Jones put down his pen. 'Ok. I'm listening.'

Speight wiped her nose on a tissue. 'Fate just seemed to throw us together when Dee-Dee got sick. Kevin felt isolated after the operation and when Dee-Dee was going through chemo, and I was lonely. Malcolm is away every month, and when he *is* here, he's always working. That's the reason I go away on my own most of the time.' She pointed to the photo of her and her husband. 'The one of me and Malcolm is from our honeymoon *ten years ago*; the last time we had a proper holiday together. I was comforting Kevin here one night when things were particularly tough for him and Dee-Dee, and, well, a friendly hug turned into something more. It snowballed from there. We wanted to stop, we tried a couple of times, but we were drawn to each other. Lost souls married to the wrong people.' Speight looked sad as she dabbed her eyes once more.

Jones said nothing, feeling awkward.

'Will you have to tell my husband, Sergeant?'

He closed his notepad and put it in his jacket pocket. 'No. All I'm interested in is verifying Kevin's alibi. What you get up to in your own home is none of my business.'

Speight let out a nervous chuckle. 'Pity. It might have been easier that way. I've known our marriage is over for a long time. It's just a shame it took this for me to admit it to myself. God, it'll break his heart.'

Jones had enough of this conversation. 'Like I said, that's your business.' He stood up. 'Anyway, I think my twenty minutes are up. I should be going.'

Moments later, as he was about to step outside, Speight grabbed his arm. 'Thank you, Sergeant.'

He looked at her, puzzled.

'For your discretion. I really do appreciate it.'

Jones smiled awkwardly, then turned away and walked down the path.

35

I t was a bright February morning, cold but mercifully dry. Phillips trod carefully over the icy path, which had been freshly gritted, and could hear a hypnotic drone, muffled but audible, coming from the open door to St Patrick's Church. The street beyond the gates was lined with cars – she guessed they belonged to those making the noise. As she tentatively stepped inside, she stopped a moment behind the glass doors that had been fitted to insulate the cavernous space from bitter winter winds and the incessant Manchester rain.

Through the glass, she could see a line of people in the centre aisle, queuing for communion. Those that had already taken it were filing back down the right and left flanks. Standing at the altar was Father Maguire, dressed in full robes and, for the first time, she observed him as a Catholic priest. Gently opening one of the double glass doors, she stepped inside the main body of the church, which was as warm as she remembered, and took a seat on the back pew, where she waited until the service was over.

As the parishioners began to file out, she remained seated, watching closely as each one passed her position accompanied by a soundtrack of whispers and clanking walking sticks. Midweek mass was clearly an advocacy of the older parishioners. When the last of the attendees had left, she followed them through the main door before ducking down the side of the church to the main house.

Maguire answered her knock promptly. He was wearing his usual garb of black shoes, trousers and white-collared shirt.

He greeted her with a warm smile. 'Inspector Phillips. Back so soon?'

'Sorry to bother you, Father, but I wondered if I could pick your brain with something?'

'Of course, do come in. I'll break out the cafetière again.'

A few minutes later, she found herself back in the familiar surroundings of the kitchen on one of the rock-hard chairs, drinking surprisingly good coffee. Maguire noticed her appreciation.

'I tried a different blend, Colombian. Do you like it?'

'I do, actually. Best cup I've had in a while. And I drink *a lot* of coffee.'

'I must confess, I was never really bothered by it. More of a tea man, but this new contraption—' He tapped the cafetière lid. '—has really changed my view. I think I'm a convert.'

Phillips flashed a smile. 'Interesting choice of words, Father.'

'Ha, yes. Indeed.'

'I was surprised there were no hymns at the service today. Is that normal?'

'Yes, no hymns at the weekday masses unless it's a festival, like Ash Wednesday or Good Friday. Organists cost money and we're a bit strapped for cash, so we save the hymns for prime-time on Sundays.' Maguire chuckled. 'But I'm guessing you're not here for insights into the logistics of running a Catholic Church, are you, Inspector?'

Phillips rested her cup on the table and pulled her notepad from her jacket pocket. 'No. I guess I'm not.'

'So, how can I help the Greater Manchester Police today?'

'Do you know a man named Richard, or Ricky, Murray?'

'Little Ricky? I do. How is he?'

'I'm afraid he's dead, Father.'

The priest's face dropped. 'Oh dear Lord, no. What happened?'

'We think he may have been murdered by the same person that killed Susan, Deidre and Betty.'

'Little Ricky? That makes no sense, but then I guess none of it does.'

'What was he like?'

Maguire took a long swig of coffee before replying, still looking shaken. 'Well, he was quite small – hence the nickname – and a little overweight, as I recall. The other children used to tease him about that, actually, as if his nickname were accurate in regard to his height and ironic in terms of his weight.'

'What kind of person was he?'

'He was a bit of a mixture, really. I remember when he was old enough to take his first Holy Communion – which is around seven years of age – and he was a cheeky wee scamp. Always running around the church grounds after mass and very involved in the kids' church group. But a few years later he changed. I often wondered if he'd maybe started puberty early. He seemed to adopt the traits of a teenager overnight, you know – moody, introverted and withdrawn, that type of thing. And that's how he stayed, for at least a couple of years, anyway. Ironically, when he *did* become a teenager, he opened up a little more, though never with quite the same zest as when he was little. But you could at least get him to make eye-contact and have some semblance of conversation.'

'Do you know if he was friends with Matt Logan?'

'I wouldn't say best friends, but I occasionally saw them hanging around together at church discos and things like that when they were both still quite young. As I said, once Ricky got to a certain age he wasn't interested in other people. Neither was Matt, come to think of it.'

'What were his parents like?'

'*Parent*, Inspector. His mum brought him and his younger brother up on her own after his father left her for another woman. Ricky and Aaron were very young at the time.'

'Was she ever abusive towards him?'

'Eileen? Heavens no. She was a wonderful mother to Ricky. Did her very best for both the boys in difficult circumstances. She must be devastated. I'll make sure I call round and see her this week.'

'I'm sure that would help. Sadly, she was the one who found his body.'

'Oh, dear God in heaven! Poor Eileen. He was the absolute apple of her eye. Even now.'

'*Even now*, Father?'

Maguire took a moment to answer. 'I'm sure I won't win any awards for political correctness, Inspector, but when Ricky admitted he was gay, she took it very badly at first; cried for months. She prayed for his soul constantly, and hoped he would see sense and realise it was just a phase.'

'Because the church doesn't agree with homosexuality, right?'

'No. It considers it sinful and against God.'

'Like priests molesting innocent children?' The words spilled from her mouth before she could stop them.

Maguire forced a smile before responding. 'In all walks of life there are bad apples, Inspector. It doesn't mean the whole church is rotten. As you saw with your own colleagues a few years back, no organisation is beyond reproach.'

Phillips's mind flashed back to Chief Constable Blake. She

had to admit, he had a point. 'I'm sorry, Father, we seem to be veering off point here. If we can get back to Ricky?'

'Of course. What else can I tell you?'

'Had you seen him recently?'

'He was a regular at mass with his mum every Sunday, and in the summer he'd often help out with the Cubs and Scout troops that meet in the church hall on Wednesday nights. He sometimes acted as a chaperone on trips away.'

'Do the Scouts not meet in the winter, then?'

'They do, but Ricky wasn't not a fan of the cold, and the church hall is freezing during the winter months. He preferred to get involved when it's shorts and T-shirts weather.'

Phillips made a note in her pad before pulling out her phone and bringing up the picture of the Lourdes group. 'Did Ricky attend this trip, like the other victims?'

Maguire took the phone and examined the image once more. 'No. I'm pretty sure he missed that one. If I remember rightly, he was due to go, but pulled out at the last minute.'

'Do you know why?'

'It was a very long time ago, Inspector.' Maguire tapped his temple, the smile returning. 'I'm afraid my memory isn't quite as sharp as I'd like it to be.' He topped up Phillips's mug with coffee.

She took another sip, then, placing the mug back on the table, turned her attention back to her notes. 'I can't recall if I asked you this already, but did you go on that trip?'

Maguire stared at the image again. 'I'm pretty sure I didn't.'

'Did you *not* want to go?'

'Actually, I did. If I remember it rightly, I think my first visit to Lourdes came the following year. It was very expensive, and the church couldn't afford to pay for the children to make the trip, so it was funded by the parents and parishioners. We ran special events and collections throughout the year. We only ever sent the most promising kids over – those that scored top grades in R.E. and who we believed would continue as part of the church in the future.'

'So why send middle-aged Betty Clarke then?'

'Ah yes, wonderful Betty. For a very good reason, actually. Whenever girls went away overnight with the church, a female chaperone was required – particularly on that trip, as I recall, since some of the group were approaching puberty. Far too tricky for a couple of awkward priests to deal with, if you get my meaning.'

'Right, I see. So, who took Ricky's place when he pulled out?'

'I don't think anyone did, to be honest. It was the very last minute when he dropped out, so I think it was too short-notice to change the tickets.'

'You must have been disappointed.'

'I was. Not just for me but for the parish as a whole. A lot of money wasted. Still, knowing his mother Eileen, I'm sure it had to be a valid reason for Ricky not to go.'

Phillips shifted her weight in the chair, attempting in vain to get comfortable. 'Can we go back to Susan Gillespie?'

'Of course, but before we do, can I ask when the body will be released?'

'It's still with the coroner at this stage, so I'm afraid I can't say. As soon as he's completed his verdict, her undertakers will be notified.'

'In that case, I'll wait for them to call. Sorry. Back to Susie, Inspector.'

'The night she was killed, you said she was here, organising a cleaning party. Was that a normal event for her to be involved with?'

Maguire nodded. 'She was active in all events regarding the church, Inspector, so yes, she cleaned the church with the other ladies once a month. Although, that evening was an additional session because of the repair work we'd had done to the office after the break-in.'

Philipps frowned. 'Break-in? When was that?'

'Now you're testing me. Forgive me for asking, but what day did Susan die?'

'Monday the twenty-eighth of January.'

'Right, in that case, the workmen were here on the Friday before, and the break-in was about three weeks earlier.'

'How did they get in?'

'They came through a window straight into the office at the back of the house, during evening mass on a Sunday.'

'Was anything taken?'

Maguire rubbed his chin with one hand. 'Not really. I think they must have been disturbed.'

'Why do you stay that?'

'Because they took the top drawer of the bureau with them – the entire thing – then dumped it in the grounds. It was empty when we found it.'

'And what was missing?'

'Some files, a bit of petty cash. Nothing of value.'

'How much cash?'

'Twenty pounds max. Hardly the crime of the century.'

'Do you remember what the files contained?'

'Just some tax information for the accountant.'

'And who is your accountant?'

'Noel Gillespie.'

Phillips raised an eyebrow. 'How long has he been doing your books, Father?'

'Well, his family have been looking after St Patrick's for many, many years. It started with his dad and Father Donnelly – long before my time – then Noel took over when he retired. I saw no reason to switch when I became parish priest.'

'Was there anything in the stolen files that would be of value?'

'No. It was just a record of the collections for the last twelve months. You know, the names of those who made donations. We need to keep track of that.'

'Did it include their addresses too?'

Maguire nodded.

Phillip's pulse quickened. 'I don't suppose you kept copies, did you?'

Maguire smiled. 'Indeed, I did. I have digital copies on the computer in the office. Would you like to see them?'

'Yes, that would be very helpful.'

Maguire pulled back his chair and stood up. 'Follow me.'

As Maguire opened the office door, she was struck by the strong scent of air-freshener that hung thick in the air. It reminded her of her grandma's house, like an old lady's perfume.

Maguire took a seat at his desk and booted up the PC, and a moment later the screen buzzed into life. He was surprisingly adept, zooming through a sequence of folders until he found what he was looking for. 'Here it is, Inspector. Last year's cumulative totals for donations per parishioner, including their names, addresses and residential status. Apparently HMRC think even the church might not be immune to laundering money, so we have to keep records of who is giving us what. Just in case they want to audit us.'

'Could you print me a couple copies?'

'Already on it.' The printer on the desk suddenly sparked into life as the rollers positioned themselves noisily. Soon the printed pages began to slowly emerge from the machine.

Maguire grabbed a plastic A4 folder and placed the pages inside it before handing it to Phillips. 'Three copies. One for good luck. I do hope it helps, Inspector.'

Phillips scanned the pages. It didn't take long to find what she was looking for. She glanced back up at Maguire and smiled. 'Do you know, Father, this might be just what I'm looking for.'

36

Phillips knew Brown had yet another 'PR management' briefing scheduled first thing that morning. She was keen to use the time without him to debrief on the 'off-the book' Noel Gillespie and Kevin McNulty enquiries. Each of the team had arrived promptly and gathered in a private meeting room adjacent to the incident room. Outside, an array of freshly seconded uniformed officers had filled the desks and the incident room was humming with activity.

'Ok, guys. I've no idea how long Brown will be in his briefing, so let's crack on. What did you find out yesterday?'

Jones spoke first. 'McNulty's alibi stacks up. Speight confirmed they've been having an affair.'

'Do you reckon McNulty gave her the heads-up you'd be coming?' asked Bovalino.

'I don't think so. She seemed genuinely surprised. I almost felt sorry for her. Says her marriage is a sham and she and McNulty were brought together by their shared heartache. I think she genuinely has feelings for the guy.'

Bovalino scoffed. 'Doesn't look like he feels the same way. Not if he hadn't warned her we were coming.'

Jones agreed. 'I suspect, with that little toad, it was just about getting his end away.'

Entwistle eagerly held up a sheet of paper in his hand. 'And I have fresh information to back that up. I ran McNulty's plates through the ANPR database for the last couple of months. I got loads of hits – and not just between home and the airport.'

Phillips, perched at her favourite spot on the edge of her desk, was intrigued. 'Really? Where else?'

Jones jumped in. 'Let me guess. Cheetham Hill?'

Entwistle grinned. 'Got it in one, Jonesy.'

Jones's didn't return his smile. Instead, he leaned forwards at his desk. 'That's *DS Jones* to you.'

Entwistle flushed with embarrassment. 'Sorry, I didn't mean to offend you, I—'

Phillips cut across him, waving her arm. 'Pay no attention, Entwistle, he's winding you up.'

Jones and Bovalino burst out laughing, high-fiving each other.

'Had you then, sunshine,' said Jones, pointing at the rookie.

Ordinarily Phillips would have allowed the banter to continue. It was good for the team morale, but they were short on time this morning. She told Entwistle to continue.

'Turns out he's been up in Cheetham Hill *a lot* in the last couple of months, so I ran the whole of last year. His car has been tagged in that area every couple of weeks, each time when he was supposed to be on shift at the airport. So, I checked in with his bosses and it turns out he suffers from severe migraines and is off quite regularly. That said, their view is he's a good worker when he's actually there. He even does overtime to make up for being off, so they let it slide. They often struggle to get people to work weekends and holidays, so he comes in handy.'

'Do we think the affair with Speight is a cover, then?' Phillips asked.

Entwistle shook his head. 'Looking at the logs, there is one Thursday every month where his car doesn't appear anywhere on ANPR, regular as clockwork. Each of those days coincides with Malcolm Speight's trips to Denmark.'

'When the husband's away...the wife will play,' Bovalino joked.

'So not only is he shagging his wife's best mate once a month, he's also getting it on with professionals every couple of weeks? He's an even bigger shit than I thought,' said Jones.

Phillips was keen to move on. 'Whatever his moral compass, McNulty's off the list of suspects then?'

'Looks that way, Guv,' said Jones.

Phillips turned her attention to Bovalino. 'What about Gillespie?'

'Alibi checks out, Guv. His receptionist confirms they were "working late..."' Bovalino made inverted commas in the air with his fingers, 'and the security log shows he set the alarm at 9 p.m. the night Murray was killed.'

'The receptionist could have used his fob easily enough, though,' Jones mused.

'True, but I also checked CCTV on Cheadle High Street. You can clearly see him walking from the front of the office around to the car park at the rear just after nine. His car emerges with him at the wheel a few minutes later.'

'So, Gillespie's out too,' said Phillips a split second before the meeting-room door burst open.

Brown observed them suspiciously from the doorway. 'Is this a private meeting or can anyone join in?'

Phillips did her best to appear deferent. 'Morning, sir. Just gathering the troops ready for you.'

Brown looked surprised by her comment and stepped inside, leaving the door to slam behind him. He pulled up a chair and straddled it backwards – his favoured position.

'Right, Phillips. So what have you got on Logan?'

'Nothing major, I'm afraid sir, other than the fact he and Murray were friends.'

'*Friends*? How?'

'The church group. I called in to see Father Maguire and he was very helpful. Turns out Ricky was part of the same group in the photograph, he just didn't go on that trip.'

'So, they are all still connected?' said Entwistle.

Phillips nodded. 'Yep, and the way Maguire describes Murray's change in demeanour at a certain age mirrors the way Thomas Dempsey described Logan's change in behaviour around the same time. I think Ricky Murray was also abused.'

'Assuming Logan *was* actually abused,' argued Brown.

'Happy, fun-loving kids who suddenly become introverted, isolated and difficult to communicate with – years before puberty – sounds like the hallmarks of abuse to me.'

'Maybe the other kids were the abusers? It's not unheard of. Could Logan be a victim and this is his revenge?' said Bovalino

Phillips shook her head. 'I'm not so sure, and after talking to Father Maguire, I'm not convinced the photograph is the only link. He told me the reason why Susan was cleaning the church that night. Apparently, the church was broken into a few weeks earlier and the ladies were getting the office back in shape after the workmen had been in to make some repairs. Hardly enough damage to warrant a cleaning *party*, but as two of the team were octogenarians, I'm pretty sure Gillespie would have been doing most of the work that night.'

'And what has any of this got to do with the four unsolved murders currently on our plate Inspector?' Brown said sounding exasperated.

'I'm coming to that.'

'I wish you bloody would!'

Phillips ignored the jibe. 'Maguire reckons that whoever did it must have been disturbed, because they only got away with twenty quid and a file they lifted, along with the entire top drawer of his bureau.'

'They nicked a drawer? That's a first,' said Jones.

'Yeah, I know, and I don't believe they were disturbed. I think they got exactly what they were looking for.' She retrieved the printed copies from Maguire's PC, passed one to Brown, another to the guys, who huddled around it, and kept one for herself. 'These are the church's donation records for every parishioner who gives regularly. It contains the names and addresses of Susan Gillespie, Deidre McNulty, Betty Clarke and Ricky Murray.'

Jones scanned the long list of names. 'Jesus. That can't be a coincidence, can it?'

'I don't believe in coincidences. I'm sure it's linked.'

'This is all very enlightening, of course—' Brown's tone was laced with sarcasm. '—but what does this list have to do with catching the killer?'

Phillips turned the page around to face him. 'This list was one of the items stolen during the break in at St Patrick's Church. A month after it was taken, four people on it were ritually murdered in exactly the same way. I hate to tell you sir, but there's a chance that any one of the *two hundred* names listed here could be our next victim.'

The colour drained from Brown's face as Phillip's words landed. He steadied himself against a nearby desk, leaning on its edge. 'Two hundred?' he echoed, in almost a whisper. 'That's all I fucking need.'

'So how would you like us to proceed from here, sir'

Brown didn't reply, appearing lost in his own thoughts. No doubt thinking what damage this might do to his career.

'*Sir?*' repeated Phillips, louder this time.

Brown turned his head to face her but appeared distant. 'What?'

'How would you like us to proceed from here?'

The DCI seemed suddenly aware of all eyes trained on him and stood bolt-upright, back to full bluster. 'Find out where Logan was on the night of the burglary. As we've got nothing concrete to hold him for the murders, we'll have no choice but to let him go in a couple of hours. So, let's see if we can get him on breaking and entering. It'll give us a chance to hold him for another twenty-four hours at least.'

'Yes sir,' said Phillips.

Brown ran his hand through his hair and straightened his tie before heading for the door. 'I have to brief the Chief-Super on this new development.'

When Brown had disappeared out into the corridor, Bovalino chuckled. 'Delivering the news to Fox that there could be two-hundred-plus potential victims? Rather him than me.'

'You're not kidding. She's going to tear him a new arsehole,' said Phillips.

Jones laughed and rubbed his hands together. 'And it couldn't happen to a more deserving bloke, could it?'

J ust after 11 p.m., Matt Logan finally unlocked the door to his tiny room at the hostel. He closed it behind him, flopped down on the single bed and shut his eyes. *Another long day at the office*, he thought, and allowed himself a wry smile.

He was drifting off to sleep when, a few minutes later, there was a knock at the door. Then it opened tentatively.

He spied one of the volunteers peering through the gap. 'All right, fella?' Logan called everyone *fella*; it saved having to remember names.

'You okay, Matt?' said the volunteer.

Logan sat upright. 'Yeah, just a bit knackered.'

'You fancy a smoke?'

Logan nodded and the volunteer stepped inside, finally revealing the name badge on his chest, which read *Trevor*.

'Tough day?' Trevor took a seat on the grey plastic chair next to Logan's bed.

'You could say that.' He took one of the cigarettes offered, lit it and enjoyed a deep drag before leaning back against the wall. 'You not having one?'

'Just put one out, but when I saw you come in, I thought you might need one. So, where you been the last few days?'

'Ashton House.'

'The police station?'

'Yep.'

'What were you doing there?'

'You won't believe this; I was arrested on suspicion of murder.'

Trevor let out a nervous laugh. He stared at Matt uneasily. 'Seriously?'

'Deadly. They were looking at me for those Cheadle murders.'

'That's hardcore! How the hell are you connected with them?'

'I used to know the victims – in a previous life.'

'Bollocks, you did.' Trevor laughed and slapped his leg, stopping as Logan fixed him with a steely glare before taking another drag of his cigarette.

'I wasn't always a junkie, you know.'

Trevor raised his arms in defence. 'Sorry, Matt. I didn't mean to offend you.'

'It takes more than that to offend *me*, fella, but you should never judge a book by its cover. Not everyone, or everything, is always as it seems.' A wry smile spread across his face.

'How long did they keep you there?'

'Two days. They started with the suspicion of murder arrest, then when they couldn't find enough to charge me, they re-arrested me yesterday on suspicion of burglary – to hold me for another twenty-four hours. They hadn't counted on me having a cast-iron alibi for the first murder, as well as the night they reckon I broke into my old church in Cheadle.'

'Really? That's lucky.'

'No luck needed when I've got Dannielle. She'll say anything I want her to.'

'Dannielle? is that your girlfriend?'

'*I wish.* Nah, she's my old cellmate's sister. Lives in Levenshulme. In fact, you probably know her brother, Mitchy. He stays here sometimes.'

'As in David Mitchell?'

'That's him. He backed up my story too. Mind you, the issue with Mitchy is juries don't like junkies as alibis. Whereas Dannielle, well, she's an upstanding member of the community. Has a job at the Town Hall and everything.' Logan chuckled.

'And she lied for you?'

A cunning smile crossed Logan's face. 'Lied? No. Let's just say, she backed up my story.'

'So, what happens now? Are you free and clear?'

Logan took another drag from his cigarette, letting the smoke billow from his nostrils as he spoke. 'No chance. I've got form. They think I know how to get into houses without being seen.'

'Is that what you were inside for?'

'Yeah. I did a few stretches for burglary when things got tough on the outside. I was in and out like a bloody yo-yo for a while.'

'Well, you're here now, so they obviously didn't have enough to charge you then?'

'Not yet. But you can bet they'll be doing everything they can to find *something*.'

Trevor sat forwards in his chair, his expression grave. 'What you gonna do, then? I mean, murder? That's serious. They could put you away for the rest of your life.'

Logan shrugged his shoulders. 'I know that, but what can I do?'

Trevor appeared frustrated. 'Well, you can't just sit here and do nothing, Matt. If you think they're going to come after you, then you've got to take control of the situation and do something – *anything*.'

'How?'

'I don't know, but you can't let them send you down if you're innocent. What a waste of a life.'

'That's my life all over, fella.' Logan took one last drag from the cigarette before pressing it into an overflowing ashtray on the bed stand.

Trevor stood up. 'Look, I'd better be going, I'm due to finish at midnight and I need to finish my rounds before I go. You going to be ok?'

'Yeah, I'll be fine. It'll all work itself out in the end.'

'Well, at least take a couple more of these.' Trevor opened the packet of the cigarettes.

Logan scooped out a few fingerfuls. 'Thanks fella, very good of you.' He placed them on the bed stand.

'You're welcome. And let me get you a fresh one of those...' Trevor left the room, returning a minute later with a clean ashtray and replaced the full one.

Logan looked him up and down. 'You know, you look really familiar. Were you in a band or something?'

'For a while, yeah. Did a few gigs in Liverpool but we never played in Manchester. And it was a *long* time ago now.'

'I definitely wouldn't have seen you then. I've always made it a policy to stay out of Liverpool.'

Trevor laughed. 'Like so many Mancs before you.' His expression turned grave. 'Seriously, Matt, don't let them send you down for this. Life in Hawk Green is no way to spend your days. Don't give in. Like I say, you've got to get the upper hand while you still can; take control before they do.'

Logan groaned as he lay down on his back and closed his eyes. 'I'll have a think about it, fella,' he muttered without conviction.

Trevor headed for the door.

'Switch the light off on the way out, will you?'

'No problem,' said Trevor.

A moment later, the door closed and the windowless room was plunged into darkness.

'I'm sure I can come up with something, fella,' he whispered as he began to drift off to sleep.

38

S tarting her day with a post mortem was always a challenge, made all the more difficult this morning as Phillips had been partnered with Brown. Over the years, she'd learned the hard way that it was best to watch proceedings without breakfast, though she still struggled with the noise of slicing flesh, organs being scooped onto weighing scales and, where necessary, bones being drilled or sawn apart. Thankfully this morning had been a straightforward procedure that Chakrabortty had completed in just a few hours.

'So, Doctor, Murray's cause of death is essentially the same as the other three, then?' said Brown.

'Very close, but there are a few differences. The first three victims were suffocated with plastic bags, whereas Murray was strangled whilst the bag was over his head.'

'I don't understand.'

Chakrabortty explained. 'Well, in the cases of Gillespie, McNulty and Clarke, each victim died of asphyxiation – essentially, the plastic bag placed over their heads deprived them of oxygen. In Murray's case, the killer pulled the plastic bag over his head, but also used their hands to squeeze his neck until he stopped breathing. Heavy bruising on the trachea and vocal cords indicate consistent pressure was applied for some time.'

'So, are we looking at a copycat then, Tan?' asked Phillips.

'I don't think so, but I can't be one hundred per cent sure. The tetryzoline in Murray's system was also a first.'

Brown already seemed to be losing patience. 'Tetryzoline? What the bloody hell is that?'

Judging by the expression on her face, Chakrabortty had the same dislike for Brown as the majority of the GMP. She stared him in the eye, her features hard and unflinching, her voice clipped. 'Tetryzoline is a drug found in eyedrops. If administered in large enough quantities, it can cause nausea and vomiting, and occasionally diarrhoea. In some cases, it can also be used as a sedative.'

'Do you think that was how Murray was subdued?' asked Phillips.

'I don't believe so. We found the same quantities of benzodiazepines, methoxyflurane and chloroform in his blood as the others.'

'Information that hasn't been released to the press,' said Phillips.

'Exactly, Jane. So, despite the differences in the method of death, there's a very good chance Murray was killed by the same person as the first three.'

'Right,' said Brown. 'Now that we've established that life-changing information, did you find anything that can *actually* help us identify the killer?'

Chakrabortty didn't respond to Brown's sarcasm. 'Nothing. As per the others, the body was wiped down with benzalkonium chloride.'

'A cleaning agent, sir,' Phillips explained.

Brown shot Phillips a look. 'I know what it is, Inspector. I'm not a total idiot.'

Phillips suppressed her grin as she watched Brown's face begin to turn red. 'Of course not, sir.'

Chakrabortty caught Phillips's eye and smiled briefly, straightening her face instantly as Brown turned back to her. She continued her deadpan delivery. 'We found traces of Latex gloves on the body, but again a generic brand found in most chemists across the country. Whoever your killer is, he may have adjusted his method of killing, but his attention to detail when cleaning up after himself is exceptional. He leaves nothing behind. I've never seen anything quite like it.'

'You sound like you admire the guy?'

'DCI Brown, in the ten years I've been doing this, I've yet to find a killer so thorough in their attempts to clean up after themselves.'

'So, we're still no closer to finding our killer, then?' said Brown curtly.

'From a pathological point of view, no, we're not.'

PHILLIPS CHUCKLED TO HERSELF, following at a distance as Brown stormed across the wet car park like a petulant child, his collar turned up against the rain. He said nothing as she unlocked the doors and got in the driver's side.

'Well, *she's* absolutely no fucking use.' Brown slammed the door unnecessarily hard as he took his position in the passenger seat next to her.

Phillips switched on the ignition. 'She can only find what the killer leaves behind, sir.'

'Exactly. Are you telling me that the killer left nothing behind whatsoever? No fibres, no spit, no sweat?'

'If he had, then Tan would have found it.'

'Bollocks. It's there, she just can't be arsed to look for it. All she's interested in is getting that body off the slab as quickly as possible and clearing her caseload.'

Listening to his hypocrisy, Phillips struggled to stay quiet.

'I've a good mind to speak to the coroner and demand a second post mortem.'

It was an empty threat and Phillips knew it. The coroner, Dr Thiel, was a powerful and strong-willed woman who had trained Chakrabortty, and they were still close allies. Brown had no idea how to handle strong women. She was confident he would rather eat his own hand than take Theil on himself.

Just then, Brown's phone rang. 'Aw shit, the Chief Super. That's all I need,' he said, glancing at the screen. He answered it, his voice suddenly turning light and jovial. 'Hello ma'am.'

Phillips looked away as if distracted, but trained her ears on the conversation. From what she could tell, Brown was getting a dressing-down.

'No, ma'am. No forensics as yet, but we are working on it.' He suddenly sounded very subservient.

Phillips could just about hear the agitated voice of Chief Superintendent Fox on the other end of the line.

'Of course. Right away. I'll be there within the hour, ma'am.' The phone went dead.

'Everything ok, sir?' From experience, Phillips knew the answer only too well.

Brown forced a thin smile. 'Fine. Just the Chief Super looking for an update. She wants to see me as soon as we get to Ashton House.'

Phillips steered the car towards the exit. 'Right, sir. Best not keep her waiting.'

Aside from the sound of the engine as they navigated city centre traffic, the car was silent for a few minutes. Brown finally spoke. 'What are you doing when you get back to the station, Phillips?'

'Catching up with the team.'

'Cancel it.'

Phillips looked puzzled. 'Sir?'

'Cancel your catch-up. You're coming with me to see the Chief Super. It's about time she had an update on what you and your team have been doing to catch this guy.'

My team, is it now? thought Phillips. She knew exactly how the meeting was going to go.

39

Chief Superintendent Fox was a thirty-year veteran of the force and had spent her entire career in the Greater Manchester Police. Openly proud of the fact that she had worked her way up through the ranks from WPC, she had a formidable reputation for getting results, and her conviction rates were second to none. On the face of it, Fox appeared relaxed and jovial, but for those unlucky enough to land on the wrong side of her, her temper was legendary. Urban myths abounded that battle-hardened coppers had been reduced to tears when pulled up in front of her.

When Brown and Phillips entered her office on the top floor of Ashton House, Fox was sitting in uniform behind her large smoked-glass desk, reading a thick report. Her reading glasses were perched on the end of her overly tanned and prematurely wrinkled nose, the brown skin accentuated by her badly bleached blonde hair. Phillips had always wondered how someone on a Chief Super's salary could find a way to look so cheap.

Fox glanced up briefly before scribbling something in the margin and moving the file to the edge of the desk. 'DCI

Brown... *and DI Phillips*? I wasn't expecting you, Jane, but please take a seat.' She smiled widely, but her eyes remained cold and black.

Taking adjacent seats, Brown and Phillips sat down opposite her.

Fox's smile remained intact. 'So, where are we at with the Cheadle murders?'

Clearly nervous, Brown stuttered slightly as he spoke. 'W-well, ma'am, we've confirmed the fourth murder was likely the work of the same killer as the previous three.'

Fox's smile began to slip. 'You've confirmed, or it's likely? Which is it?'

'Well, ma'am, without forensics, it's impossible to say with complete certainty, but we're very confident we're looking at the same person for all four murders.'

Fox tapped her pen on her teeth while she stared at Brown. 'Very confident? Well, that's an improvement.'

Phillips almost felt sorry for him as she watched Brown shrink in Fox's presence, but she knew it wouldn't be long before he threw her to the lions – or in this case, *the Fox.*

'And what about the suspects we interviewed last week. Where are we at with them?'

'We're pretty certain Logan is our man,' said Brown.

Fox sat back in her high-backed leather chair. 'Really? That's good news. When are you planning on charging him?'

'Well, *typically* the CPS want more than we've presented on him at the moment.'

Phillips listened as Brown began to shift blame to yet more people connected to the case.

'If I may, ma'am,' she cut in, 'the CPS need more evidence because Logan has an alibi for murder one, and as yet there's no forensic evidence to link him to any of the other crime scenes.'

Brown shot her a murderous look.

Fox appeared confused. 'So how he is our number one suspect, then?'

Phillips opened her mouth to speak but was cut off by Brown. 'Ma'am, he knew all the victims intimately. He has form for burglary and has experience working with chemical compounds. He was also seen getting onto a tram headed for East Didsbury ninety minutes prior to the fourth murder, which took place just five hundred metres from the tram station. The same station where he was spotted on CCTV an hour before Ricky Murray was killed.'

Phillips wasn't giving up. 'But we can't be sure it was actually Logan, sir.'

'And we can't be sure it *wasn't* either!' Brown said without looking at her.

'So what about his alibi? How reliable is it?' asked Fox.

Brown scoffed. 'He has two: one a junkie called David Mitchell. The other is Mitchell's sister, Dannielle Tierney. Wife of Jason Tierney.'

Fox raised an eyebrow. 'The bank robber?'

'The same. She's a born liar and hates the police. She'd say anything to piss us off.'

Fox folded her arms and pressed her head into the soft leather. 'I remember her from Tierney's trial. Shouting about injustice in front of the press pack when he was sent down. A vile creature. You're right not to trust her. What about the other two you had in – the brother and the husband?'

Phillips was impressed Fox had retained so much detail about the investigation. Then again, Brown was rarely out of her office, briefing her on every tiny development as soon as they came up.

'Nothing of note, Ma'am. The brother stands to inherit Susan Gillespie's estate and Kevin McNulty was having an affair. Good motives for each, but both have water-tight alibis. Plus, neither fits the profile.'

What profile? thought Phillips. Brown hadn't provided any form of profile, which really could be helpful in identifying their killer.

'So, Logan's our only candidate for it at the moment?'

'Yes ma'am,' said Brown.

'What about the chap who had the near miss in Fallowfield. Has he seen anything else?'

'Dempsey? Nothing ma'am. Uniform have been checking in on him each evening and have had nothing significant to report, other than he was having panic attacks and had been signed off work.'

Fox appeared deep in thought for a moment. 'Ok. So how confident are you that you can get a case in front of the CPS that will put Logan away?'

'Very,' said Brown.

'With respect, ma'am, I'm not so sure.'

'You never bloody are, are you Phillips?' sneered Brown.

'What's that supposed to mean?'

Brown turned to face Phillips, his eyes almost feral. 'It means, Inspector, that we have a suspect who is known to the victims, explaining why at least two of them may have let him in. He's a convicted burglar, so knows how to get into the houses of those that didn't, *and* has experience of working with chemical compounds. He's also a junkie caught on CCTV in the vicinity of the fourth victim's home at the time of the murder. Yet, even with all that, you still refuse to believe that Logan could be the killer.'

Fox's gaze shifted to Phillips. 'DCI Brown makes a compelling argument, Jane.'

Phillips could feel the investigation slipping away into Brown's incompetent hands and felt sick to her stomach. 'With respect, ma'am, we have no concrete evidence that puts Logan at any of the murder scenes.'

Brown immediately cut in. 'And whose fault is that? *You* and your detectives have been on this case for almost two weeks and we're no further than when I walked into Gillespie's lounge room that first morning.'

'You're the SIO on this, not *me.*'

'Exactly, and for good reason.'

Fox raised her arms to break up the fight, her voice measured yet authoritative. 'The fact of the matter is, we need a result on this quickly, especially as the latest development suggests his next victim could be any one of two hundred St Patrick's parishioners. The eyes of the world are on us, and we appear no further ahead in this investigation than we claimed to be at your press conference. In fact, some might say we've gone backwards. That's not good for any of our ambitions within the force. DCI Brown, I'm inclined to agree with you that Logan looks like a good fit. I think the entire focus of the investigation should be on finding the evidence to charge him.'

'But what if it's not Logan?' Phillips protested.

'As I said, Inspector Phillips, I think a swift conclusion to this case will be best for all of us.'

Phillips knew she was beaten. 'Of course, ma'am.' The words stuck in her throat.

Fox's smile widened farther, and when she spoke again, her tone was motherly, just short of condescending. 'I know all about your purist methods, Jane, and I'll admit they have been very effective in the past. But perhaps, in the modern world of policing, that's where they must remain – in the past. As you pointed out, DCI Brown is the SIO on this case. Whether you agree with him or not, he must have your full support as well was that of the team. Do I make myself clear?'

Phillips gritted her teeth. 'Yes ma'am.'

'Thank you, ma'am' said Brown triumphantly.

Fox's smile vanished instantly. 'Right, I have a report to finish for the Chief Constable.' Returning her glasses to the end of her nose, she retrieved the file. 'Dismissed,' she said without looking up.

Phillips rose to her feet and hurried out of the office. She couldn't bear to look at Brown, let alone speak to him.

As she stormed down the corridor he called after her. 'Where are you going *Inspector*?'

'Out!' she shouted over her shoulder before ducking down the stairs and out into the car park.

She had to get away, and she needed a drink.

40

D espite their best efforts, the Greater Manchester Police was still without a name on the charge sheet for the four murders. And tonight, if everything went according to plan, he would deal with victim number five – the *wildcard.*

He called it that as it wasn't part of the original plan, and despite chastising himself for going off piste with Ricky Murray, he had come to the conclusion that an additional victim would be of benefit at this stage of the game. It was a risk, of course he knew that, but one he believed was worth taking. Besides, he reasoned, any risk was mitigated by his own brilliance and unrivalled ability to hide in plain sight.

Circumstances had changed. Phillips and her crew had begun pulling the pieces together, making connections faster than he had anticipated, and it was time to throw in a curveball. Something that would send shockwaves through the team and buy him time to complete his mission before leaving this place *forever.*

HE HAD ENJOYED the hour-long walk to tonight's location. Moving quietly through the dark, cold streets of Manchester, he had taken in the world around him. Watched people living out their lives behind closed curtains, no doubt glued to their televisions, with no idea that the 'Cheadle Murderer' was outside their window, prowling their street.

He arrived at his destination and deftly climbed over the ten-foot-high wall, dropping silently into the flower bed below.

The hairs at the back of his neck tingled as he stared at the large French doors to the rear of the house. Unlike those of his other victims, this residence had been fitted with a sophisticated network of security lights. If anything crossed within three metres of their sensors, the garden lit up like a football stadium – something he'd learned whilst watching the house the previous night. Thankfully, in a neighbourhood filled with wandering cats and hungry foxes, he'd had plenty of opportunities during his time in the shadows to assess their sensitivity, range and timing. He'd identified a blind spot running down the edge of the path that led to his current position, standing on the rock-hard, frozen flower bed in the far corner of the garden, cloaked in darkness.

As he listened to the commuters returning home around him, he smiled contentedly and settled in. Everything he needed lay carefully packed in the rucksack between his feet. Cupping his latex-gloved hands together over his mouth, he gently blew on them in an effort to keep warm, his eyes locked on the house and its occupant, clearly visible through the glass doors up ahead.

'Tick-tock, tick-tock,' he giggled to himself.

41

W hen she finally made it home, Phillips was past the point of hunger.

Earlier, bumping into Jones as she stormed across the car park, she had shared the events of her delightful day with Brown – including Ricky Murray's post mortem, the lynching in Fox's office plus her unquenching thirst for the blood of their totally incompetent DCI. Thankfully for her sake, Jones had suggested that, rather than act on those urges, they should head off for a drink in her local. It was the first sensible thing she'd heard all day. A couple of glasses in, Jones had called Bovalino and asked him to join them, but he had declined, citing his urgent preparation of the family rally car for an upcoming race that weekend. Entwistle had purposefully not been invited. As much as he was proving useful, and was growing on them both personally, he was still too new for the kind of anti-Brown chat that had dominated their conversation for the last two hours.

Finally, when they'd grown weary of examining Brown's long list of failings as both a copper and a human being, Jones had done the sensible thing and taken a taxi home. Phillips however was not finished. After leaving the pub, she had dropped into the uber-trendy independent grocery store at the end of her street – owned and operated by a couple of 'reformed' investment bankers – to pick up a couple more bottles of white wine. She regularly paid a premium for the privilege of knowing her wine was organic and fair-trade, but, in truth, it was close to home and easier than going anywhere else.

Making her way into the kitchen, she fed the cat and deposited one of the bottles in the fridge, then carried the second into the living room and poured herself a large glass. Switching on the TV, she took a long mouthful, savouring the crisp edge to the flavour, and relaxed back into the sofa.

'Why do I do it, Floss? Why do I allow myself to work for such an incompetent wanker like Brown? Why?'

If Floss was listening, she didn't show it, instead purring loudly as she stuffed her face in her food bowl, never once looking up.

Phillips smiled. 'Oh, to be a cat.'

Browsing through the endless TV channels, she eventually landed on back-to-back re-runs of *Seinfeld*, then put her feet up on the sofa and lay back. A moment later, Floss jumped up onto her lap, kneading her paws up and down methodically, preparing the 'ground' where she intended to make her bed.

Soon, they were both fast asleep.

Phillips's heart jumped in her chest as she came awake with a start. Floss leaped from her lap and scurried over to the armchair on the other side of the room.

Sweat covered the back of Phillips's neck and she put her hand to the bullet wound in her chest, which was throbbing. For a moment she was back in that house, on the floor with the gun pointing directly at her. She could almost hear the blood coursing through her veins as she took a moment to orientate herself, trying to locate the noise that had woken her. Right on cue, there it was again.

She shook her head and chuckled. The Cheadle murders had clearly set her on edge. 'The front door. Is that all it was?'

She got up and walked out into the hallway. Ahead, she saw a large figure through the mottled-glass panel in the top half of the ornate front door. He appeared to be staring straight at her. Instantly, adrenaline surged through her body as panic started to fill every pore of her skin.

'Who is it?' She tried her best to sound calm when the opposite was true.

The person responded, but the voice was muffled and she couldn't make it out.

'Sorry, who is it?' she repeated, chastising herself for not having a spyhole fitted in the door.

The man knocked again just as Phillips engaged the chain. Taking a deep breath, she opened it a fraction, casting her eyes over a heavy-set man wearing a black anorak. He had turned away from her towards the street, and his face was hidden by the hood.

'Hello?' she said tentatively, her tongue clicking in her bone-dry mouth.

The man turned around, his face still cast in shadow. 'Hello Jane.' His voice was deep and low as he pulled his hood down. 'Have you missed me?'

Her heart jumped into her mouth. '*Marty*? Jesus, you scared the shit out of me!' Her relief was palpable.

'Sorry, Jane,' Marty Michaels said with a cheeky grin.

'Marty, it's late. What are you doing here?'

'You invited me.'

'I did? When?'

'The other day. When you replied to my text about not taking you out to the theatre. You said I should come over one night after work.'

'Well, I didn't mean tonight.'

'Oh...right. I figured it was an open invitation. I was just on my way home from the studio and thought I'd see how you were.'

Phillips opened the door fully and headed back to the kitchen, shouting back at him without turning, 'You wanna drink?'

He stepped inside. 'Coffee please,' he called after her.

SINCE BEING THROWN TOGETHER JUST over six months ago during the murder investigation that had almost cost Phillips her life, she and the outspoken radio – and now TV – host, Marty Michaels, had become friends. Not the type of friend you see every week, but on occasion, often when she was feeling anxious about the events that had almost killed her.

As Phillips prepared his drink, she noted how well Marty looked. He'd lost a tonne of weight since she first met him, and since cutting back on the booze, his skin appeared to glow. He'd even managed to tidy up his trademark dishevelled hair, in part due to his new-found career in front of the camera.

'You're looking well, Marty,' she commented.

'Thank you. It's amazing what giving up the early mornings does for your mental and physical health. Now I'm out of it, I can see I was living on the edge of burnout for almost twenty years.'

Phillips passed him his coffee and headed through to the lounge room, taking a seat on the couch. Marty followed and sat down in the armchair opposite.

'So, what was all that about then?' he asked, looking at her curiously.

'What was what about?'

'At the front door. You looked like you'd seen a ghost.'

Phillips took a gulp of wine before answering, 'It's nothing. Just these Cheadle murders have got me on edge. You know how it is.'

'Do I?'

'What's that supposed to mean?'

'Do I really have any idea what's going on in your head, Jane? Does anyone?'

'I told you. It's just work stuff. It's a stressful job. You know that.'

Marty stared at her for a moment without saying anything, which made her feel even more uncomfortable. She knew what he was doing.

'Cut it out,' she warned.

'What?'

'Trying to read me, assessing my non-verbal cues. I know you too well, Marty. And I know how to do that shit far better than you. It's my job, after all.'

Marty smiled and raised a hand. 'Guilty as charged!'

Phillips changed the subject. 'I saw your new TV show the other day.'

Marty sat forwards in his chair. 'Really? What did you think?'

'Well, I didn't actually watch the show, but I did see the advert for it. I'm recording it. How's the ratings?'

'Really good. The first couple have gone down very well with both the audiences and guests. The network bosses are talking about commissioning a second series already, which is brilliant.'

'So you're well and truly back in the big time, then?'

Marty took a sip from his coffee. 'Looks that way,' he said nonchalantly.

'Good for you.' Phillips took another swig of wine as a wave of anger washed over her without warning. She fought to keep it under wraps, but try as she might, she couldn't help thinking how he'd fared far better than she had since their shared ordeal.

'How's your work?' he asked, seeming genuinely interested, for a change.

Phillips shrugged. 'My career is going in the complete opposite direction to yours.'

'Why? What's going on?'

'Coppers have long memories, Marty, which means I'm still taking flack for helping you.'

'But I thought all was forgotten and everything was back to normal now? It's been six months, for God's sake.'

'Yep, it has. Six months of shitty remarks behind my back. People calling *me* a bent copper. *Me*? I'm not sure I'll ever get back to DCI; and to top it all, I'm working for someone with the policing ability of Inspector Clouseau. Plus, an ego that's even bigger than yours – if you can believe that.'

Marty said nothing for a moment. Then a smile crept over his face. 'Wow. Has he really got an ego bigger than mine?'

Phillips laughed. 'Sorry Marty, I didn't mean that.'

'Yes you did, and honestly, I don't mind. Therapy has taught me to appreciate my ego rather than suppress it. It's kept me at the top of my game for over twenty years, so it can't be all that bad, can it?'

'Good point.'

'But seriously, Jane, I'm worried about you. You look like you're suffering.'

She took another mouthful of wine. 'I'm fine.'

'"Fine with wine" more like it,' he quipped.

On the couch, Phillips pulled her knees close to her chest like an awkward teenager. 'Oh, please don't start on my drinking again.'

Marty moved towards the edge of the armchair. 'Look Jane, I get it. I really do. I buried myself in whiskey for years after Dad and David died. And when Rebecca left me, well, I virtually lived on the stuff. But it can't fix you in here.' He pointed to his heart. 'Or in here,' he added tapping his temple.

Phillips avoided his gaze and stared into her glass. There was a long moment of silence.

'Are you at least seeing the therapist from work?' Marty asked after a while.

Phillips buried her head behind her knees so her words were slightly muffled. 'I've been a couple of times, but work is crazy busy at the minute.'

'And what does she think?'

Phillips lifted her head. 'She thinks that after what happened, I'll have issues with PTSD for the rest of my life, but that it's manageable.'

'And what do you think?' Marty's voice was soft and reassuring.

For a moment, Phillips wondered if he was using one of his well-honed interview techniques.

'What do *I* think? I think I'm a copper with a very stressful job. Some days I'm fine, while others I'm not. Sometimes I feel like I did on that horrific night in that house, a gun pointing at my head – trapped, terrified and powerless.' She forced a smile as she fought back the tears.

'The drinking won't help long term, Jane, I promise you that.'

'No, but it's helping me now.' She jumped from the sofa and headed into the kitchen, a moment later returning with a replenished glass in hand.

Marty let out a sigh then stood up. 'That looks like my cue to leave.'

Phillips placed the wine on the coffee table in the middle of the room. 'Probably best.'

He leant in and kissed her gently on the cheek. 'Please take it easy, Jane, that's all I'm asking. I really do care about you, you know.'

'Thanks.' She swatted away a tear from her cheek, then forced a smile. 'Come on, I'll show you out.'

When they reached the door, Marty zipped up his anorak and pulled on his leather gloves.

'I meant to ask, how's things with Becky?'

Marty scoffed lightly. 'Your guess is as good as mine. Sean's agreed to the divorce at least, so that's something.'

'Which leaves the door open for you again, right?'

'Theoretically. But does she really want to take me back after everything that's gone on?'

'You don't know until you ask.'

Marty flashed a knowing smile. 'True. But what if she said no? I don't think I could bear to lose her twice. At least, as things stand, I can live in hope it *could* happen one day, and hope is a powerful thing. If I knew for certain it couldn't, it'd break my heart.'

Phillips patted him gently on the chest. 'I used to work with a great copper from Newcastle called DCI Campbell. He always used to say: "Shy bairns get nowt."'

Marty looked confused. 'And what the hell does that mean?'

'Quiet children get nothing...and the loud ones get everything. If she doesn't know you *want* her back, how can you ever *get* her back, Marty?'

'Sounds like a smart man, that Campbell.'

'Yeah, he was. You could do a lot worse than follow his advice.'

Marty smiled. 'Only if you at least think about following mine.'

'I'll *think* about it, Marty. I promise.'

'Well, I can't ask for any more than that, can I?' He leaned forwards and hugged her tightly. 'Look after yourself, Jane,' he whispered in her ear.

She held his hug for a long moment. 'I will,' she replied

before pulling back the door for him. 'Now bugger off and let me get some sleep, will you?'

Marty stepped out onto the front step, then pressed the key fob to his car, causing the lights to flash on his enormous SUV parked out on the street. He turned. 'Sleep well, Jane.'

She nodded. 'Goodnight, Marty,' she said, closing the door and locking it behind him.

The next moment, the cat appeared at her feet, snaking between her legs. She checked her watch. 'Look at that, it's only eleven-thirty, Floss. Fancy a nightcap? One more won't hurt.'

42

Phillips woke with a start as Floss jumped from her lap with a meow. *Dé jà vu*, she thought to herself, rubbing her eyes.

Rousing herself, she stood up slowly from the couch to see that the timer light connected to the free-standing lamp in the corner of the room had switched itself off. As had the TV, indicating she'd been asleep for some time. Stepping into the darkened kitchen, she spied the digital clock on the cooker. It read 3.08 a.m.

'Not again,' she muttered.

Opening the fridge, the room around her illuminated as she pulled out a carton of fresh orange juice and gulped it down loudly, attempting to quench her raging thirst.

'Floss?' she called between gulps. *'Flossy...?'*

Taking one final mouthful of juice, she replaced it on the shelf and closed the fridge door, plunging the room back into darkness. As she flicked on the main kitchen light, she noticed cold air running across her bare feet. Her eyes swivelled to the backdoor to see that it was slightly ajar.

'That's odd?' She stepped closer to get a better look. 'I'm sure that was locked.'

She reached out and grabbed the door handle. It was wet from the rain that had blown in through the gap, indicating that it had been open for some time.

A sudden noise from behind startled her, causing her to jump. She spun around to see a meowing Floss. 'Jesus, don't creep up on people!' She bent down to stroke the cat. 'You almost gave me a bloody heart attack.'

She locked the back door, then switched on the security lights at the rear of the house and looked out into the garden. She must have opened it for Floss when she returned from the pub and forgotten to close it. 'Too much wine is making you ditsy, Jane.' She flicked off the lights again. 'Not a great combination.'

Floss had her nose in her bowl again as Phillips walked back into the kitchen, conscious of the two empty wine bottles on the kitchen bench. Marty was right – her drinking *was* getting out of hand. At that moment, the remorse was almost crippling. 'Gotta start looking after yourself, Jane. Because if you don't, it's a slippery slope.'

Casting the empties into the recycling bin, she pulled a tumbler from the kitchen cabinet and filled it from the cold tap. 'Come on, Floss, time for bed.'

She switched off the kitchen light and walked into the hall. Cold air now came from the front door, which was also ajar. 'What the hell?'

She placed her glass of water on the window ledge and flicked on the hall light. Nothing happened. Her heart pounding, she switched on her phone and, using the screen as a torch, shone it up at the light fitting to see that the bulb had been removed.

Panic clawed at every fibre of her being. She needed to take action but was frozen to the spot, fear paralysing her. A cold sweat trickled down her back as she fumbled with her phone and opened up the contacts page. 'Please be there, Jonesy,' she whispered into the darkness.

'There's no need for that, Jane,' said a deep male voice from behind her.

Phillips spun round. A large man stood in the darkness of the kitchen, his sweater hood up and some kind of mask across his face. His right hand gripped something by his side.

She froze for a moment and stared at him. Her heart was now pounding so fast she thought it might explode. Then her instincts kicked in. Breaking free from her paralysis, she threw herself towards the only possible exit, the unlocked front door. Her attacker must have guessed her plan, for he was on her in an instant. He rammed his fist into the back of her head, She stumbled forwards, hit her face on the heavy wooden door and fell to the floor. Blood poured from her nose as he knelt and grabbed her from behind, expertly hooking his left bicep around her throat and squeezing tightly.

His right hand holding a spray dispenser came into view. She knew immediately what it was and used every ounce of her strength to punch it from his grasp. It landed on the floor and rolled down the hall.

He loosened his grip momentarily, allowing her room to move her head, and she attempted to catch sight of the man standing above her. But in the darkness of the hallway, she couldn't make him out. Strangely, she was acutely aware of the scent he was wearing, Gucci Guilty. It was Marty's favourite.

Her attacker decided against retrieving the dispenser. Instead, he rolled onto his back like a cage fighter and pulled Phillips on top of him, his legs wrapped tightly around her middle. The more she fought, the tighter his grip became until finally she couldn't move an inch.

'Let it happen,' he whispered softly in her ear as his arm pressed hard against her neck. She tried to place his voice but the pressure on her temples was overwhelming and spots began to dance across her vision.

Trapped on the floor of her own hallway, she had never imagined this would be how she would die.

'Let it happen,' her attacker repeated. 'Let it happen.'

Phillips clawed at his thick arm, her feet kicking out in all directions. Opening her mouth, she managed a faint scream.

'Sshhhh.' He clasped his hand over her mouth and gripped her tighter.

She writhed underneath him, forcing him to adjust his grip over her mouth. It was all she needed. Opening her jaw wide, she clamped her teeth down on his index finger. He screamed out and loosened his grip, enough for her to ram her elbow into his crotch. Crying out, he let go of her.

Phillips didn't hesitate this time. She dragged herself to her feet and ran into kitchen. At the counter, she grabbed the biggest blade from the knife block and turned, ready to face her assailant again.

From her position, she couldn't see the front door, only the darkness at the end of the long hallway. She wheezed loudly, trying desperately to get air through her damaged throat. Her blood pounded in her ears.

A minute passed and she remained glued to her spot in the kitchen, knife in hand, staring at the blackness of the hallway. *Where is he?*

Finally, with no sign of him, she inched forwards and peered into the hallway. At the end, the front door was wide open and rain was blowing in from outside. Tentatively she moved down the hallway, knife ready. When she made it to the doorway, she stared out into the night to see her front gate banging in the wind. He was gone.

Overwhelmed with relief, she leant back against the wall and slid down it, the effects of her injuries causing her to pass out before she hit the floor.

43

J ones woke to the sound of his phone vibrating on the bedside cabinet. Next to him, his wife remained fast asleep. He picked up the phone. Bov's ID flashed up. It was 4.27 a.m., so it had to be urgent.

'What's up, Bov?' he whispered as he got out of bed and headed into the en suite bathroom. Switching on the light, he caught sight of his puffy red face in the mirror, his hair pointing in all directions.

'It's the guv. Someone just tried to kill her.'

His eyes widened in disbelief. 'What the fuck? Where?'

'Her house. Two hours ago. Uniform are with her now. She's in bad shape and can hardly speak. She had to use a silent 999 call to alert the operator.'

'Bloody hell!' Jones ran a hand through his hair. 'How did you hear about it?'

'My mate Hendricks from uniform was first on scene and called me.'

'Right. Look, I'll meet you at hers ASAP.'

'No point. According to Hendricks, they're just about to load her into an ambulance. She needs an MRI.'

'It's that bad?'

'Dunno at this stage, Jonesy. Probably standard procedure. I'm only ten minutes out, so I'll let you know when I get there.'

'Good man. I'll be with you in twenty.'

Jones ended the call. Scooping yesterday's clothes up in his arms, he tiptoed out the bedroom and downstairs, trying his best not to wake his wife, and hurried to get dressed.

Thirty minutes later, Jones pulled into the car park of the Manchester Royal Infirmary. Traffic had been light, but still busy for 5 a.m., and the heavy rain hadn't helped.

Dumping his car in a parking bay reserved for uniformed police vehicles outside the A&E department, he rushed through reception, following directions from Bovalino's text message, and headed towards a treatment room at the end of a long corridor.

Inside, he spotted his partner's large frame step out through the curtains of one of the cubicles. 'Bov...'

Bovalino turned towards him, his huge shoulders sagging. 'Who would do this to the guv?' He nodded towards the curtain. 'Fucking animal, Jonesy.'

Jones swallowed hard and stepped through, coming face to face with Phillips. She lay on the bed, which was set at a forty-five-degree angle, her eyes closed but already blackening from a broken nose, which was hidden under an oxygen mask. Her neck was a mixture of purple and dark red bruises.

'Jesus Christ, Guv,' he whispered, stepping in close enough to hold her hand.

Phillips's opened her eyes and smiled at him weakly.

Jones leaned forwards. 'We're going to get this bastard, Guv,' he said as Bovalino joined him.

Phillips nodded slowly, then closed her eyes again.

'Too fucking right, we are,' Bovalino said through gritted teeth. 'And when we do, I'm going to tear his arms off and feed them to him.'

Phillips didn't react, her eyes remaining closed.

Jones watched her a few moments. Then, with a heavy heart, he gestured for Bovalino to follow him out of the cubicle. Stepping out of earshot, he whispered, 'Do we think this is the same guy as the Cheadle murders?'

Bovalino shrugged. 'Not sure. She's been out of it since I got here. Hendricks said she could hardly speak when they arrived at the house, but he was sure she was trying to say "Guilty Marty", over and over.'

'*Guilty Marty*. What the hell does that mean?'

'The only Marty I can think of is Marty Michaels. Could she be talking about him?'

Jones shook his head. 'I doubt it. I'm not his biggest fan, but I can't see Marty doing something like this to the guv. Not after what they went through together. No, it can't be him. They're friends. She was just talking about him the other day.'

At that moment, a wiry, young male doctor arrived and introduced himself as Dr Henry. Jones and Bovalino shared their own credentials.

'How's she looking, doctor?' Jones asked.

Doctor Henry glanced at the chart in his hand before answering. 'Well, she can breathe on her own, which was our main concern when she was admitted. However, we will need to do more tests to ensure there's no serious internal damage to her throat and larynx. They took the brunt of the trauma. We'll also X-ray her skull. She's suffered a broken nose and we need to make sure there's no fracture to the skull or serious damage to her cheekbones, which can cause all manner of complications. And, of course, there's the psychological trauma. She's been through a horrific ordeal. We'll be admitting her for the remainder of the tests, and keep her under observation for a couple of days.'

Jones let out a sigh of relief. 'Good. I was hoping you were going to say that. Knowing the guv, she'd discharge herself at eight o'clock this morning and head into the office.'

'No chance of that. The pain relief we've administered is very strong. She won't be going anywhere without the use of a trolley and a porter for some time.'

'Because of the nature of the attack, we'll station a couple of uniformed officers to guard her twenty-four-seven,' Jones informed the doctor.

Henry's expression suggested he wasn't a fan of the plan. 'The hospital is quite secure, Sergeant. I'm sure that won't be necessary.'

Jones stepped closer, his expression grave. 'A Detective Inspector in the Greater Manchester Police has been attacked in her own home by someone we suspect could be involved in a series of violent crimes. None of the previous victims have survived, meaning DI Phillips is our only living witness. We intend to protect her. First, from any potential follow-up attack, and second, from the press, who will swarm round your hospital like flies on shit once this gets out. So, she'll need a private room, and two officers will stand guard at all times. Are we clear on that, doctor?'

Dr Henry held Jones's gaze before glancing at Bovalino, who was standing directly behind his partner. He forced a smile, his bleached white teeth gleaming under the fluorescent lights of the A&E. 'As you wish. We'll see to it right away.' With a curt nod, he left the room.

Jones turned to Bovalino. 'Has a SOCO team been dispatched to the guv's yet?'

'No, not yet.'

'Right. Call Evans and get him over there immediately. And send Entwistle to keep an eye on them too.'

'Got it.'

'I'll call Brown, then I'll arrange for uniform to guard the guv. Once they arrive, you and I can get over to her place and see what the hell went on there.'

44

As soon as Jones and Bovalino pulled up outside Phillips's house, they were greeted by a sea of channel-branded news cars and trucks, some of whom were already broadcasting from outside the police cordon.

The two got out of their vehicles. 'How did this lot get here so quickly?' said Bovalino.

'Gossip travels fast in the GMP. It's hard to keep a lid on anything these days, especially when it concerns the guv. The press love her. Bloody vultures.'

As they approached the cordon, a few reporters peeled away from the press pack and approached them.

'Detective, can you tell us if DI Phillips was attacked last night?'

'Is it true DI Phillips fought off the man responsible for the Cheadle murders?'

'Did the GMP release their prime suspect in the case just hours before DI Phillips was attacked?'

By now they were surrounded by the rest of the pack, who continued to bombard them with questions. Bovalino pushed his way past them, then a uniformed officer raised the police tape and they ducked under it and into the relative quiet of the white SOCO tent at the front of the house.

Inside, Entwistle greeted them in his white overalls. 'Am I glad to see you two,' he said, looking relieved. 'I've never seen anything like that out there.'

'It's never easy once this lot get involved,' Jones replied grimly. 'God knows what their presence will do to Brown's state of mind.'

Bovalino pointed through the tent flap and across the street. 'I think we're about to find out.'

Jones turned to see Brown rooted to the spot on the other side of the police tape, a host of logo'ed microphones under his nose. From where they stood, it was hard to hear what he was saying but, judging by his facial expression, he was deeply uncomfortable.

Jones zipped up his suit, then pulled on protective shoe covers. 'Great. That's all we need.'

A minute later, Brown managed to extricate himself from the crowd and entered the tent, 'This case just keeps on getting better, doesn't it?' he muttered disconsolately.

A chorus of lacklustre 'sir's greeted him.

'What have we got, then?'

'We've just arrived, sir,' replied Jones. 'But from we can ascertain so far, the guv was attacked in her home in the early hours of the morning. We believe she fought back and that her attacker escaped undetected. Sometime later, she used a silent 999 sequence to alert the police to her situation. A uniformed team arrived within ten minutes to find her unconscious on the floor. No forced entry.'

'No forced entry? Could this be the same guy?'

'We can't rule it out, sir, but Phillips has made a lot of enemies over the years.'

'Quite. Ok, what else?'

'That's all we know so far.'

'That's it?'

'Like I said, sir, we arrived just a few minutes before you did.'

The little Scotsman stepped closer to Jones. 'I don't know if it's escaped your notice, Sergeant, but half the world's media is now camped outside our latest crime scene. We need to tell them something positive, for Christ's sake.'

Jones locked his eyes on Brown's, both fists clenched in his latex gloves. What he wouldn't give to knock the little weasel on his backside right now, but that wouldn't help find the guv's attacker any quicker. 'You could try telling them that DI Phillips survived a horrific attack in her own home last night. That she's lucky to be alive, and being treated in hospital. That we wish her a speedy recovery...*sir*.'

The penny appeared to drop for Brown, and his demeanour suddenly softened. 'Of course. Sorry, how is she?'

'Looks like a broken nose, a nasty cut above her eye, plus damage to her neck and throat. He beat her up pretty badly. She can hardly speak.'

'My God, that terrible.' Brown almost sounded concerned. *Almost.* 'Still, at least it'll stop her giving me earache all the time.' Brown forced a chuckle.

The team stared at Brown in silence, his attempt at humour clearly misjudged under the circumstances. Apparently sensing their disapproval, he grabbed a SOCO suit and stepped into it, looking as ridiculous as ever in the billowing overalls. 'Right, let's see if we can finally catch this bastard, shall we?'

Jones didn't need an excuse to get away from Brown. Exiting the tent, he walked into the house with Bovalino and Entwistle following closely behind.

Inside, senior pathologist Andy Evans stood in the kitchen at the end of the hall. 'Anything we need to know, Andy?' asked Jones.

'Looks like all the action happened right here. From what

we see so far, the attack took place between where you're standing and the front door.' He pointed to the floor. 'All the scuff marks and blood are centred around this area.'

'Did we get any of his blood?'

Evans shook his head. 'Can't say for certain until we test it, but from the blood spatter patterns, it's consistent with one victim and matches the type of blood loss you'd see with a broken nose.'

'Ok. Any other fluids that might give us a chance at DNA?'

'Nothing as yet—'

At that moment, Brown strode down the hall. 'What have I missed?'

Evans shuffled forwards so Brown could see him. He appeared to be the only man on the planet keen to impress him. 'I was just saying, sir, that most of the action appears to have taken place in the hallway, where you're standing. As of yet, we haven't found anything that might identify our man.'

Judging by his expression, this wasn't the news Brown was hoping to hear. 'For fuck's sake, Evans. One of our officers suffered a brutal attack in a confined space – yet you and your team say there's no evidence of the man involved. Surely there must be something he left behind?'

Jones watched Evans's face fall like a child being told he wasn't good enough by a disapproving father. 'We can only find what they leave behind, sir.'

'That's what *you lot* always say.'

One of Evans's forensic team appeared now, slightly out of breath. 'I think you should see this, Andy.'

Evans turned to face him. 'What is it, Denning?'

'We found a cigarette butt inside the perimeter of the garden. It looks fresh.'

Brown didn't hesitate. 'Show me, sonny.' Accompanied by Denning, he marched through Phillips's kitchen and out into the garden.

The rest of the team followed, stopping at the end of the path by a wooden gate that opened through a concrete wall. Jones noted it was padlocked from the inside.

Denning crouched and used a gloved finger to point to the cigarette butt almost hidden from view on top of the soil at the base of the wall. 'It was hard to spot at first because of all the plants, but the good news is that the shrubbery covered it from any rain we had last night, so we should still be able to pull DNA from it.'

'Excellent work, sonny.' Brown sounded excited.

Jones looked up at the garden wall. 'Any chance it could have been tossed over from the alley?'

Denning stood up. 'It's possible, but unlikely it would land so close to the wall. That's a good ten feet high, which means you'd need a decent trajectory to clear the wall from the alley. In which case, the butt would land much closer to the path.

'Any footprints?' asked Bovalino.

'No, that's the odd thing. The soil has been turned over, you know, with a garden fork or something.'

Bovalino screwed up his face. 'He did that, yet left a cigarette butt behind? That's a bit careless, isn't it?'

'Not to mention the fact it was freezing last night. That soil would've been like concrete,' said Jones.

Brown cut in. 'Well, if it's the same guy as the Cheadle murders, it looks like his usual plans for finishing off his victims were scuppered by Phillips fighting back. He obviously left in a hurry. He's finally messed up and left something behind. Excellent work, Denning. You too, Evans.'

Jones wasn't so sure. A brutal murderer, who so far had left no trace, suddenly leaving a cigarette butt behind after removing his footprints from the mud? It seemed out of character for their guy.

'How long before we can check for DNA?' Brown asked Evans.

'It's not the quickest of processes, I'm afraid, but I'm sure, with this being an attack on a copper, we can pull some strings at the lab and have results in a few days.'

'And what if we're simply trying to match one suspect whose DNA is already on file?'

'Much quicker. Tomorrow, under the circumstances.'

'Tonight, sonny.'

Evans smiled awkwardly. 'I'll do my best, sir.'

'That's what I like to hear!' Brown was all smiles now. He headed back into the house, draping his arm across Evans's back as they walked together and shared a private joke.

Jones turned away and watched while Denning took photos and measurements of the cigarette butt and surrounding areas. He checked his watch: 11.40 a.m. He figured they should have completed Phillips's tests by now. Hopefully she would be up for answering a few questions about her attacker.

He tapped Bov on the arm. 'Fancy coming to see the guv?'

'Bloody right, I do.'

Jones pulled Entwistle close to him, out of Denning's hearing. 'You buying this cigarette stuff, Entwistle?'

'Seems a bit sloppy for our guy, if I'm honest. Not to mention convenient for the investigation.'

'Good lad. Neither are we. Head back to Ashton House with Brown and let us know as soon as the DNA results come in.'

'Gotcha.'

'Me and Bov are off to visit the guv, see if there's anything she can remember about last night. She's the key to catching this guy. I can feel it in my bones.'

45

Phillips was sitting up in the bed in her private room when Jones and Bovalino flashed their IDs and stepped past the two uniformed officers stationed at her door. Hooked up to a multitude of machines and an intravenous drip, she broke into faint smile when she saw them arrive.

'How you feeling, Guv?'

'Like I've been hit by a bus, Jonesy. He really did a number on me, didn't he?' Her voice was husky and strained, thanks to the damage to her throat.

Bovalino stood at the end of the bed and rested his hands on the metal frame. 'You're lucky to be alive, that's for sure.'

Jones grabbed a couple of chairs and both men sat down as Phillips took a sip of water through a straw, wincing slightly as she did so.

'Are you up for talking, Guv?' asked Jones, observing her.

Phillips nodded, though obviously still in pain.

'Can you tell us what happened last night after you and I left the pub?'

Phillips filled them in on her journey home via the grocery

store to get more wine, and how she fell asleep on the couch with Floss before being woken up when Marty Michaels paid her a visit.

'Marty?' Jones sounded shocked.

Phillips nodded. 'Remember that message where he blew me off for Rebecca? When I replied, I asked him to call in one night after work. He did that last night.'

Bovalino leant forwards. 'Interesting. Do you remember what you said to the attending officers when they arrived at the house?'

'No, what?'

'According to Sergeant Hendricks, you kept saying "Guilty Marty" and pointing to your neck.'

'Was he the man that attacked you, Guv?' asked Jones.

Phillips let out a husky chuckle. 'Don't be silly. Marty wouldn't hurt me. No, I was referring to the attacker's scent I could smell. I could have sworn it was Gucci Guilty.'

Bovalino looked confused. 'How does Marty fit in with that?'

'It's his favourite aftershave. His ex loved it, and he still wears it every day.'

Jones frowned. 'You're sure it wasn't Marty, then?'

'Positive. This guy was much more agile. He moved incredibly quickly – his arms and legs were wrapped round me in a flash. Marty's too lazy to stay in that kind of shape.'

'So what happened, Guv?'

Jones and Bovalino listened intently as Phillips talked them through her movements after saying goodnight to Marty, how she woke up on the couch at 3 a.m. and found both her doors open, and was then attacked by the man in her hallway.

'Do you think it was the same guy who's behind the church murders?' asked Jones.

Phillips nodded. 'One hundred per cent.'

Bovalino's face twisted into a grimace. 'What I don't get is, why attempt to strangle you when he's used a sedative to knock out all the other victims? Why not use that on you?'

Phillips shifted her weight on the bed. 'He had it with him. From my brief glimpse, it looked like a small dispenser about the size of a nasal spray. Once he'd grappled me to the floor, he tried to turn it on me. Luckily, I managed to punch it out of his hand. I was fighting with everything I had, so I guess he thought better of letting me go to retrieve it. Decided to choke me instead.'

'And did you get a look at his face, or anything else that might help us identify him?' said Jones.

'No. He wore a dark hoody, so his face was covered in shadow, and he had some kind of mask across his nose and mouth.'

'Mask? What, like a clown?' asked Bovalino.

Phillips laughed, but stopped immediately with a sharp wince. 'That's it, Bov. Put out an APB on Ronald McDonald. He's our killer.' She patted the edge of the bed nearest to him.

Bovalino reddened slightly. 'Sorry, Guv. When I think of masks, I immediately think of clowns. I bloody hate clowns.'

'It was hard to see fully because of the hoodie, but it looked like a surgeon's mask. You know, the ones everyone was wearing in London when the bird flu hit a few years ago.'

Jones lowered his voice to avoid being overheard by the uniformed officers at the door. 'You know Brown is still convinced it's Logan, don't you? He's got Evans working up a DNA match as we speak.'

'DNA match on what?'

'A cigarette butt found in your garden, by the gate.'

Phillips appeared confused. 'Cigarette butt? What, and he thinks my attacker left it behind?'

'He's certain,' said Bovalino.

'But that doesn't make any sense. Our guy is meticulous and methodical. He's killed four people without leaving a single speck of evidence, and now he's suddenly leaving a cigarette behind?'

'Our thoughts exactly,' said Jones.

'And besides, the guy who did this to me didn't smoke. He smelt fresh and clean. If he'd had a cigarette before he attacked me, I'd have smelled it. You know how I can smell stale smoke a mile off.'

Jones smiled, recalling her regular complaints about the smell inside his car. He might have quit a year ago, but the odour was still noticeable under the air-fresheners. 'So how did it get there?' he asked.

'Maybe the wind blew it in? It was pretty brutal last night,' Bovalino replied.

Phillips closed her eyes a moment and let out a small grimace. 'Maybe, Bov. We'll have to see what Evans and the team get from it.'

'Are you ok, Guv?' said Jones.

'Yeah, just the painkillers wearing off. I'll get the nurse to give me some more in a minute.'

Jones stood. 'We better leave you to get some rest. The nurse said we shouldn't stay too long. There are two uniform coppers at your door, just in case our guy decides to try and finish what he started.'

'Very reassuring, Jonesy,' Phillips said with another grimace. 'Send the nurse in on your way out, will you?

Jones patted her on the wrist. 'Will do, Guv. Rest up. We need you back in one piece ASAP.'

'Yeah,' Bovalino chimed in. He pointed at Jones. 'Or one of us two will be going down for DCI Brown's murder.'

46

It was a frustratingly slow afternoon for the team as they waited for developments from forensics. Jones and Bovalino finally lost patience and decided to canvas Phillips's neighbours to see if they had seen or heard anything helpful, as well as taking another look at the crime scene. They'd left Entwistle with strict instructions to keep an eye on Brown, who was hungry for Logan's blood and itching for a result. As soon as any news came in, he would call them.

An hour earlier, Brown had looked very pleased with himself as he headed upstairs to share the latest development with Fox, who had recently returned from a meeting at the Town Hall. He was back now, a spring in his step.

'You still here, sonny?' he asked the young police officer.

'Yes sir,' Entwistle replied. 'Just catching up on paperwork.' He was actually compiling a dossier at Jones's request of all the evidence that pointed to – as well as against – Matt Logan. Entwistle knew that if Brown found out, he'd be finished in the murder squad. At the same time, he'd come to realise what Bovalino had meant that day when he told him there were two types of coppers. He wanted more than anything to be the 'thorough and determined' type as opposed to 'quick and easy'. In the imaginary fight for his soul, Phillips and the guys had won. Brown had lost.

At around 6.45 p.m., Entwistle headed to the canteen to grab something hot before it closed for the night, or else he would be forced to eat packet sandwiches out of the machine. As a former university-level athlete, he tried to eat healthily, but since joining the team it wasn't always easy, what with the long hours and shift work.

Sitting alone, he was finishing his vegetable curry and rice when Brown appeared looking like a man at the airport, late for his plane.

'There you are, Entwistle. You need to come with me right away. We've got a match on Logan's DNA to that cigarette we found.'

'Right, sir.' He pushed his plate aside and followed Brown out of the canteen. 'Where are we going?'

'Following a tactical unit to Logan's hostel in Cheetham Hill,' Brown replied over his shoulder.

'Shall I call Jones and Bovalino and ask them to meet us there?'

'No, sonny. This one's on us. The new broom showing the old guard how it's done. I don't want them involved. Are we clear on that?'

'Very good, sir,' said Entwistle without feeling, as Brown burst through the door to the car park like a gunslinger in a Western.

The drive from Ashton House to Cheetham Hill normally took twenty minutes, but under blue lights they made it in half the time. When they arrived, they pulled up next to the armed response unit, alongside dogs with their handlers, plus a couple of uniform teams. Having compiled a sizeable dossier on Logan, Entwistle couldn't help but feel it was all a bit unnecessary. The Logan he'd researched in such detail was anything but dangerous.

Brown barked out his orders with the confidence of a man about to apprehend the UK's highest-profile serial-killer since the Yorkshire Ripper, and the tactical team made their move. Surprisingly, Brown waited outside. 'No sense getting in the way, sonny,' he said when Entwistle asked him if he would be leading the team in. *That's a first.*

In less than three minutes, Brown was given the all-clear from the tactical unit and headed inside. Entwistle followed closely behind. As they approached Logan's room, the demonstration of manpower became even more apparent. Burly men in stab vests and helmets, and carrying automatic weapons, cluttered the small corridor that housed Logan's tiny room.

With Logan now safely secured in handcuffs, Brown wasted no time in inserting himself into the picture, talking loudly but, somehow, managing to say nothing worthwhile. As Entwistle stepped in next, he couldn't believe this tiny space was where Logan called home. Even harder to comprehend, in his mind, was that the criminal mastermind who had ritualistically murdered four victims using sophisticated chemical sedatives was the same man who sat on the end of the bed in a dirty old Manchester United football top and black tracksuit bottoms. His eyes were like saucers, and a repetitive moaning sound came from the back of his throat.

Entwistle took a closer look. 'He's as high as a kite, sir.'

'Well, let's get him back to the station and sober him up, sonny.'

Kneeling in front of Logan, Entwistle lifted the man's drooping chin. Drool fell from the corner of his mouth and his eyes had begun to roll so intensely, they appeared totally white.

Entwistle checked his pulse. 'Sir, his heart rate is dangerously high.'

'A side-effect of the drugs, no doubt.'

Logan's body began to shake, slowly at first but quickly building.

'Seriously, sir, I think he's about to start fitting. We need to get an ambulance right away.'

Brown appeared to care less. He pulled on latex gloves. 'Nonsense. One of the first-aiders can see to him at Ashton House.'

'Sir,' Entwistle inserted as much authority into his tone as he could. 'I've seen this before when I was in Leeds. It looks like he's taken Spice. If we don't do something fast, his heart will literally explode before we can even get to Ashton House.'

The seriousness of the situation finally dawned on Brown, and a look of panic flashed across his face. His prime suspect risked dying before he could take the credit for convicting him. 'Call the paramedics now. Get this man some help!'

IT TOOK the paramedics almost an hour to stabilise Logan in the ambulance. In the meantime, Brown enlisted Entwistle's help to go through Logan's room. It hadn't taken long to find what Brown was looking for: cigarette stubs that matched the one found at Phillips's house, a pair of latex gloves and a surgeon's mask, all neatly boxed under his bed.

'We've got the bastard!' Brown held the box triumphantly in one hand and slapped Entwistle on the back with the other. 'Well done, sonny. This is going look great on your CV.'

Entwistle forced a smile. Great on Brown's diversity stats, more like.

A uniformed officer entered the room. 'Sir, they're ready to take him to A&E now.'

'Thank you, Sergeant.' Brown was clearly enjoying himself as he turned to Entwistle, looking like the hero of the day.

'Right, sonny. I'll finish up here with forensics. You go with Logan to the hospital. He speaks to nobody but you.'

'Should I inform Jones and Bovalino now, sir?'

Brown shook his head firmly. 'Not at this stage. I'd like a clear run at this myself.'

'Yes sir.'

'And I want to know the moment he comes around. You got that?'

'Understood, sir.'

'All right, away you go.' Brown turned back into the room, clasping his hands together enthusiastically.

Entwistle travelled in silence in the back of the ambulance as the paramedic continued to monitor Logan's condition. Within ten minutes, they arrived at Manchester Royal Infirmary's A&E department, situated on the ground floor of the same hospital where Phillips was recovering. The irony was not lost on him.

In one smooth movement, Logan was whisked into the emergency intake area, where the paramedics officially handed him over to the medical staff. Thirty minutes later, when he was safely in the hands of a full medical crew and undergoing myriad tests, Entwistle took a moment to step outside and catch his breath. It had been an uncomfortable few hours.

Standing in the bitterly cold night air, he contemplated calling Jones, but knew it would be career suicide to go against Brown's orders. Still, he also knew that leaving Jones and Bovalino out of the loop would mean he was finished with the team. Pacing up and down, he prayed for clarity. He considered heading upstairs to see Phillips but, having heard Jones and Bovalino's account of her injuries, thought better of it. He needed to figure this one out on his own.

Pulling his collar up and stuffing his hands in his pockets to protect him from the bitter wind, he walked out onto Upper Brook Street and looked for inspiration. But it wasn't forthcoming, and he felt trapped and confused. What was he going to do? Whichever decision he chose, he was screwed.

He came up to an empty bus shelter and took a seat out of the wind, leaning back against the cold glass and closed his eyes, his head swirling.

Sometime later, he heard a soft Mancunian voice. 'Are you all right, lovey?'

He opened his eyes to see that a middle-aged lady had taken the seat next to him. She wore a thick coat and scarf over a navy-blue uniform. 'You look upset. Have you been in the hospital?'

'Er, yes... Well, kind of.'

'Somebody close to you?'

'No, not at all.'

Her brow furrowed and it felt like she could sense his anguish. 'You know, it never ceases to amaze me the power of the human spirit. We can find ourselves caring for souls we hardly know.'

'Sorry?' Entwistle wasn't sure if she was referring to him or herself.

She pointed towards the hospital. 'I've been a nurse for over thirty years, and I've seen that look on your face a thousand times. Let me tell you, it'll be ok, because it's rarely as bad as you think it is. People have a way of pulling through. Just have faith and never give up hope. It'll all work out right in the end, you'll see.'

In that moment, Bov's words on Entwistle's first day came into sharp focus: 'There are coppers who will not rest until they get the *right* result. You need to decide which kind of copper *you* want to be.'

Entwistle jumped to his feet. 'Thank you. That's exactly what I needed to hear.'

The lady smiled, appearing a little surprised by his sudden change in demeanour. She patted him on the arm and wished him well, then he hurried back in the direction of A&E, pulling out his phone as he walked. He selected the number he wanted and pressed the call button.

A moment later, it was answered.

'Jonesy, it's Entwistle... The shit's hit the fan with Logan.'

47

Entwistle followed Jones's instructions and headed upstairs to Phillips's room to brief her on the events of the evening so far. Entering her cubicle, he was shocked by the state of her injuries and, for a moment, contemplated turning away. Then she opened one eye and, staring at him questioningly, beckoned him over. Jones had been correct. She wanted to know what was happening with the case.

Ten minutes later, and fully up to speed, she sat in silence for a long moment, deep in thought. 'The case against Logan appears compelling: a positive DNA match, latex gloves, a surgeon's mask – all found in his room. With his record, any jury will find him guilty.' Phillips's voice was still gravelly.

'Looks that way, Guv.'

'But I'm still not convinced he's our guy. The man who attacked me was agile and strong. Logan is off his face most of his waking life. I'm struggling to believe he's our killer.'

'Could someone be setting him up, Guv?

'Possibly. But who, and why?'

'The real killer?'

'It would make sense, but how the hell did they get Logan's

cigarette butt into my garden?' Phillips zoned out again, deep in thought.

Entwistle shifted uncomfortably in his seat after a couple of minutes silence. 'Guv, are you okay?'

Phillips turned to him and smiled. 'Sorry, bad habit when I'm thinking. My mum still goes mad when I stare off into space like that, but I get it from my dad. They used to fall out over it all the time, especially on summer holidays. Dad always claimed he was thinking, but she swore he was ignoring her. Mind you – if you ever met my mother, you'd understand why.'

'That reminds me, Guv.' He pulled a folded sheet of A4 paper out from inside his jacket pocket and handed it to Phillips.

She scanned the page. 'What's this?'

'The manifest for the St Patrick's minibus that travelled to Lourdes with Logan, Gillespie, etc. on board.'

Phillips squinted at it, reading through the detail.

Entwistle shared his findings. 'According to Father Maguire, Ricky Murray pulled out of the trip the night before and no-one replaced him, right?'

'That's what he said.'

'Which means there would've been six people on this manifest: Father Donnelly, Betty Clarke, Gillespie, McNulty, Matt Logan and Thomas Dempsey.'

A dawn of realisation appeared on Phillips's face. 'Yet, according to this list, *seven* people travelled.'

'Exactly, Guv. So, either Maguire's lying or someone else snuck onto that trip without him knowing.'

Entwistle pulled out his phone, opened his photos, and selected the picture of the Lourdes trip. He handed it to her. 'Since I came across that manifest, I've been staring at this picture non-stop, convinced I've been missing something I couldn't quite put my finger on. Then it occurred to me:

everyone on that trip is either dead or has been interviewed about the murders, right?'

'Right.'

'Except one.'

Phillips looked puzzled. 'Who?'

Entwistle tapped the phone screen. 'The person *taking* the photo, Guv.'

Phillips eyes seemed to double in size for a moment. 'Entwistle, you're a bloody genius! Why didn't I see that?' Years ago, she would never have missed such an obvious link. Her drinking had clearly taken its toll on her performance as a detective.

'It's the missing link, Guv,' the young officer said proudly. 'We find the cameraman, maybe we find the killer.'

'So, what do you wanna do, Guv?'

Phillips thought a moment. 'Where's Brown now?'

'He went home after I told him Logan would remain in hospital overnight for observation. Gave me strict instructions to call him, and only him, as soon as he was ready to be discharged. He wants to meet us at the station to start the interview process. The thing is, Guv, he's also given me instructions to leave Jones and Bovalino out of the loop.'

Phillips scoffed. 'Of course he did. With victory in sight, he doesn't want to share the limelight.'

'Apart from with his mixed-race protégé.'

'You catch on fast.' Phillips chuckled. 'How's Logan looking by the way?'

'He'll live. Standard effects of Spice. Elevated heart rate, raised temperature, delirium. Once it leaves his system, he'll be back to normal.'

Phillips pulled back the sheets and instructed Entwistle to help her off the bed. 'I need to pee.'

A few minutes later, he heard the toilet flush and Phillips re-emerged from the en suite bathroom, her hair now pulled back in a ponytail. She seemed brighter, more alert. 'Okay, here's what we'll do. You go back downstairs and plant yourself next to Logan. Do not leave his side for anything. You need to pee, do it in a bottle. You got that?'

'Yes, Guv.'

'As soon as he's fit to talk, call Brown *first*.'

'Guv?' Entwistle appeared confused.

'It covers your arse. I may choose to take risks but you're just starting out. No sense making an enemy of Brown so early on. He'll only turn up in ten years and try his best to fuck your career. Trust me, I have first hand experience of it.'

'Ok, Guv...thanks.'

'After that, you call me. I'm not being discharged until the morning – I'll come down and talk to Logan before you take him back to Ashton House. If he can help us identify the person taking the photo, I'll use Jonesy and Bov to help track them down whilst Brown is distracted with the Logan interview.'

'Sounds like a plan, Guv.'

Phillips sat back down on the bed and grimaced. 'Yeah. Let's hope it works out, otherwise an innocent man will go to jail and I'll be well and truly fucked.'

48

Logan lay with his eyes closed in a private room almost identical to the one Phillips had just emerged from upstairs. An armed guard stood to either side of the door as she stepped inside to question him, Entwistle at her side.

Logan looked gaunt, his skin grey and waxy. His chest was exposed above the waist, revealing his bony frame. His thin, wiry arms were full of needle marks. It was just after 8.00 a.m. and Brown was expecting Logan and Entwistle at Ashton House within the hour. Phillips had no time to waste.

She moved next to his bed. 'How are you feeling, Matt?'

He opened his eyes and turned his head slowly towards her, taking a moment to look her up and down. When he spoke, his voice was a low murmur. 'I've been better.' He closed his eyes again.

'So how long have you been taking Spice?'

He took time to answer, his eyes remaining shut. 'On and off for a couple of years. It's cheap.'

'Do you remember what happened before you came to hospital, Matt?'

'Not really. I have a hazy memory of lots of coppers in my room, but I can't tell you if that was real or I dreamt it.'

Phillips dragged out the chair next to the bed, its metal legs screeching across the polished floor as she took a seat. Entwistle remained standing at the foot of the bed. 'I'm afraid it was real Matt. *Very real*, and you're in a lot of trouble.'

He made no effort to respond.

Phillips continued. 'A cigarette containing your DNA was found in my garden after I was attacked at home two nights ago.'

Logan opened his eyes wide, a look of shock on his face. '*My* DNA?'

'Yes, and all the evidence points to *you* attacking me.'

He shifted his position in the bed, sitting up to attention. 'Me? Why would I attack you?'

'That's what I'm here to find out, because the evidence is pretty damning. As well as your DNA on the cigarette, officers found latex gloves and a surgeon's mask hidden in your room.'

Logan appeared incredulous. 'That stuff's not mine!'

'So how do you explain the fact we found it all packed in a box under your bed?'

'Under *my* bed?'

Phillips looked across at the rookie. 'You saw it for yourself last night, didn't you?'

He nodded. 'Yes, Guv.'

Logan's bloodshot eyes focused on Entwistle. 'Seriously, I don't know anything about a box or masks or latex gloves – or any of that stuff.'

'So how did it get into your room?' said Phillips.

'I have no bloody idea. I swear on my life, I don't know anything about any box under my bed.'

'What about the cigarette? Bit of a coincidence the same brand was found in the ashtray in your room, isn't it?'

'What brand? I smoke roll-ups.'

'No, Marlboro Reds.'

'They can't be mine. I don't smoke packet fags. They're too expensive.'

'So how do you explain the fact we found Marlboro Reds in your room?'

Logan raised his hand to his temple, the saline drip in his hand clattering against the bed frame. 'Fucking hell, I'm being set up.'

'Come on, Matt, you don't seriously expect us to believe that fairy story, do you?'

Logan looked desperate now. 'The guy that works at the shelter gave them to me. I swear he did.'

'Well, isn't that convenient?' said Phillips sarcastically.

'Honestly, you have to believe me. There's a guy comes in my room sometimes. He offered me some Reds the other night. It was after I'd been locked up. He saw me come back to the hostel and came to say hello. Gave me some of his fags.'

Just then, a young-looking nurse walked into the room pushing a trolley. 'Time for one last blood pressure check before you're released, Mr Logan.'

Phillips shot Entwistle a look, who took the initiative and asked to speak to the nurse outside. She looked confused but followed him out. Phillips continued her questioning.

'So, can you describe this man?'

'Yeah, yeah. He's a tall fella, looks arty, kinda like a musician. Started working there a couple of months back.'

'What's his name?'

Logan took time to answer, as if sifting through his patchy memory. 'Fuck, I've forgotten.'

Phillips was losing patience, or at least that's what she wanted Logan to think. 'Come on, Matt. If this guy is real, he has to have a name. For your own sake, it's very important you remember.'

Logan closed his eyes and screwed up his face, 'I think it was something like Kevin, or Nigel, or Trevor...'

'Kevin? Was it Kevin McNulty.'

Logan didn't respond.

Phillips pressed him again. 'Matt, was it Kevin McNulty?'

Logan looked back to Phillips, his face forlorn. 'I honestly can't remember.'

'But you're sure he could have been called Kevin?'

Entwistle walked back into the room, assuming his position at the end of the bed.

'I can't be a hundred per cent sure. I just recall it was one of those names people used to take the piss out of back in the day. You know, with women in the eighties, you got lots of Sharons and Traceys, Well, his name was like that for a guy...like a Kevin or Nigel or Trevor.'

'Are you sure you can't remember which one it was?'

Logan shook his head and Phillips believed him. She glanced at Entwistle, who gently tapped his watch. Time was running out.

She pressed on. 'Ok, so where were you the night before last?'

'Er, it's all a bit blurry, but two nights ago I think I was with Mitchy and his sister Dannielle.'

'And they'll vouch for you, will they?'

Logan nodded enthusiastically. 'Damn right they will.'

Phillips turned to Entwistle. 'Make sure you talk to them today.'

He made a note in his pad.

'And pass me your phone, will you?' She held out her hand and Entwistle duly obliged.

'Ok, Matt, I want you to look at this for me.' Phillips handed him the Lourdes picture on Entwistle's mobile. 'Do you remember seeing this picture before?'

He nodded. 'You lot already showed it to me.'

'Can you identify each of the people in the shot?'

Logan looked closely at the picture, tapping a grubby finger on the screen in time with each name. 'That's Mrs Clarke, that's me, Susan Gillespie, Deidre McNulty, Thomas Dempsey and —' He stopped at Father Donnelly for a moment. 'You know who that is.'

Phillips handed him the travel manifest. 'This document states how many people travelled on that trip to Lourdes. As you can see, it says there were seven people on the minibus.'

'So?'

'How many people are in that picture, Matt?'

Logan counted them slowly. 'Six.'

'Yet there's seven people listed here.' Phillips tapped the manifesto. 'We know Ricky Murray pulled out the night before the trip, so someone went in his place. Someone who we think took that picture.'

Logan swallowed hard.

'I don't believe you killed these people, Matt, and I don't think you attacked me either. But I do strongly sense all four murders are connected to that trip. Everyone who went on it has been accounted for, except one. I believe they're the key to finding the killer. Who was it, Matt? Who went to Lourdes instead of Ricky?'

'I can't say.'

'Can't or won't, Matt?'

'Both.'

'Come on, Matt. Help us out here. We're trying to stop a killer.' Phillips was losing her patience for real now.

Logan folded his arms, a look of defiance on his face, 'After I got sent down for the third time, none of my family and friends gave a flying fuck about me. They left me to rot in there. But one person didn't abandon me. They visited me every couple of weeks, brought me treats, listened to my problems. They really looked out for me. And when I got out, they helped me get into the hostel, helped out with money, drink and cigarettes. They're the reason I'm still alive. That's why I can't, and won't, say. If they've done something they shouldn't have, then that's down to them and their own conscience. I owe them, and I'm not a grass.'

Phillips struggled to keep her temper in check. 'Matt, do you understand that we have enough evidence to send you to prison for the rest of your life, and a DCI who is hell-bent on putting you there? Helping us find that missing person is your only hope of proving you didn't kill those people.'

Logan shook his head firmly. 'I've told you, I'm not a grass.'

Phillips became increasingly incensed listening to his 'code of the street' bullshit. 'Jesus, Matt, you could be going down for four murders you didn't commit, while the real killer walks away scot-free. Don't you care what happens to you?'

Logan shrugged his shoulders. 'I've had enough of life on the streets. I'm better off in prison. At least I'll get respect there for murder.'

'Come on, Matt, that bollocks. Nobody wants to go to prison. Tell us, who was the seventh person on that trip?'

Logan fixed her with a steely glare, his voice measured now. 'The document must be wrong. There were only *six* of us on that mini-bus, and *six* of us on that trip.'

'So you're sticking to that story?'

'Yes I am.'

Phillips sighed, exasperated. 'Right, have it your way, but you're making a big mistake. Entwistle, get that nurse back in and get him discharged. Time for him to face whatever Brown has in store for him.'

Entwistle hurried out of the room.

'You're going to regret this, Matt.'

Logan looked at Phillips with sad eyes. 'So? What's new, Inspector?'

49

The cold morning air felt good against her face, despite her still tender wounds. The sun was shining, but the walkways outside the Manchester Royal Infirmary had still been given a liberal covering of salt to melt away any hidden ice patches. It was a relief to be discharged. Phillips had never liked hospitals, and after spending months in the MRI recovering from a gunshot wound, she had vowed to do everything she could to stay away from them. That was before someone had tried to strangle her in her own home.

With Logan staying silent on the identity of the photographer, and now en route to Ashton House, she needed answers quickly before Brown sent the wrong man down. She was tempted to bring in Father Maguire for questioning, considering he'd potentially lied about who had replaced Ricky on the Lourdes trip, but she wanted all the facts before she played that card, and she had a good idea where she could get them.

Pulling out her phone, she selected Jonesy from her favourites and hit dial. Phillips had briefed Jones the previous night on their plans to talk to Logan.

He answered in a just a few moments. 'Guv. Everything ok?'

'Yeah, I'm fine. Glad to be out, that's for sure.'

'How did it go this morning?' he asked hopefully.

'Not great. He's staying quiet on the identity of the photographer. Says whoever it is, he owes them and he's not a grass. Usual criminal brotherhood bullshit.'

'That's crazy. Brown has enough to put him away for good. He'll die in prison.'

'I told him that but he's not having it. Says he'd rather do time than let this person down. Plus, he says he's had enough of living on the streets and actually *wants* to go back inside.'

'Jesus. How messed up does your life have to be to want that?'

'I know. Poor sod.'

'So, what next, Guv?'

'We need to identify the photographer before Brown pins all four murders on him. Which, with the evidence and Logan's desire to go back to prison, won't take long. So, the clock is ticking. Where are you and Bov?'

'Ashton House.'

'Ok. we need to talk to Father Maguire and find out what he really knows. Can you pick me up?'

'Sure, from the MRI?'

'No. Thomas Dempsey's place. It's only a fifteen-minute walk from here and it makes sense to get as much info as possible before confronting Maguire.'

'Gotcha. Bov's got some paperwork to finish up, but we should be with you by ten. That okay?'

Phillips checked her watch; it was 8.50 a.m. 'Yeah, that works. I'll see you then.'

50

Phillips stood under the small porch and knocked on Dempsey's front door. Uniform had reported he'd become somewhat of a recluse in the last week, having been signed off from work with anxiety and panic attacks. After her own troubles over the last twelve months, she could empathise.

He took a few moments to open the door on the chain. 'Hello?' he said, peering out of the darkened hall.

'Hi, Tom, it's Detective Inspector Phillips. Can I come in for a minute?'

Dempsey looked out onto the street before unlocking the chain and opening the door fully. 'Have you caught him yet?'

'No, Tom. Could we perhaps talk inside?'

He nodded, guiding her through to the living room, where he took a seat on the armchair while Phillips took the adjacent sofa.

'How you holding up?' she asked

'Good days and bad days, to be honest,' he said with a thin smile.

'I understand you've been signed off work?'

'Yeah, I keep having panic attacks when I go outside. Not great for a postman.'

Phillips's heart went out to him and she found herself placing a comforting hand on his knee, 'I know these days everyone says it, but I do know how you feel. I went through the same thing myself after a major trauma last year.'

Dempsey appeared close to tears, his dark eyes searching hers. 'Does it get better, Inspector?'

'In time, yes. But it might be worth talking to someone. You know, professional help?'

Dempsey wiped a lone tear from his cheek. 'Therapy?'

'Yes.'

'I'm afraid I can't afford therapy on my wages, Inspector.'

'What about work? A lot of companies offer confidential support to their employees.'

'Really? I'm not sure the Post Office does.'

'Or you can always get it on the NHS.'

Dempsey scoffed. 'Yeah, in about a year. The waiting lists are huge for that kind of thing.'

Phillips sensed he really wasn't keen. 'Whichever route you take, Tom, it can't hurt to look into it, can it?'

Dempsey nodded without conviction. He changed the subject. 'What happened to your face?'

Phillips instinctively touched her temple around one of the cuts. 'Our mutual friend broke into my house and decided to use me as a punching bag a few nights ago.'

'Jesus Christ. Why the hell would he do that?'

'I don't know, but I'm hoping you might be able to shed some light on it for me.'

Dempsey looked confused 'Me? How can I help?'

Phillips pulled out her phone and placed it in front of him.

'You recognise that picture, don't you?'

Dempsey retrieved his glasses from the top of the fireplace before returning to his seat and picking up the phone. 'It's the

Lourdes trip. Your colleagues showed it to me when they first paid me a visit.'

'Do you recognise the people in the photo?'

Dempsey nodded and reeled off their names in order.

'Do you remember Ricky Murray?'

'Little Ricky? Yeah, I do. I heard about him on the news the other night. I still can't believe he's dead.'

'Did he go on that trip to France with you?'

Dempsey paused briefly, deep in thought. 'No, but I'm pretty sure he was supposed to. I have a vague memory of him pulling out at the last minute. I think he got sick or something.'

'Did anyone else take his place?'

Dempsey shrugged. 'I assume so.'

'But you can't say for sure?'

'Not really. I'd have been about eleven at the time. All I cared about was going on holiday to France. I wasn't really paying attention to who might have come in at the last minute.'

'I guess not. Look, I know I'm going back a long time, but do you remember who took this photo, Tom?'

Dempsey examined it again. 'I do. It was Seamus Maguire, although you probably know him as Father Maguire.'

'From St Patrick's?'

'That's the one. He was a young seminarian – you know, like a priest in training. He'd have been a teenager, or maybe in his early twenties, at the time.'

'And you're sure it was him?'

'Oh yeah. I only went on one trip abroad with the church, and he was definitely on it.'

So Maguire had been lying the whole time.

'Do you know anything about allegations of abuse made against a priest from St Patrick's?'

Dempsey shifted in his seat uncomfortably, then nodded.

'Could you tell me about them?'

'I can't be certain, but I'm sure it started on that trip to France.'

Phillips looked down at her notes. 'You told DS Jones and DC Bovalino that you suspected Father Donnelly had been inappropriate with Matt Logan, that he'd potentially kissed his genitals.'

'That's correct.'

'Besides Logan's conversations with you about this, was there anything else that lead you to think he was telling the truth about Donnelly?'

Dempsey stared at the floor for a long moment before answering. 'It might be nothing...'

'What might be?'

'I'm really not sure I should say this. It was a long time ago and I may be remembering it wrong.' Dempsey appeared even more anxious than before.

'Please, Tom, tell me. It could be important.'

'I'm sure it was totally innocent, but each night Donnelly would send Seamus, I mean Father Maguire, to collect Matt at bedtime, when we were all in our pyjamas, and take him to his room.'

'Donnelly's room?'

'Yeah. Matt would be gone about an hour and come back crying and upset. We used to ask him what was wrong, what had happened, but all he would say was that he was a sinner and God was punishing him.'

'And did you see any signs that Donnelly might be abusing any of the other kids?'

'I don't know for sure, but he always seemed to single Ricky out for special attention as well.'

'What do you mean by special attention?'

'You know, private meetings in the vestry. Father Donnelly would insist on giving him confession in the church house as opposed to the confessionals in the main church. He told Ricky he was special in God's eyes.'

'Did he ever abuse you, Thomas?'

Dempsey shook his head vigorously. 'No, thank God.'

'And what about Maguire? Was he abusing any of the children?'

Dempsey's brow furrowed. 'I couldn't say for sure, but he definitely brought Matt to Father Donnelly when the two were living in the same house at the time.'

'Is there any way to prove Maguire was involved?'

Dempsey laughed. 'I doubt it. The Catholic Church covers their tracks very well when it comes to child abuse, Inspector.'

At that moment, Phillips felt a trickle of liquid run down her right nostril and onto her upper lip. Touching her finger to it, she saw blood on the tip. 'Oh shit. Could I get a tissue?'

'Of course.' Dempsey looked a little panicked at the sight of blood. He jumped up and rushed out of the room, returning a moment later with a large kitchen roll in his hand.

'Thank you.' Phillips smiled awkwardly and pulled off a couple of pieces, placing one against her nose. 'The doctor warned me this could happen while it's healing.'

She tilted her head back and pressed the towel against her nose, as hard as she could stand, to try and stem the bleeding. After a couple of minutes, it finally stopped.

'Would you mind if I clean up a little?' Her fingers and face were now covered in dry blood.

'No, no, not at all. Please come this way.'

She followed him into the narrow hallway.

'The toilet is upstairs on the landing, straight in front of you. You can't miss it.'

Phillips thanked him and followed his directions. Once in the bathroom, she washed her hands and face, watching the bloody water circle around the basin before disappearing down the plughole. Grabbing a towel off the radiator, she dabbed it gently against her swollen nose...and was struck by a very familiar smell. She inhaled again, and stared at her battered reflection in the mirror. *It couldn't be?* Unlocking the bathroom door, she stood at the top of the stairs and listened to the sound of Dempsey in the kitchen below. She heard plates clattering, and guessed he was filling the dishwasher.

The small landing had two rooms running off it; the front and back bedrooms. Treading lightly, she peered into the back room, which was sparsely furnished and almost military-tidy. It smelt stale and unused. Closing the door again, she could still hear Dempsey moving about downstairs as she made for the front bedroom.

Cautiously, she stepped inside. This was obviously Dempsey's bedroom, and although still lacking in the softer touches, it at least had a few pictures on the walls and a photograph of a white-haired elderly woman in a frame next to the bed. A small desk and chair housed a laptop to the side of a large mirrored wardrobe opposite her, reflecting into the room. Moving quietly, she followed her instincts and opened the wardrobe, revealing a hanger rail with pristinely pressed shirts and a number of branded postman uniforms.

On the shelf above was a selection of grooming products, including beard oil and hair wax. Standing next to them was a distinctive silver and chrome bottle of aftershave: *Guilty* by *Gucci*. She pulled off the top and took a sniff. There was no mistaking it. Coincidence? Almost twenty years of policing had taught her there was rarely any such thing as a coincidence.

Spotting a black rucksack on the floor of the wardrobe, she bent down and opened it. Inside, was a packet of latex gloves, several clear plastic bags, black gaffer tape, a surgeon's mask – and a hand-sized spray dispenser.

Phillips's heart beat fast as adrenaline coursed through her veins. *Holy Fuck!*

She had to get out of here fast. Replacing everything carefully, she zipped up the bag and put it back where she'd found it. Desperately trying to control her breathing, she stood back and closed the wardrobe door. As it shut, she came face to face with Dempsey's reflection in the mirror. He stood in the doorway behind, watching her.

Their eyes met and a malevolent grin spread across his face. 'Oh dear, Jane. It looks like you've discovered my little secret.'

He stepped into the room. 'I suppose it's time to finish what I started.'

Phillips's survival instincts kicked in. She charged at him. The unexpected nature of her attack catching him off guard. Pushing him in the chest, she managed to squeeze past him.

He reached out and grabbed her by the hair, but her momentum continued to drive her forwards. She cried out as he ripped a chunk of hair from her head. Racing to the top of the stairs, she threw herself down them and, reaching the ground floor, rushed to the front door.

She turned the knob, but the door was deadlocked. Turning around, she saw Dempsey casually making his way down the stairs, as if wandering down for breakfast.

'It's no use, Jane. You can't escape this time.' His voice was measured and calm.

Phillips ran into the kitchen and raced towards the back door. Again, it was deadlocked.

Strolling in behind her, Dempsey stood, watching, in the doorway.

'Jones and Bovalino will be here any minute,' she said panting.

'No they won't, Jane.'

'I'm telling you, they're on their way. I asked them to meet me here at ten o'clock.'

Dempsey checked his watch and smiled wickedly, 'That doesn't give us much time, does it? We better get cracking.'

'Give yourself up, Dempsey. It's the only way out of this mess.'

Dempsey shook his head. 'Actually, Inspector, my plan is still very much alive, and neither you nor your fellow officers can stop the grand finale. As far as I'm concerned, *that* is the only way out for me.'

He took a few steps closer.

Phillips grabbed a saucepan from the drying rack, causing Dempsey to chuckle.

'Oh come on, Jane. Don't be silly.'

She swung the pan over her shoulder, ready to strike. 'Get back,' she warned him, but he kept coming closer until he was only a few feet away.

He lifted an outstretched arm. 'Give me it, Jane.'

Phillips swung the pan, aiming for his head. Dempsey ducked like a pro boxer. Then, springing upwards, he rammed the top of his head into her already broken nose. The pain was agonising. Head spinning, she knew she was no match for him. In an instant he had her on the ground, landing hard on top of her. Before she could catch her breath, his arms and legs were wrapped around her and her throat once more locked inside the vice-like grip of his bicep. He squeezed hard and she could feel her neck being crushed. Slowly, Dempsey moved onto his knees with Phillips still locked in his grip. Soon he was up onto his feet, dragging her by the neck into the hallway and towards the lounge room.

Just then, the doorbell rang. If it was Jones and Bovalino, they were early.

Dempsey clasped his hand over Phillips's mouth. 'Quiet,' he whispered.

After a long pause, the bell rang again, followed by a loud banging on the door. Then Phillips's phone began to ring loudly in her pocket. A second later, the letterbox shoved open and Jones's South London drawl rang out.

'Guv? Are you in there?' For a moment, nothing happened, then she heard Jones order Bovalino to kick the door in.

When Bov's boot hit the door, Dempsey released Phillips and pushed her towards the front door. She turned to follow him, but a heavy kick to her stomach dropped her to her knees. Winded, she rolled on the floor, gasping for air, as the sound of the front door being repeatedly kicked echoed down the hallway.

Dempsey ran through to the kitchen. He fumbled with his keys and eventually unlocked the back door and rushed into the yard. Phillips lifted her head to see him burst through the gate and into the alley behind.

The front door finally caved and Bovalino rushed in, followed by Jones.

'Dempsey's the killer!' she managed to say, pointing towards the back gate.

Jones and Bovalino didn't hesitate. Rushing past her, they sprinted down the hallway, through the kitchen and into the yard. A moment later, they had disappeared down the alleyway.

51

B y the time Jones and Bovalino returned, Phillips was
finishing up a call with Brown.

'Yes sir. We'll wait for you here.'

Bovalino was out of breath, his dark hair thick with sweat.
'We lost him, Guv. It's a maze of alleys and lanes back there.'

'He probably had an escape route planned,' Phillips replied.

'What did Brown say?' asked Jones.

'He reckons Logan is on the verge of confessing to all four
murders, so this is a bit of a curveball for him.'

Jones looked incredulous. 'A curveball? Surely even *he*
wants the right man, not just any man?'

'He will once he figures out how to spin it to his advantage.
From the way he was talking on the call, I think he's already
told Fox that Logan's ready to confess. You know what she's like;
she's probably already fed that up the chain to the Chief
Constable.'

A knowing smile appeared on Jones's face. 'Which could
make them both look bad to the top brass if Dempsey *is* our
guy.'

OMJ RYAN

Bovalino winked. 'That won't help his chances of promotion.'

'And that's not good for any of us.' Phillips sighed. 'At least promotion gets him out of the squad.'

Jones chuckled. 'Maybe we *should* just let Matt Logan confess then, Guv?'

Phillips laughed. 'Tempting, I grant you.'

'What happens now?' said Bovalino.

'Brown has suspended the interview with Logan. He and Entwistle are heading over here now. He wants to see the evidence for himself.'

'And to ensure he's at the centre of catching Dempsey.'

'*Exactly*, Jonesy. Right, let's see if we can figure out what Dempsey plans to do next.'

'Surely he'll try and run, Guv,' said Bovalino.

'I don't think so, Bov. He was adamant his *grand finale* was still to come.'

Jones appeared confused. 'What the hell did he mean by that?'

'I don't know, but we better find out, and fast.'

Jones handed out latex gloves as Phillips pulled out her phone. 'Time to call Entwistle and sort out a search warrant for this place.'

While they waited for clearance, Phillips brought the guys up to speed on Dempsey's claim that Maguire was the seventh person on the Lourdes trip, and involved in helping Donnelly molest Logan.

'Do you believe him?'

Phillips shrugged. 'I don't know what to believe. I have to admit, I never suspected meek and mild Thomas Dempsey could be the killer. He was very convincing.'

Bovalino scratched his head. 'I don't get it. Uniform have been checking on him every night.'

'True, but they were only checking to see if he was safe.

They weren't checking to see if he actually stayed in the house when they weren't around.'

Jones nodded. 'They checked him the same time every night between 8 and 9 p.m. After we put the detail on him, both attacks happened either side of that. Ricky at 4 p.m., and you in the early hours of the morning. Clever bugger. He faked his own attack to create the perfect alibi for himself – the police.'

Phillips's phone rang. It was Entwistle, telling her the warrant had been approved, and that he and Brown were en route to the house.

She gathered the team in Dempsey's bedroom. 'Right, let's get started in here.'

Pulling the black bag out of the wardrobe, she passed it to Jones, who carefully emptied the contents onto Dempsey's bed and started bagging them. Seeing the surgeon's mask, cable ties and the rest of his paraphernalia laid out in front of her sent a shiver down her spine. She had come very close to being victim number five.

Meanwhile, Bovalino was attempting to log on to Dempsey's laptop, but struggled to get beyond the password.

Phillips wandered over to help the huge man, hunched over the desk. 'You locked out?' she asked.

He turned to face her with a scowl. 'I bloody hate technology, Guv.'

'Yeah, but Entwistle loves it. Give him a call and see what he can do to help.'

Over the phone, Entwistle walked Bovalino through how to connect his mobile to the laptop in a way that had allowed him to download Special Branch technology and gain remote access. Keying in a code that appeared on his phone, he bypassed the password and logged straight in to Dempsey's laptop. As the home screen opened in front of him, Bovalino grinned like a Cheshire Cat. 'I bloody *love* technology.'

Phillips tapped him on the shoulder. 'Take a look and see if there's any digital forensics that can prove he's our guy. The murder kit is one thing, but without his DNA at the crime scenes, a decent lawyer will rip that to shreds. Especially considering I found it without a warrant.'

With Phillips standing behind him, Bovalino opened the hard drive and began scrolling through various folders within the system whilst Jones continued examining the wardrobe and bagging any evidence.

Phillips spotted something. 'Go back to the last screen,' she said.

Bovalino obliged.

'There, that folder marked "SP Photos". Open that.'

Clicking on the folder, myriad thumbnail images of residential houses appeared. Bovalino began clicking through the photos. 'Jesus, that's outside the front of Susan Gillespie's. That one is McNulty's and that's Clarke's.'

Each was time-stamped approximately two weeks prior to the date of each murder. Bovalino continued scrolling until an image popped up that made Phillips's blood run cold; the back of her own home, dated within the last week.

'The bastard was in my garden taking pictures and I never saw him. How the hell did he get over the wall without triggering the security lights?'

'This guy is something special, that's for sure,' said Bovalino.

At that moment, Jones walked over and presented Phillips with a Cheetham Hill Hostel name badge. 'Check this out, Guv.'

Phillips examined the badge. On it, she read the name: *Trevor*. 'Logan said the guy who gave him the cigarettes was either called Kevin, Nigel or Trevor. I guess it was Trevor.'

'All Dempsey needed was access to Logan's ashtray to pull out the butt we found in your garden,' said Jones.

Phillips passed the badge back. 'He didn't stand a chance against this guy, did he?'

'Jackpot!' said Bovalino loudly.

Phillips turned back to the laptop. 'What it is, Bov?'

'This is Dempsey's browser history from the two weeks leading up to the first murder, Entwistle told me how to access it. If I use this filter, it brings up the most frequently searched words...' Bovalino pressed the return key. 'Well, look at that.'

Phillips read from the screen. 'Catholic Church abuse, historical Catholic abuse, surveillance techniques, special forces methods, police protocols, chemical compounds, human sedation, animal sedation, airborne sedatives, DNA testing, trace DNA, forensics, amateur forensics, how to beat forensics, surgical equipment...bloody hell.'

'This guy's crazy, Guv,' said Bovalino.

'And look what else I've just found in the wardrobe.' Jones passed Phillips the original list of parishioner names stolen from St Patrick's, complete with full addresses, phone numbers and, in some cases, emails. 'Look: Gillespie, McNulty, Clarke and Murray have all been circled. This is his murder list, Guv.'

Phillips looked down at the names and once again zoned out, allowing her thoughts to crystallise.

Jones smiled. 'She's got the look, Bov.'

Bovalino turned away from the laptop and watched, waiting for her to come back to them. A moment later, oblivious to their comments, she began summarising what they had.

'Here's what we know: Dempsey is smart, meticulous and determined. He's managed to create and deliver a chemical compound capable of incapacitating his victims, and to all intents and purposes, he's self-taught. He's mastered surveillance and understands forensic techniques well enough to commit his crimes undetected. He's killed four people that we know of and attempted a fifth. Aside from me, the victims are all connected to the trip to Lourdes and, in his own words, he has a grand finale planned. Based on the crime scenes and victims so far, he's big on rituals and symbolism. Each killing was drama personified, each body staged, so the grand finale would need to be suitably extravagant to live up to its billing. So, what is it, guys? How's Dempsey going to finish it all?'

Jones picked up the list of parishioners and began scanning the names for anything they might have missed. Phillips turned back to Bovalino and asked him to open up the oldest image in the stack. She tapped the screen with her gloved finger, 'What do you reckon that is, then?'

Bovalino scrutinised the photo a few moments. 'It's taken from pretty far away, but if I had to put money on it, I'd say it looks like a church service.'

Phillips pointed at the remaining thumbnails on the screen. 'Keep going. There's a bunch of them.'

The big man flicked through the photos one at a time, stopping at one taken from a nearer position. 'It's a funeral service. Look, you can see the hearse in the background.'

'When was St Patrick's broken into?' asked Phillips

Jones pulled out his notepad and flipped through the pages. 'Sunday the 13th of January.'

'These photos were taken the week before that. You can see from the timestamp on the screen.'

'So?' said Jones.

'So, Father Donnelly's funeral was around that time. And if you look at the sequence of pictures, look who attended this particular funeral.'

Jones stared at the screen. 'Gillespie, McNulty, Clarke, Murray – and it looks like Maguire, all dressed up.'

'He must have conducted the mass,' mused Phillips.

'Could Donnelly's funeral be the link?' asked Bovalino.

Phillips stared at the screen, trying to piece it all together. 'Noel Gillespie told us he was at that same funeral, but there's no shots of him or anyone else, for that matter, in Dempsey's photos. Just those *five* people.'

Jones glanced back at the parishioners list. 'It's the church, Guv. Look here.' He turned the list to Phillips. 'Each one of the victim's names is circled on here. The only other name circled is *St Patrick's* at the top.' He frowned. 'Is he's going to do something to the church? Set it on fire, perhaps? That would be a pretty grand finale.'

Phillips wasn't convinced. All of the murders had been up close and personal so far. The church was inanimate, bricks and mortar. No; it had to be something else, *someone else*. Then it came to her. She focused back on the images on the laptop. 'Who is the only person in all these photos who's still alive *and* we believe was on the Lourdes trip, besides Dempsey?'

Jones peered at the screen. 'Father Maguire.' He turned and stared at Phillips. 'Shit, Guv, *Maguire* is his grand finale. He's the final kill.'

Phillips was already on her way out of the room. 'And we've got to get to him before Dempsey does.'

Bovalino reached for his phone. 'Jonesy, you go with the guv. I'll call uniform and get them to secure the house. I'll follow on once they arrive.'

As Phillips and Jones rushed out, they were greeted by an unhappy DCI Brown walking briskly up the path.

'This had better be good, Inspector?' he said in a clipped tone.

Phillips strode towards the little man. 'Can't stop now, sir. We think we know who Dempsey's last victim will be.'

Brown looked incredulous. 'I beg your pardon?'

'I'll explain later,' Phillips shouted, running towards her car with Jones alongside her.

Brown spun around and followed her. 'You'll explain *now*,' he demanded.

Phillips reached her car and turned to face him. 'Sir, we're running out of time. If you want to know what's going on, come with us. I can brief you in the car.'

'I'm not going anywhere. And neither are you, Inspector. That's an order.'

Phillips held the driver's door open, one foot already in the car. 'A man's life is at stake. If Dempsey gets there before us, his death will be on us. Sorry, but with respect, sir – fuck your orders.'

She jumped in the car, followed by Jones, and gunned the engine. A moment later, tyres screeching, they sped away towards St Patrick's Church.

52

It had been an unusually busy morning for Father Maguire, with a continuous flow of parishioners filing through for confessions since 10 a.m. He was feeling the weight of unburdening so many sins in such a short space of time and was looking forward to a sandwich at lunchtime. He'd forgotten to put on his watch but was sure it was almost midday and the end of confession. It had been five minutes since anyone had entered the confessional, and it looked like he had no more sins to hear.

He stepped out and checked the clock at the back of the church. It was 11.53 a.m. *Excellent.* The vast space was empty and blissfully quiet, with just one solitary soul kneeling in prayer a couple of pews away. Maguire watched a moment, then, walking over to him, placed his hand gently on the man's shoulder.

'Are you here for confession?'

The man looked up with sad, dark eyes, and nodded.

Maguire produced a warm smile. 'You're my last of the day. Join me when you're ready.' He turned around and took his place in the confessional once more. A minute passed, then the door opened on the other side of the screen and the man knelt down, the silhouette of his large frame visible through the mesh.

The man cleared his throat before speaking. 'Bless me, Father, for I have sinned. It has been over thirty years since my last confession.'

'In that case, I'm glad you've found your way back to the Lord, my son, for He is always with us. And what would you like to confess?'

There was a short pause on the other side of the screen, then the man spoke. 'Father, I have committed a mortal sin.'

'Go on.'

'In fact, I have committed many mortal sins.'

Maguire's tone was sympathetic. 'Come on now. I'm sure you've not done anything that serious. Mortal sin does, after all, mean to take a life; to kill someone.'

'Yes, Father.'

Maguire was taken aback. 'I'm sorry. Are you saying you've taken a life?'

'No, Father, you misunderstand. I haven't taken *a* life. I've taken *four*.'

Maguire was sure he must have misheard. 'I beg your pardon. Did you just say you've killed four people?'

'Yes, Father.'

Maguire wasn't sure if the man was joking or insane. Either way, he was keen to bring the confession to a close. 'Well, my son, the good Lord forgives all our sins, no matter how grave. As long as we repent, there is a place for us in heaven—'

'Did Father Donnelly repent?'

'What did you say?'

The voice from the other side deepened. 'I asked you if Father Donnelly repented before he died?'

Maguire was beginning to feel uncomfortable with the line of questioning. 'I'm sure he did. He was a man of God, after all.

I'm sorry; what does any of this have to do with *your* confession?'

The man ignored his question. 'If he did repent, then he must have confessed to molesting Matt Logan, Ricky Murray and Thomas Dempsey?'

'Is this some kind of sick joke?'

'It is sick, but I assure you it's no joke, Father.'

Maguire had had enough. 'I'm afraid I'm not prepared to continue with this. I'm going to have to ask you to leave the confessional and the church.' The man remained silent on the other side of the screen, though Maguire could hear him breathing. 'Didn't you hear what I said? I would like you to leave.'

'But you haven't absolved me of my sins, Father. I can't leave until I have repented and you have granted me forgiveness.' The tone of the voice sent a shiver up Maguire's spine.

'Look, I don't know what you're playing at, but this is completely inappropriate. I will not countenance such a conversation in the house of God. If you don't leave, I shall be forced to call the pol—'

'Bless me, Father, for I have sinned,' the man said, his strong, measured voice cutting Maguire off. 'I confess to torturing and murdering Susan Gillespie, Deidre McNulty, Betty Clarke and Ricky Murray.' He paused, his breathing the only sound in the deadly silence. 'I ask you to grant me God's forgiveness, for I am the angel of vengeance known as the Cheadle Killer, and I'm here to send you to hell.'

Panic overcame Maguire as he heard the door to the confessional opposite him open. A shadowy figure stepped out, his slow, heavy footsteps echoing around the empty church. When they stopped outside his door, Maguire pinned himself back to the wall in a feeble attempt to get away.

The door creaked open. 'Hello Seamus. Remember me?' The man's hulking frame filled the doorway, his cold, dark eyes locked on Maguire, his fists clenched at his side as he stepped inside the confessional. 'It's time to repent, Father.'

Maguire raised his arms to protect himself but it was no use as the large man smashed his fist into his face, over and over, until everything went black.

53

Thomas Dempsey dragged the priest's bloodied body through the church, through the sanctuary and into the vestry. He secured him to a large mahogany chair in the centre of the room using a length of nylon twine he'd found in a toolbox in the church's garage moments before entering the building.

Father Maguire was out cold, and Dempsey was short on time. Looking at his watch, he reasoned Phillips and her team would arrive sooner rather than later. It didn't matter, though. In fact, their presence would actually help him execute his plan in a way he couldn't do alone. Still, he needed to get a few things done before they turned up, so he slapped Maguire's face a couple of times to wake him up. It did the trick and the priest began to stir.

'Welcome back, Seamus.'

Maguire opened his eyes. Startled, he attempted to get off the chair before realising he was strapped in.

Dempsey stood in front of him, smiling. 'We have unfinished business, Seamus, so let's get cracking, shall we.?

He rubbed his hands, then strode across the room and

retrieved the toolbox. He placed it on a nearby chest of drawers, opened it and began slowly removing the tools.

'I planned to kill you the same way as the others, but the police have got all my gear now, so I'll just have to improvise.'

'W-what are you going to do?'

'I told you, Seamus. I'm going to send you to hell.'

'But, why? I don't know you.'

Dempsey turned to face him. 'You don't, do you? But maybe you remember me as a chubby, vulnerable little boy in *Winnie the Pooh* pyjamas? An eleven-year-old who you persuaded to follow you to Father Donnelly's room on the trip to Lourdes, so he could rape me.'

Maguire looked incredulous. 'You're *Winnie*? But you're so big, and Thomas was so—'

'*Small?*' Dempsey nodded. 'It's amazing what you can do with steroids and time in the gym. When Father Donnelly finally got bored of me and moved on to his next victim, all I wanted to do was die. I couldn't live with the shame, the self-loathing, the guilt. *Guilt?* Can you imagine *I* felt guilty for what *he'd* done to me? Like I'd somehow caused it. I planned to kill myself a couple of times, but in the end I couldn't go through with it. I knew it would've broken my mum's heart, but what actually stopped me was my fear that suicide was a mortal sin. Can you believe that? Even after all the abuse, I was still scared of going to hell if I killed myself. So, eventually, I decided that if I was stuck in a living hell, it would be *my* hell and I was going to take back control. To become someone no-one would ever victimise again. So I created this...' He waved a hand up and down his body. 'And do you know what, Seamus? Since then, nobody has.'

'Please, Thomas, I beg you. Don't hurt me. I didn't know he was abusing you. I swear it.'

Dempsey stood motionless, staring coldly at Maguire. 'Like

you didn't know he was abusing Matt Logan and little Ricky Murray as well? You're a liar, Seamus.'

Maguire's eyes oozed panic, his words coming out in double-time. 'I was a young seminarian in training. Father Donnelly was a very powerful and influential man within the church. I promise you, I never knew what went on in his room. I just did as I was told.'

'Cut the crap, Seamus. You knew exactly what he was doing. Not only did you let it happen – you helped him get away with it. Then, after a lifetime of abusing kids, he dies and gets off scot-free. That bastard even received a hero's funeral. A monster who, at the very end, was lauded by you and the church, and the very same people who turned a blind eye to my abuse.'

'That's not true.'

'Oh, fuck off, Seamus. *I was there*. I saw it with my own eyes, for God's sake.'

'You were at Donnelly's funeral? I didn't see you.'

Dempsey laughed loudly. 'I don't know if it's escaped your notice, Seamus, but I killed four people without leaving a trace. I think I can sneak in and out of a funeral without being seen. No, I was there, and I witnessed the abhorrent re-writing of history. Susan's eulogy, pontificating about what a wonderful servant of God he was: "Such a brilliant man". Dee-Dee and Mrs Clarke saying bidding-prayers for his soul. And Ricky, crying like a baby at the back. I thought he was upset, but it turns out he was crying because Donnelly was finally dead.'

Beads of sweat ran down the side of Maguire's face. 'Father Donnelly had a weakness, but deep down he was a good man.'

Dempsey pulled out a pair of pliers and pointed them at Maguire. 'He was an evil predator who abused his power as a Catholic priest. He raped me, and God knows how many others, inside the grounds of this fucking church.'

'He wouldn't do that. Not in the house of God.'

'He would and he did, and you were complicit in it.'

'I wasn't, Tom, as God is my witness.'

'There you go again, bringing God into this. You just can't stop lying, can you?'

'I'm not lying, Tom. I swear I'm not.'

'Enough!' Dempsey screamed, causing the priest to jump in the chair. He inspected the claw hammer in his hand before placing it on the chest of drawers. His voice was measured when he spoke next. 'Do you know why I killed each of them in different parts of their houses?'

Maguire shook his head, his eyes locked on the hammer.

'Because that's where he used to rape me. In the lounge, in the bedroom, in his car – even in the bath.' He pointed towards the church house. 'The same bath you probably use to this day.'

Maguire opened his mouth to speak, but struggled to find the words.

'Do you know where else he raped me, Seamus?' Dempsey slowly pulled out a large screwdriver from the toolbox.

'No.' Maguire was barely audible.

'Right here in this vestry, on that very seat you're sitting on. The exact spot, Father Seamus Maguire...*where you're going to die.*'

54

Phillips and Jones leapt out of their car and ran headlong up the slippery wet path towards St Patrick's church. As they reached the main door, her phone rang. It was Brown.

They stopped and stared at each other.

'Well, are you going answer it?'

Phillips let it ring out. A moment later, it rang again.

'You better answer it, Guv. It'll only make things worse if you ignore him.'

'We really don't have time for this. Dempsey could already be in there with Maguire.'

'Seriously, Guv, I think you should answer it.'

She knew Jones was right. 'Sir?' she said, reluctantly answering it on the fifth ring.

On the line, Brown's raging voice was almost incoherent. Wincing, she held the phone away and switched it to speaker so Jones could hear.

'...furthermore, you will stand the fuck down and you will wait for the tactical firearms unit to arrive. Do you understand me, Inspector Phillips?'

'How long will that be, sir?'

'As long as it bloody well takes. If Dempsey is as dangerous as you claim, you and Jones are not equipped to take him on. Doing so may well endanger the life you're trying to save, as well as your own.'

'But sir, Dempsey knows we're onto him. If he is inside, he won't waste any time. We have to go in before he kills Father Maguire.'

'No, you do not. What you have to do is follow fucking orders for once in your life!'

Phillips looked at Jones, who silently gave Brown the 'V' sign and nodded towards the church. It was all she needed to know. He was with her.

'Sorry, sir, what did you just say? You're breaking up.'

'Don't pull that crap with me, Phillips.'

'It's a terrible line, sir. I can't hear you.'

'Stay exactly where you are, Phillips, and wait for TFU. Stand down. That's an order.'

'Nope, sorry, I've lost you.' Phillips ended the call and put the phone on silent before pushing it deep into her coat pocket. 'Looks like it's just me and you, Jonesy.'

Jones shrugged. 'I never wanted a long career. Police pensions are overrated anyway.'

'Are you sure? Brown's beef is with me, not you.'

Jones's face became serious. 'There is no you or me, Guv, just the team. That's all that matters. Fuck Brown. He can do what he likes.' Phillips smiled briefly, but Jones continued. 'So how do you want to do this?' He glanced at the church. 'It's a big building. He could be anywhere.'

Phillips thought quickly. 'You go round the back and through the house. I'll check out the church. You see anything suspicious, holler.'

'Got it!' Jones turned and headed over to the other side of the building.

A moment later, with her phone relentlessly vibrating in her pocket, Phillips opened the outer door to the church and stepped inside the large porch. Moving quietly through the inner doors, she entered the chapel. All was silent inside, and she stopped a moment to survey the cavernous space. She spotted something glistening on the wooden floor and bent down to take a closer look. She dabbed at it and inspected her finger. It was fresh blood, and there was a lot more leading towards the altar.

The noise of the inner doors opening behind her made her jump. She spun around to see Entwistle stride towards her.

'What are you doing here?' she whispered.

'Couldn't let you and Jonesy take all the glory, now could I?' Entwistle looked around the church. 'So, what now?'

She pointed ahead. 'There's a trail of blood running up the centre aisle towards the vestry. Let's try that first. We can get access to the house that way too.'

Phillips started walking towards the altar when a blood-curdling scream stopped her in her tracks.

'It's coming from the vestry, Guv.' Entwistle ran past her, stopping a moment later and turning to face her. 'Guv?' He looked confused.

Phillips was frozen to the spot. Narrowly surviving a point-blank shooting had been harrowing enough; the flashbacks, the nightmares, the panic. She'd learnt to live with them over the last six months. However, the attacks by Dempsey had left her with fresh, crippling wounds that ached inside and out. As much as she wanted to charge in and save Maguire, her feet would not move. She stood like a statue, her breathing shallow, her body weak.

Another loud scream echoed around them.

'Guv! We have to get in there.'

'I-I can't...' she mumbled.

Entwistle stared at her a moment longer, then sprinted

towards the vestry. Reaching it, he kicked the door open and launched himself inside.

Phillips heard shouting and what sounded like a scuffle, then two heavy thuds in close succession. The silence returned.

Phillip's heart beat like a manic bass drum, her mouth bone dry.

'Inspector Phillips, so good of you to join us,' Dempsey called out from within the vestry, his bellowing tones bouncing off the walls of the church. 'I'm afraid your little friend has had an accident; overwhelmed by Christ, you might say.' His laughter echoed around her.

Next, Phillips heard Father Maguire's terrified voice. 'He's killed the young lad! He's says he's going to kill me. Please... you've got to help me.'

Phillips's mind flashed back to Dempsey's house. She could almost feel Dempsey's thick arm wrapped around her neck. The fear, like a living thing, holding her in a vice – she couldn't put herself in that position again. Brown was right; it was time to let the TFU run the show. *She was finished.*

She took a step back but stopped suddenly, recalling Jones's words from just a few moments ago. *There's no you or me, Guv, just the team. That's all that matters.* Repeating the phrase out loud, she turned around and headed for the vestry door. 'Do it for the team,' she repeated like a mantra.

Stepping slowly inside, Phillips surveyed the scene. Entwistle was lying face forward in a heap on the floor, a pool of blood collecting under a deep gash on his temple. Above him stood Dempsey, a huge gold crucifix – bloodied at one end – in his hand. Behind him sat Maguire, his arms and legs secured with rope to a large chair. His two front teeth were missing, and blood seeped out of the side his mouth.

Dempsey followed her gaze. 'A tooth for a tooth, Inspector.'

'Thomas, please stop this.'

'I'll stop when it's over. And please, call me Tom.'

'When will it *ever* be over, Tom?'

Dempsey's demeanour changed. 'When this evil bastard atones for his sins.' He pointed at Maguire, then threw the crucifix across the room, where it landed with a heavy thud on the thick green carpet.

'Look, Tom, I know you were one of Donnelly's victims, just like Logan. I know what he did to you. I can never take that pain away, but this isn't the answer. Killing Father Maguire won't make it right.'

Dempsey's chest heaved. 'No, but it will make it *fair*. He helped Donnelly abuse me. I trusted Seamus, looked up to him like an older brother. And what did he do? Delivered me, an innocent little boy, to that monster's bedroom. He's as guilty as Donnelly.' He picked up the claw hammer in his right hand.

'You don't want to use that, Tom.'

Dempsey stared down at the rusting tool in his grip. 'Do you like it? I think this used to be Donnelly's. I have a vague recollection of him doing DIY about the place when I was little. I found it in the toolbox in the garage.'

Phillips raised her palms gently. 'Put the hammer down and I promise you, Tom, we can reopen the case against Donnelly. Show the world who he really was. And if Father Maguire had anything to do with abusing you or any other kids, I'll make sure he goes to prison for a very long time.'

'Prison's too good for this scumbag.' Dempsey pressed the top of the hammer against Maguire's temple, causing him to flinch. 'He needs to die, like the rest.'

Phillips was doing everything she could to appear calm and in control when the exact opposite was true. 'No Tom, he doesn't. He needs to face justice and be held accountable for his actions.'

Dempsey laughed. 'A Catholic priest, accountable? That's a joke. They've been covering up their crimes for centuries. They're not about to change now.'

'Maybe not, but the *world* is changing. More and more cases of historical abuse are coming to court and those abusers are going to prison. Think about it, Tom. If he dies, the lies, the deceit, the horrific abuse – it all dies with him. If you let him live and you help us put him on trial, the whole world will know what he and Donnelly did to you and Logan...and *all the others.*'

For a moment, Dempsey said nothing, staring into space. 'Do you know what they used to call me?'

'Who, Tom?'

'Susan, Dee-Dee and the others. They had a nickname for me.'

'No, I don't.'

'Winnie.' Dempsey snorted. '*Winnie.* And do you know why?'

'No, Tom.'

Dempsey placed the hammer head against Maguire's temple again. 'Because the first night this bastard delivered me to Donnelly's room in France, I was wearing hand-me-down *Winnie the Pooh* pyjamas. Mum didn't have much money, so she got them from a church jumble sale. I was naïve, I thought they were great until I put them on and all the kids started laughing at me. They said I was a tramp wearing someone else's clothes – pyjamas that little kids wear.'

'Kids can be cruel, Tom.'

'I cried my eyes out and ran from the dorm – and bumped into Father Seamus.' He shoved Maguire's head sideways with the hammer. 'This devious prick told me to ignore the other kids. That they were just jealous because I was *special*. So special, in fact, that Father Donnelly had asked to see me privately in his room. He had a special gift for me, and Seamus would take me to see him. *Me* special? After the others had been so cruel, I was over the moon. I couldn't wait to see what

Father Donnelly had for me.' Dempsey paused, clearly struggling with the memory.

'Tom, I'm so sorry.'

Dempsey steeled himself once more. 'He raped me that
night for the first time, and then every week after that for
almost three years. And do you know what the worst part of it
was?'

'I can't imagine.'

'The kids never, ever called me Thomas or Tom after that
night. Just Winnie. A name that constantly reminded me of that
horrific night and what Donnelly did to me.'

'Is that why you killed them?'

Dempsey wiped a tear from his cheek. 'In part, I guess, but
not that alone. No. They died because, at some point, they all
knew what he was doing to me and not one of them said
anything to anybody, ever. They could have stopped what was
happening to me, but instead they looked away. They sat back
and did nothing whilst Donnelly stole my life.' Another tear
ran down his face. 'So I stole their lives. A fair trade, as far as
I'm concerned.'

At that moment, Phillips's phone began to vibrate in her
jacket pocket.

'I need to get that, Tom.'

'No phones,' Dempsey said firmly.

The phone continued to buzz loudly.

'If I don't answer it, they'll send the TFU guys in and they
will shoot you, Tom.'

'Do you really think I'm afraid to die, Inspector? That's how
this ends. Maguire dies, and then I do.' The phone stopped.
Sadness flashed across Dempsey's face. 'I won't kill me; they
will.'

Phillips was confused. 'Who's they?'

Dempsey pointed to the window. 'Your marksmen. I've
studied your protocols and I know that, with a police officer as

my hostage, if I refuse to negotiate, it's only be a matter of time before they give the shoot-on-sight order.'

Phillips gaped at him. 'Why would you want that?'

'Because I've wanted to die since that first night in France. But I still have this stupid, ingrained fear that suicide is against God.'

'And killing Father Maguire isn't?'

Dempsey shook his head. 'No, I don't think it is. Like the Bible says, "an eye for an eye, a tooth for a tooth".'

Phillips's phone began to vibrate again.

'Please let me answer that, Tom. I need to get Entwistle some help. He's just a young copper starting out. He's in a bad way and your fight's not with him.'

Dempsey stared at Entwistle's prostrate body. Blood continued to pour from the gash on his head. He nodded. 'Okay, answer it.'

He stepped behind Maguire, the hammer ready in his hand.

Phillips took the call. 'Yes sir, I have eyes on him now... No sir... No sir... Yes sir... That's correct sir, please just give me five more minutes... Thank you sir...and we'll need an ambulance for DC Entwistle. He's sustained a serious head injury... Yes sir...thank you, sir.' Phillips ended the call.

'Ready to storm the castle are they, Inspector?'

Phillips nodded. 'That was the head of the TFU. As you predicted, this is now a hostage situation and they have eyes on us through each of these four windows with snipers ready to fire on his command. He's given me five minutes to talk you down before he authorises a shoot-on-sight protocol.'

'In that case, I'd better get this over with.' Dempsey spun the hammer in his hand like a tennis player spinning a racket.

'Listen to me, Tom. You don't have to die. Stop this now and help me bring Donnelly and Maguire to justice.'

Dempsey stared at Phillips a long moment, then walked

behind Maguire and placed a hand on his shoulder. He nodded softly. 'There's merit in what you want to do, Inspector, and I really do envy your optimism. That's something I lost thirty years ago. The truth is, the church will always find a way to protect its own. This man will never pay for his crimes and I'll never get justice. No, I'm sorry Jane, Maguire dies.' Dempsey raised the hammer high above his head.

Phillips launched herself at him just as his arm plunged, knocking him backwards. The hammer missed Maguire by mere millimetres. It fell from his hand and landed on the carpet.

A single shot rang out and glass splintered across the room as Phillips wrestled Dempsey to the floor, attempting to subdue him. But it was no use; he was too strong. Pushing her onto her back yet again, he clambered to his feet and, reaching down to pick up the crucifix, ran headlong towards Father Maguire. 'See you in hell, you bastard!'

A loud scream filled the room as Phillips, who had grabbed the claw hammer, swung the spikes deep into Dempsey's Achilles tendon, stopping him in his tracks.

Another shot rang out, this time catching Dempsey in the chest. He staggered a few feet, then slumped to the floor – next to the kneeling Phillips, who clutched the bloodied hammer tightly in her hands – and rolled onto his back.

'Guv! Are you ok?' Jones yelled, banging on the door – apparently locked – that lead from the vestry to the house. 'Guv!'

Beside her, Dempsey remained motionless, coughing up blood and staring into the distance. He was trying to say something, but Jones's shouts and banging were drowning him out.

She moved her ear closer to his mouth.

Through bloody bubbles, he was praying. 'Our Father Who art in heaven...hallowed be Thy name...'

'Thomas Dempsey – you're not going anywhere.' Phillips

jumped up and ran over to the door to let Jones in. He halted when he saw the scene.

'We need an ambulance... Now, Jonesy!'

'Yes, Guv.' Jones raced across the vestry and through the church to alert the medics waiting outside.

Phillips knelt beside Dempsey, and was alarmed to see he had stopped breathing. 'Don't you die on me, Tom. Not after everything we've been through.' She started CPR.

Above her, still tied to the chair, Maguire looked on. 'Let him die, Inspector. It's what he wanted.' His words were slurred through his missing front teeth.

Phillips finished giving Dempsey mouth to mouth and started chest compressions. 'You'd like that, wouldn't you?' she panted. 'Clears everything up nicely between you and Donnelly.'

She repeated mouth to mouth as Maguire continued behind her. 'He was insane. A total fantasist. I never did any of the things he said I did. I have no idea what he's talking about.'

Just then, a group of TFU officers charged into the room in formation, guns cocked at the ready. They were followed by two paramedic teams, who split up and immediately started working on Dempsey and Entwistle.

Jones followed them in, reaching out his hand to help Phillips to her feet. 'You've got to stop doing this to us, Guv.' He was smiling, 'We really thought we'd lost you again.'

Phillips blew out a sigh of relief. 'Tell me about it.'

'Please... Can somebody please help me out of this chair.' She turned to see Maguire tugging at his restraints as more uniformed officers entered the room.

She picked the pliers off the floor and handed them to Jones. 'Cut him loose, will you?'

While Jones cut through the ropes, Phillips stepped behind Maguire. As soon as he got to his feet, she yanked his arms roughly behind his back. 'Seamus Maguire, I am arresting you on suspicion of being complicit in the sexual abuse and rape of Thomas Dempsey. You do not have to say anything, but it may harm your defence if you do not mention, when questioned, something which you later rely on in court. Anything you do say may be given in evidence.' She turned him around to face her.

Maguire's crooked, toothless smile greeted her. 'You can't prove anything, Inspector. It's Dempsey's word against mine, and it looks like he'll be needing the last rites soon enough. Would you like me to oblige?'

Phillips stepped in closer, struggling to contain the emotions boiling inside her. 'I know Thomas wasn't your only victim, *Seamus*. And while you have some kind of hold over Matt Logan, he *will* tell me what you and Donnelly did to him all those years ago, and I will put you in prison for a very, very long time.'

Maguire scoffed. 'Matthew? I was like a father to him. Everyone else gave up on him, but I never did. We have a special bond you wouldn't understand. He would never say anything against me, you can be sure of that.'

Phillips held his gaze. 'I'll tell you what you can be sure of, shall I? No matter how long it takes, I swear in this house of God that the world *will* finally hear the truth about you and Donnelly – and all those like you, hiding in plain sight. Because that's what matters now – *the truth*.' She pushed him towards Jones. 'Get this monster out of my sight.'

EPILOGUE

ONE MONTH LATER

GMP Headquarters
Ashton House

'So, what are the chances of you getting back to DCI, Guv?' Jones asked when Phillips returned to the squad room after her meeting with Chief Superintendent Fox.

She flopped into her office chair and, placing a thick Manila folder on the desk next to her, patted it with her hand. 'Well, I've just spent an hour putting my case forward as to why I deserve it.'

'Like catching the Cheadle Killer single-handed?'

Phillips reclined in the chair and smiled. 'That's very kind of you, but it was hardly single-handed. Anyway, Brown took all the credit, didn't he?'

Bovalino folded his thick arms with a scowl. 'No surprises there, then.'

'Like I say, I've made my case. Now it's up to Fox and the review board to decide.'

Bovalino continued. 'God, I hope you get it, Guv. We can't have another prick like Brown coming in and making our lives miserable.'

Phillips smiled widely. 'Thank God he got his promotion to Superintendent, hey?'

'So he's back in uniform then?' asked Jones.

'Yep. That's the protocol in his division. He's not a detective anymore, so he has to wear it.'

Bovalino let out a chuckle. 'Can you imagine it? Teeny-tiny Fraser Brown back in uniform – he'll look like a fucking kids toy!'

All three laughed loudly before Phillips brought it back to business. 'Anyway, more importantly, I spoke to the guys at the CPS today about Dempsey.'

Bovalino sat to attention. 'And what did they say?'

'Because he's pleading guilty to all four counts, it looks like they're willing to look at reducing the length of his sentence *if* he testifies against Maguire.'

'That's good news,' said Jones.

Bovalino cracked his knuckles. 'D'ya think he's a credible witness, Guv?'

'Credible? I'm not so sure. But compelling? *Absolutely*. If Dempsey stands up in front of a jury and tells his story, Maguire's going to Hawk Green until he's a very old man. Plus, having now heard that Maguire was complicit in his abuse with Donnelly, Matt Logan's agreed to testify against him too. And since his arrest hit the news, more and more victims are coming forward each day.'

Jones frowned. 'My biggest worry is that the church will try and cover it up.'

'I'm not sure they can this time, Jonesy. With the recent high-profile cases in the US, these kinds of stories make worldwide news now. And I'll personally make sure Don Townsend gets all the exclusives he needs to get the story out there. You know what he can do when he's got the bit between his teeth and, thanks to social media, he'll make sure the whole planet knows what monsters Maguire and Donnelly really were.'

Bovalino shook his head. 'I know Dempsey killed four people – he even tried to kill you, Guv – but I can't help feeling sorry for him. Does that sound crazy?'

'Not at all, Bov.'

Jones nodded. 'I'm with you, Bov. I don't think I've ever felt so conflicted about a case in my life. When I look back at the crime scene photos, it's hard not to see Dempsey as a calculated, cold-blooded killer. Then I read the historical claims of abuse and what he went through, and all I see is a little boy whose life was destroyed by evil men. Evil men abusing the trust of a whole community, pretending to be doing God's work. It's sickening.'

Phillips patted him on the shoulder. 'I know, Jonesy, I know. But it's the world we live in.' She got up from her chair. 'Right, I don't know about you guys, but it's home time for me.'

Bovalino looked surprised. 'You not coming to meet Entwistle, Guv?'

Phillips looked confused. 'Entwistle? Did I miss a meeting?'

'Remember, I mentioned it last week. We're meeting him for a few drinks in town,' Jones told her.

'More than a few!' boasted Bovalino, his hand waving in an imaginary drinking motion.

Jones continued. 'It's a welcome back party. His sick leave finishes this week.'

Phillips nodded. 'It's coming back to me, but you'll have to count me out, I'm afraid. I've got somewhere to be.' She picked up her car keys and headed for the door.

Bovalino played it camp. '*Ooh*, check you out. Anyone we know – someone special, is it?'

Phillips reached the door, but stopped for a moment. 'Nope, no one special.'

'Well, he's a lucky man, whoever he is,' quipped Jones.

Phillips stepped out into the corridor, a wry smile creeping across her face. As she headed for the car park, her phone beeped. Pulling it from her pocket, she continued walking and looked down at the diary reminder that had appeared on the screen. 'COUNSELLING – DR BARTON – 30 MINS'.

'No one special, Bov...*life-changing*, maybe.' She smiled as she opened the double doors at the end of the hall and took the stairs two at a time.

ACKNOWLEDGEMENTS

The support I received from so many people made this book possible, and I'd like to take a moment to thank them.

As ever, my biggest supporter is my wife, Kim, who gave me the courage to quit my day-job and follow my dream of being a full-time author. Even in the most frightening moments that followed, she never faltered. Thanks, Babe.

My son, Vaughan, who inspires me every day to be playful and to have fun.

My coaches, Donna and Cheryl from 'Now Is Your Time,' who helped me to let go, and trust in the Universe's plan for me and my writing.

My dad, who kept reminding me to have patience and let things happen as they should.

Mum, my brother, Simon, and sister, Suzanne, for their faith and support. They each resisted telling me to get a real job.

PC James Eve and Simon 'Harry' Harrison QC, who once again helped me understand the complexities of UK law.

My publishers, Garret and Brian, whose standards are so high I can't help but improve my craft working with them.

My editor, Laurel, who is simply brilliant.

And finally, thank you for reading *Deadly Silence*. If you could spend a moment to write an honest review on Amazon, no matter how short, I would be extremely grateful. They really do help readers discover my books.

Best wishes,

Owen

www.omjryan.com

Published by Inkubator Books
www.inkubatorbooks.com

Printed in Great Britain
by Amazon

27514216R00182